FOLLOW YOU DOWN

Follow You Down

KATIE WALSH

*To my Gram, who would have been so proud of me and
of this book.
And who would have told me to make it spicier.*

Chapter One

2025

Kate Walker wished someone had warned her about the lesser-known side effects of Botox. Namely, accidentally peeing your pants and ruining your favorite designer jeans.

Her friends had been raving about it for years. *I wish I'd done it sooner! You'll love it! Want my girl's number? She's a magician.* It was a self-care sorority every millennial woman seemed required to pledge.

What no one mentioned—and really, someone should have—is that there's a small but nonzero chance of briefly blacking out, forgetting where you are, and, well... letting go. Of your bladder.

Kate's first ever Botox appointment had started out innocently enough. It was an unusually warm mid-May Friday in Manhattan, and she sat in a dentist-like chair in a small exam room at Aurelia Aesthetics on 51st Street, anxiously scrolling Instagram and obsessively checking work emails.

She wasn't sure if she was nervous or excited. Maybe both? The second latte from this morning swam through her body, and she caught herself chewing on her nails again. She pulled her manicured finger out of her mouth and refocused on her phone. Usually, marking all her emails as 'read' and clearing her notifications brought some measure of Zen to her busy life. Today, not so much.

She'd made the appointment two months ago. Her best friend, Nikki Harper, had convinced her to take the leap over brunch, proclaiming, *"You must see Dr. Chu,"* with her usual confidence. *"She's the Botox fairy godmother. Bippity, boppity, Botox. You're thirty again!"*

It did seem like a great idea at the time. Nikki always encouraged her to take more risks and embrace experiences that might bring her joy, especially after Chris left. Kate wasn't always good at accepting that advice, but when your whole life has turned to shit and you're three mimosas deep, you're open to a lot of crazy ideas.

Sober-Kate planned to cancel but Nikki persuaded her to keep it. Which is how she ended up at Aurelia Aesthetics in the middle of the workday, despite the fact that she had a brand presentation due at 2 p.m.

At least the sleek décor in the exam room was somewhat soothing. The air was infused with the calming aroma of lavender. Kate figured if they took this much care with the atmosphere, they couldn't possibly botch up something as simple as Botox.

What is taking so long? She wondered, glancing at the elegant clock on the wall for the fifth time in ten minutes.

Kate didn't like being alone with her thoughts. It's why meditation made her itchy—mentally, emotionally, sometimes even physically. On a normal day, her mind spun in loops: grocery lists, overdue emails, that never-ending to-do list at work. But lately, her thoughts drifted somewhere darker. Like how unbearably quiet the spacious tenth-floor apartment felt without Chris. Or how working ten-hour days at her start-up probably wasn't *just* ambition. Or how she was polishing off half a bottle of Kim Crawford every night. Okay—three-quarters. Fine, the whole bottle.

Kate heard the door creak open and sat up straight, taking a deep breath. *Go time.*

But the person who peeked their head in was not the doctor. It was the front office staffer who brought her in fifteen minutes ago.

"I'm so sorry, Dr. Chu is running a wee bit behind," Ellie apologized with an unmistakable southern drawl. "Only a few more moments. And no need to be nervous *at all*. It's over really quickly!"

Kate forced a smile and nodded her head as Ellie quietly shut the door. She silently cursed herself for not canceling.

Why is she telling me not to be nervous? Kate wondered, suddenly alarmed. A tiny voice in her head whispered that maybe Nikki had downplayed how much this would hurt.

Nikki had over twenty tattoos. Clearly that crazy bitch enjoyed pain.

I'm going to be late, she thought, her Louboutin-clad foot tapping out an impatient rhythm against the chair leg. At five-foot-three, she felt like a restless kid in a grown-up seat. She caught her reflection in the large decorative mirror that covered most of the right wall. It was adorned with faux gold molding and screamed Pottery Barn.

Kate tugged gently at the skin around her eyes, studying her reflection and trying to imagine the magic of Botox in advance. Her eyes were large and deep-set, a captivating hazel with a quiet intensity that made people pause mid-sentence. Thick, inky lashes framed them—a stark contrast to her fair skin and the scatter of freckles across her nose. The freckles softened her, lent a kind of vulnerability that balanced out the otherwise brooding undertone she carried.

Even with the shadows of too many sleepless nights, she knew she looked younger than her 44 years. But she wasn't here just for the wrinkles. She knew that. This appointment was less about erasing wrinkles and more about erasing some of the pain of the last few months.

In an effort to relax, she peeled off the thin, zippered black leather jacket that served no practical purpose other than tying her outfit together. That morning, she'd rummaged through her closet in search of the perfect feel-good look and landed on her brand-new pair of bootcut Mother jeans. She felt a quiet sense of triumph for resisting her usual skinny jeans—still folded in abundance in her drawer. She could only say goodbye to so many long-term relationships in one year.

She twisted the gold bead on her Eden Hand Arts Cape Cod bracelet—a nervous habit. Nikki had given it to her as an unexpected gift years ago, before the bracelets became the must-have status symbol of every Cape vacationer. Kate wasn't much of a jewelry person, but she wore that bracelet everywhere—while working out, in the shower, sunbathing. It had even been on her wrist the day she got married. Its permanence turned out to run deeper than her wedding ring had.

She smiled at herself in the mirror, trying to produce the pesky crow's feet. Her lips were full and naturally pink. When she smiled, they revealed a row of perfectly straight and white teeth that could only be achieved with four awkward years of braces.

They're not THAT bad. If I leave now, I can make it back to work on time.

Right as Kate started to hoist herself out of the chair to dash for the exit, Dr. Chu entered. A wave of vanilla and cedar followed her in, a cloud of embodied rejuvenation.

Gorgeous and radiating confidence, the Botox fairy godmother looked just as stunning in person as she did in the "Top 30 Plastic Surgeons in Manhattan" article Kate poured over before booking the appointment. Dr. Chu was nearing 50, but didn't look a day over 30. Her perfect porcelain skin was glowing, not a wrinkle in sight, and her almond eyes sparkled with kindness.

"Good afternoon, Kate. It's so nice to meet you and welcome you to our practice. How are you today?" Dr. Chu's warm demeanor immediately put Kate a little more at ease.

"I'm doing well, thank you," Kate said, trying to sound casual.

Dr. Chu pursed her perfect lips and gave an overly sympathetic nod. "It's completely normal to feel a bit anxious, but I assure you, this will be quick and relatively painless. I see this is your first time—how exciting. Why don't you tell me what brought you in today?"

Kate winced. *Where to begin?* Should she be honest? The real reason was depressing. Her life was kind of depressing right now. Best to keep it light.

"Well, I've always been happy with my skin, but I know I'm getting older. And I'm all for aging gracefully, but I just want to feel confident and beautiful, even though I'm over forty," Kate began. A perfectly reasonable start.

Dr. Chu gave her a warm smile of agreement. "Makes sense. Is that all?"

An awkward silence followed. Kate had never been good with those. She waited a second for Dr. Chu, who seemed to be waiting for Kate to continue.

"I mean...it's been a hard year for me so far. And I feel like this might help boost my confidence?" She didn't mean for it to come out as a question. A little more than she probably needed to share. But all those things were true.

Dr. Chu nodded pensively, but didn't respond. Was she encouraging her to keep going? Kate wriggled in her chair a bit. Was more rationale and backstory required?

"I was married to a great guy for 10 years. And I have a stepdaughter, who is basically my daughter. But they're both...gone." There was more emotion in those words than she intended. Dr Chu reared back slightly, her eyebrows raising with immediate concern.

"God, that sounds morbid, sorry," Kate apologized. "They're not dead or anything. Sydney is at college in Boston, we're still close, but I miss her a ton. Chris blindsided me on New Year's Day at our favorite Greek place, telling me he wasn't happy over pitas and hummus. And I was so shocked I just kept shoving more pita in my mouth searching for the right thing to say. He was crying, I was basically choking on the pita trying not to cry, and—"

Even pumped full of Botox, Kate could see the pity building in Dr. Chu's face. She realized she'd just unloaded five months of emotional trauma to someone she'd only known for like 30 seconds. Her face flushed bright red.

"Um, anyway...I'm looking forward to having a more youthful look to start the summer." Mortified, she fixed her gaze on her lap and gripped her phone tightly. When she finally dared to look up, she was surprised to find Dr. Chu smiling, her eyes filled with understanding.

"Seems like you've had a rough year, I'm so sorry," Dr. Chu said, placing a comforting hand on Kate's. "If it makes you feel any better, I get this a lot. Many women come in here to do something for themselves after experiencing a tough time. Botox won't solve all your problems, but if it helps you feel better about yourself, it's a start, right?"

Kate managed a half-smile and let out a deep breath. *Damn, Dr. Chu was good. Really good.*

"Are you sure this is something you want to do today?" Dr. Chu asked gently. Clearly, she was also a passable therapist.

Kate hesitated, second-guessing if she was in the right headspace to make such a big decision. It was fairly off-brand for her to inject toxins into her face willingly. As she wavered, a new text message popped up on her phone. It was from her sister.

> BTW I'm taking the beach house this summer. Sorry, just makes more sense since I have a family to use it.

Wow, Lindsey. The words punched Kate straight through the phone. *In case you have forgotten, you have no family. You are alone.*

Leave it to Lindsey to casually drop reminders at the worst possible moments that she was younger, happier, and more successful at life. God only knew what she'd say if she found out Kate was getting Botox.

And it's not like Kate had even stepped foot in Cape Cod for twenty years, or even *asked* to use their aunt's house.

But it still pissed her off. Indignation replaced Kate's anxiety. *My life may be a hot mess, but my face will look younger than Lindsey's this summer. She can have the old stuffy beach house while I have a hot girl summer in the Hamptons.*

"Yes, I'd like to do the Botox today. Please." She said firmly with a smile.

Kate had no plans to be in the Hamptons, but it was more impressive than the Cape. She made a note to search for rental homes in Montauk.

Dr. Chu nodded. "Alright then! Let's get you looking younger and ready to get back out there and get your groove back. The Hamptons won't see you coming!"

Kate blanched. Could Dr. Chu read minds?

Dr. Chu called in an assistant, and the procedure began. As Kate felt a series of small pricks on her forehead, she focused on deep breathing, determined to stay calm and make Nikki proud. *This isn't so bad*, she reassured herself, relieved when Dr. Chu finished the last injection.

"All done," Dr. Chu chirped. "How are you feeling?"

"Pretty good," Kate responded as the electronic chair tilted upright. Her hands tingled a little, but she figured she'd been clenching her hands without realizing it.

"Amazing, you did great. Now let's talk about aftercare. No icing, as it can cause uneven..."

Dr. Chu's voice faded in Kate's ears, like her head was plunged underwater. A cold sweat broke out across her skin, and she felt a sudden wave of nausea wash over her.

Oh my God, I'm going to throw up. No, that can't be right. Why would I be throwing up?

"Kate—is everything ok?" Dr. Chu's concerned voice cut through Kate's swirling thoughts. Kate opened her mouth to respond, but the room started to spin. Her vision blurred.

I'm not going to throw up, she realized with dawning horror. *I'm about to—*

And everything went black.

Chapter Two

2025

*C*hris? Sydney?

Everything was black. Somewhere in the distance, Kate heard the faint whirr of a machine. A fan, maybe?

Where am I? Is this a dream?

There were voices, but they were muffled. It didn't feel like a dream. She started to feel physical sensations, a general awareness of her body. She was sitting. Somewhere. And it wasn't her bed.

What is going on...why do I feel panicked?

Kate was yanked from the abyss, disoriented and confused. Reality rushed back in with a jarring force. As her eyes fluttered open, she found herself reclined in the chair, surrounded by the anxious faces of the office staff, cold packs pressed against her forehead and neck. Dr. Chu gently patted her hand.

"Kate? Can you hear me?" Dr. Chu's voice was calm, but there was an unmistakable note of concern.

Kate blinked, struggling to clear her hazy thoughts. "I'm ok. I think," she said, trying to convince herself more than anyone else. "What... what happened?"

"You had a vasovagal response," Dr. Chu explained. "You fainted. It's common. Just relax while we check your vitals. You're OK, just breathe."

WTF is a vasovagal response? Kate tried to nod, but she was still in a daze.

Everyone who works at this med spa must be in this room right now, she thought, embarrassment soaking in. As the assistant wrapped a blood pressure cuff around her arm, something else soaked in: a warm dampness around her thighs. Specifically, in her pants.

Oh god. She glanced down in desperate denial. *Maybe the ice packs leaked?* But they weren't anywhere near her crotch. Why would they be?

She could feel the urine spreading from her jeans through to the flimsy paper liner on the chair. The only bootcuts she owned. Her skinny jeans would *never* have let this happen. This is she didn't try new things. She was punished every time she did.

Fuck. Seriously?! What else could possibly go wrong here?

Dr. Chu's eyes followed Kate's hands as she tried to reposition her jacket over her lap. She clearly wasn't as subtle as intended, because Dr. Chu seemed to notice what was unfolding.

"It's ok, Kate, that is also common," she said with a practiced, calm tone. She reached for some medical pads. "I'm sure it's not high on your list of fun experiences, but it's nothing to be embarrassed about—bladder control can be lost when you faint completely. Most of the time, people fade in and out, but you were completely out for 10 seconds."

All of that happened in 10 seconds?! Kate's already rosy cheeks burned bright red.

"I'm so sorry," she whispered, mortified, her eyes stinging with tears. She must be the most embarrassing patient in the history of Botox patients. "I can't believe this happened."

Dr. Chu squeezed her hand and smiled. "No need to apologize. I want you to take my personal number. Please check in with me later today and let me know how you're doing, ok? Take all the time you need here, don't try to get right up. Ellie will stay here and ensure you feel ok before you leave."

Ellie reappeared, as if by magic, and offered a bottle of water and sympathetic eyes. "Here, drink this slowly," she said, handing over more paper towels. "And... we've got some scrub bottoms, if that would help?"

"Yeah... thank you." Kate nodded, knowing she had no choice. "I really appreciate it." She wasn't about to parade down the streets of New York City in urine-soaked pants. Plenty of people had that covered already.

This is just phenomenal.

"Do you have a friend or family member who could meet you?" Ellie offered, retrieving a pair of scrubs from a cabinet. "It might be good to have someone with you, you know— just in case."

Kate considered that for a moment. Sydney would have been there instantaneously with a fresh pair of pants and a joke at the ready. But she was four hours away in Boston.

Nikki also lived near Boston but was often in New York for her job as the head of partnerships and collabs for a glam French luxury brand. She was the perfect best friend during Fashion Week, but as a known marketing maven in the world of sneakers, she was hard to pin down otherwise.

Who else could come on short notice? Even if her family lived closer, she'd rather take her chances blacking out again than calling her parents or her sister in Massachusetts.

That left one logical choice. She took a deep breath and sent the text.

> Hey —any chance you could meet me uptown? Now-ish? I can't really call anyone else. Sorry.

Chris replied almost instantly.

Wrapping up a meeting, what's going on? Are you OK?

Long story. Can you meet me at Aurelia Aesthetics? On 59th and Park. I just need like 30 minutes.

Ok...I have a 1:30pm though. Leaving now. What happened!?

She paused before responding. She didn't want to get into the whole situation over text, but she needed to be clear that this wasn't a contrived plea to see him.

Had a medical...issue. They suggested someone walk me back to work. In case I black out again.

What?? Jesus, Kate. Ok. I'm on my way.

Thank you. I'll meet you in the lobby.

"I have a friend coming to meet me," Kate said, signaling to Ellie that she was free to leave the room. "I'll be ok, thanks for the help. And sorry again for all of this."

When she was the only one left in the room, she peeled off her jeans and underwear, hastily shoving them into a plastic bag that Ellie gave to her. Thank god for tote bags. She could fit her wet clothes in and no one would be the wiser. She attempted the best paper towel sponge bath she could, slid on the scrub pants, and gave herself a quick once-over in the mirror.

Green hospital scrub pants, a white cashmere tank, and a leather jacket. *Not exactly Gigi Hadid over here,* she sighed. But this was New York. People might assume it was a new fashion trend.

Kate made her way to the lobby, trying to avoid any eye contact and awkward pity stares from the staff, and braced herself to see her soon-to-be ex-husband.

She hadn't physically seen him in over three weeks. Not since he collected the last of his things and handed over his key to their condo, still attached to the maple leaf key chain from their family ski trip to Stowe in 2019. Formerly *their* condo, now *her* condo. At a market value north of two million dollars, he insisted early on that she keep it as part of the separation. Whether it was a fair concession or simply guilt, it gave her solace to know she was financially comfortable. When she inevitably became a cat lady, at least she and her furry companions would have a comfortable place to live.

She fidgeted with her bracelet, standing in the lobby in her new hospital-inspired ensemble. The last thing she said to him was something along the lines of "You don't get to ask me if I'm ok. You chose this. You left me. How the fuck do you think I am."

So, yeah. Calling Chris to come and "save" her was less than ideal.

Chris Walker adjusted his tie as he stepped inside. At six-foot-one, he was notably taller than anyone else milling around and looked paradoxically dapper and awkward at the same time. His dark-framed glasses and meticulously styled hair gave him an air of quiet intelligence, a look that served him well in the high-stakes world of finance. He was the epitome of a Wall Street hedge fund manager.

At least, that was the version everyone else in the lobby saw.

Kate saw someone entirely different. She saw the guy sprawled out on their old couch in a threadbare Bentley College sweatshirt, a bottle of Sam Adams lager in hand, lazily quoting *The Office* between sips. The man who once made her laugh until her stomach hurt. Her ex-husband. Ex-friend. And in an unfortunate turn of events, her current rescuer.

He hadn't noticed her yet, so she waited a moment before approaching. Despite Chris's outward composure, there was a hesitancy in his movements that only Kate could detect. There was a tightness in his jaw, a glimmer of uncertainty in his eyes as they darted around the room. He was also cracking each knuckle, one by one, in a slow, methodical rhythm—his old tell, reserved for tense client meetings and deeply uncomfortable conversations.

A small part of her felt some compassion for him. He was not a bad guy. And he was not exactly having an easy time of this either. She often wished he had cheated. That would have been easier to understand than the quiet, undetectable dissolution of being in love.

As she stood there, feeling vulnerable, the familiar sting of betrayal crept back in. Texting him was a mistake.

Then, he saw her. The anxiousness lingered on his face—just for a second—before he smoothed it over, his expression shifting into something warmer, gentler, but still edged with hesitation. He walked toward her, hands still fidgeting as if he wasn't quite sure what to do with them.

"Hey. You ok?" he asked, his voice careful. Careful is the modus operandi of approaching someone you used to greet with an affectionate kiss.

"Hey," she replied with an equal measure of care. Despite her mixed emotions, Being in his presence was still comforting. Like a Pavlovian response. "Yeah, I'm ok."

"What happened?" he asked with genuine concern, his dark brown eyes locked on her.

She sighed audibly and looked at her watch. "Can we talk and walk? I need to get back to the office. I just need...a buddy. Per the doctor."

"Sure," Chris nodded, still looking perplexed by the random afternoon meet-up. But she he deeply appreciated how much she hated to be late. "You will eventually need to spill about why you need a chaperone from what I assume was a facial gone wrong."

She smiled, loosening up a bit. "Deal. Let's go, ok?" She started walking toward the revolving door, forcing him to catch up and follow.

"What on earth are you even wearing?" he called from behind her, catching up as they stepped onto 59th Street.

She decided in that moment to tell him that she had fainted. Beyond that, he had given up the right to hear the full embarrassing story. Before she could speak, an uncomfortable lightness surged in her head. She abruptly stopped walking and took a deep breath, closing her eyes and assessing if she was on the brink of fainting again.

"Hey...I'm sorry, that was rude. Your outfit looks nice. Are you OK? You look a little pale..."

"Yeah...yeah, I'm good. I just need a minute." She took another focused breath, trying to regain her composure. She re-hoisted the tote on her shoulder and smoothed her tousled chestnut locks, glancing across the street to ensure none of the coffee shop or souvenir store signs looked blurry.

"Have you eaten? If you're feeling light-headed, you should eat and have something to drink. Have you had an afternoon coffee yet? That'll help."

She was both annoyed and thankful that he knew her so well. Chris whipped out his phone and ordered her a croissant and iced coffee at the Starbucks near her office while she filled him in on her embarrassing run-in with Botox. Minus the part where she peed her pants.

"Wow," he said. "You know...most women around here just pop in and out on their lunch break for Botox, like they're picking up dry cleaning. I bet you that's more excitement than that office usually gets all year."

And then he started laughing, chuckling at first and then harder. She smiled and joined in. It was objectively funny, and it felt so good to laugh with him. Some more of the awkward tension melted away.

"You know Kate," Chris said as they continued to her office, looking at her softly, "You don't even need Botox."

He probably meant it as a compliment, but when he said it, it stung. He decided he didn't want to be with her anymore, so he relinquished the right to pass *any* judgement on her. He had no idea what kind of pain she was in. What she might need to feel better about her life. She didn't want to be bitter. But she was.

"Your opinion doesn't really matter anymore." She didn't look at him and continued walking a few paces ahead. "I did it for myself, because it might feel better than crying every single night over a bottle of wine because my husband decided that wedding vows were merely a suggestion, and some great yet-to-be-found love was better than spending one more second with me."

Her voice started to tremble. It came out harsher than she intended. He looked like she had physically slapped him across the face.

"That's not fair, Kate," he finally said, his voice filled with hurt. "That's what you have to say after all the conversations and tears? That's what you took away? I love you, and I think we built a very comfortable life together. But we were not *in* love. Deep down, you know that's true."

She couldn't speak—even if she wanted to. Her throat tightened, the familiar ache rising, threatening to escape as a choked sob. She just wanted him to stop talking, but he didn't.

"When I met you, you knew exactly what you wanted. You were the most driven woman I'd ever met—you had mapped out your life, and somehow, mine fit seamlessly into it. And with Sydney, you were – *are* - incredible. You jumped in with both feet and loved her like your own daughter."

Her eyes were welling up. Why did he have to bring up Sydney? It felt manipulative.

"I want to be *in love*, Kate. My dad passing last year reminded me that life is short. I want more than carefully designed and comfortable. I want passion and romance. It sounds naïve, but I want the butterflies."

You are naïve, she thought angrily to herself. *Everyone knows you are supposed to marry your best friend and create a stable and happy life. Attraction and passion are superficial and not sustainable.*

She continued to look down, furiously avoiding eye contact while quickening her pace. This was spiraling; she was spiraling. She wanted to escape.

"Kate, you are an incredible woman, friend and partner. You meticulously organized our lives. With how demanding my job is, I was so thankful for that. But I want to feel passionate love. I want YOU to be in love too, Kate. You deserve that."

She remained silent, her heart beating way too fast. This was emotional overload on an already overwhelming day.

"Why are we doing this again, Kate?" he pled. "This isn't healthy. We can't keep tearing open this wound."

"Yeah, sorry I texted," she managed to say, her voice cracking with the hurt and sadness collecting in her throat. "I'll leave you alone now. Thanks for the walk and the coffee."

"You know that's not what I meant...Kate..."

But she was already walking, nearly running, around the block to her office. He called after her, but he didn't follow. She was grateful for that.

Somehow, despite the telenovela that unfolded over the last two hours, Kate returned to the office just fifteen minutes later than planned. As she scurried past the handful of young copywriters and social media managers who graced the office with their presence on a Friday, she hoped they didn't notice her pants. If it were a Monday, one of them definitely would have stopped her to chat.

Once in her small office, she closed the door and dabbed any lingering emotion from her eyes. A light knock on her office door snapped her out of her slump.

Who needs something so badly that they'd knock on my closed door on a Friday? Was Slack down or something?

"Come in," Kate said as she popped open her laptop and plastered a forced smile .

Debra popped her head in. "Hey Kate, how are you?"

Debra Rosen, the company's COO, was a short and unassuming woman who carried herself with poise. When Kate interviewed five years ago, Debra came across as pleasant and likable, and that impression stuck. She was one of Kate's favorites—direct, but fair.

Debra doesn't usually come in on Fridays, Kate thought to herself. *Odd.*

"Hey, Debra! I'm good. What are you doing here on a Friday?" she responded cheerfully, hoping to deflect any leftover tension from her run-in with Chris.

"Just some business items I needed to be here for," Debra replied vaguely, her bold lipstick stretching into a strained smile.

Again, odd.

"Let's pop into the conference room for a bit—did you see the one-thirty I put on your calendar...? Sorry for the last-minute meeting."

"No worries! I didn't see it come through—I'll be right there."

"Great, I'll meet you in there," Debra said, already heading toward the conference room, her sleek dark blonde shoulder-length hair bobbing slightly against the collar of her crisp white shirt and tailored blazer.

As she gathered her notebook and pen, she cursed herself for missing the meeting invite and racked her brain for what it could be about. Consultants and their investors had been in and out of the office lately; it was probably just an update.

Kate navigated through the mostly empty office with just a few staffers clacking away on their computers in the HR and finance corner, headphones firmly in place. No one looked up as she walked past. It was unusually empty, even for a Friday.

She went to the small conference room in the back of the office. Kate hated that particular room. It had no windows and was always stuffy. She much preferred the larger conference rooms with views.

Why are we in here? This room sucks and there is no way the others are booked. She was about to suggest a change of location when she stepped into the room and saw Danielle, the head of HR, sitting quietly at a table. In front of her was a plain manila folder. Danielle's lips pursed gravely. The air in the room felt even heavier than usual.

The scene unfolding before her jolted Kate like a lightning bolt. She had been around business long enough to know what was about to happen.

"Hi Kate," Danielle said softly. "Have a seat." Debra closed the door behind them. "I'm afraid we have to have a difficult conversation today about your future with the company, so I want to acknowledge how hard it might be to hear this news."

Fuck, so this is seriously happening.

"We want to start by saying how much we've valued your contributions to the team," Debra said empathetically. "You've done incredible work, and this decision is not a reflection of your performance."

The well-crafted talking points fed to her were so sterile and scripted, she wanted to gag. Being unceremoniously laid off from a company she had invested the last five years of her life in felt like it should be more...dramatic. Where were their pained looks? Their tears? Was she the only one that cared about loyalty and long-term relationships?

"Unfortunately, due to company-wide restructuring, your position is being eliminated," Debra continued. "This decision wasn't made lightly."

"I'm not sure I understand why my role was chosen," Kate interjected shakily. It didn't make sense. It felt like she was in some sort of weird dream.

"We'll support you however we can through the transition," Danielle responded. "We're offering a severance package, which I will walk you through in detail, and you'll also have access to career transition support."

Kate wasn't going to let them off that easily. *Career transition support*? Were they serious? She had put blood, sweat and tears into this company--she busted her ass. Chris never said her workaholic tendencies had anything to do with their marriage ending, but it probably didn't help.

"I'm sorry." She held back a scoff. "I've been here for five years and worked my ass off for this company. I've been promoted twice. I've worked nights and weekends, and sacrificed my personal life for this company." Fresh tears were threatening to come back.

Debra sighed heavily. "The decision came down to changes in business priorities. As we shift our focus, certain roles no longer align with the company's immediate needs. We've cut most of the marketing team."

She could tell by Danielle's tense facial expression that this last part was *not* the HR-approved script. Debra went out on a limb. Kate was grateful for that kindness, but she still felt numb, as though she was watching this play out from behind a two-way mirror.

It feels so personal.

"It's not personal," Debra said, reading her face like a book. "And I really fought for your severance package to be generous. I'm sorry, Kate, I know this has been a tough year for you, and this was an incredibly hard decision. But you'll land on your feet, and I am more than happy to be a reference for you, if you need it."

Kate struggled to focus, her thoughts running wild as she tried to keep her emotions in check.

Why is this average Friday the worst day of my life?

Kate's pulse rose and her stomach churned as Debra excused herself and Danielle read through the terms of her severance.

She was so lost in thought that she wasn't processing that they were paying her three weeks of salary for every year of service as severance, as well as her bonus. Which was, in truth, quite generous.

I am unemployed. Panic was setting in. What was she going to do?

In a moment of hysteria-induced absurdity—she realized she might have to scale back her future cat posse to something more modest, like six. If she wanted to spring for organic litter. On the bright side, unemployment did free her up to become a full-time cat mom more quickly. Silver linings. She almost laughed, punch-drunk, as her brain spiraled from career crisis to feline family planning.

Danielle asked her to return her laptop and pack up her things to leave today. No transitioning of projects, no farewell lunch, no emailing goodbye to colleagues. It felt cruel and unnecessary. It's not like she was going to burn the place down.

Danielle walked her back to her office and stood close by as Kate gathered the few personal effects from her office and put them in her tote, breathing deeply to keep herself calm.

Don't cry, don't cry. Wait until you get outside, don't let them see you cry. Deep breaths.

She walked quickly out of the office, trying not to make eye contact with the handful of team members casting sad glances from their desks, very much aware of the slaughter that took place that afternoon. She couldn't bear one more ounce of pity today.

It wasn't until she was standing in the elevator, her whole office shoved into her tote, riding down to the lobby for the last time, that she finally let the tears that had been building up all day flow freely.

Chapter Three

2025

"Hey! I'm on the Acela—if I cut out, blame Amtrak. So?? How was Dr. Chu? As fabulous as she looked in that magazine? Total *queen*. I'm due for some lip filler myself—might swing by and let her sprinkle a little magic before I head home. But let's have espresso martinis first, the Starbucks Roastery just launched a new flight."

That was how Nikki said hello: a quick greeting followed by whatever else was on her mind in quick succession. Nikki always came in hot, and it was one of the things that Kate loved about her. With everything in her life unraveling, she craved something solid—comfort, consistency, a lifeline. She needed her bestie.

Only five minutes prior, Kate stopped crying and collected herself enough to make the phone call as she walked toward her condo. Public crying didn't turn any heads in New York, but it wasn't like her to be openly emotional. Kate was always the dependable, stable, buttoned-up member of her family and friend group. Except for today.

Today, she was a veritable dumpster fire, in heeled boots and a pair of hospital pants. Given the way the day was going, she'd probably run into her high school ex-boyfriend.

She hoped that Nikki was close enough to meet her somewhere in person. There was so much to unpack.

"It's um...been a long day. Are you close? Can you meet up?"

Despite the simple response and chaotic train noise, Nikki immediately knew something was wrong. Best friend Spidey senses.

"What happened. I can hear it in your voice. Tell me."

"It's kind of a long story, Nik. Better over coffee. Or drinks."

"What does that mean? I'm maybe 20 minutes out.? I swear to god. I know good lawyers if they reality-TV *Botched* your beautiful face. Ugh, I knew I should have gone with you. Give me the short version."

Kate paused. "I passed out and pissed myself at the appointment, had to call Chris to come walk me back to the office. And then got laid off."

An uncharacteristically long silence followed.

"I'm cancelling my afternoon meetings. Meet me at the Ace in 20 minutes."

* * *

Kate didn't need the extra caffeine, but a caramel macchiato was too tempting to resist as she waited for Nikki at their favorite café in Midtown. The comforting aroma of freshly ground beans mingled with the sweet scent of overpriced pastries. She inhaled deeply, letting it soothe her.

She'd snagged a coveted window seat at The Stumptown Coffee Roasters nestled inside the trendy Ace Hotel. The Ace was the epitome of upscale eclectic. Music thumped from the vibey lobby, pulsing with the beat of a house DJ.

In the five minutes since she'd arrived, she'd already witnessed a parade of hipster oddities: a man sporting bedazzled cowboy boots and a white fur coat ordering a latte, a pair of Madison Avenue girls in matching Miu Miu loafers debating over pastries, and an eightyish year-old woman in a silk tiger-print blouse and pillbox hat picking up her tea. Kate's macchiato might have been overpriced, but at least the people-watching was free.

She glanced at her phone while she waited. Lindsey's text still sat at the top— ignored, unanswered.

A familiar pang of sadness bubbled up; one she'd learned to swallow over the years. She didn't have the kind of relationship where her sister was her first call in a crisis. That was the stuff of TV sisters. As kids, they'd been close—matching pajamas, whispered secrets under covers—but puberty separated them like oil and water.

Once high school hit, Lindsey became a certified beauty while Kate excelled at school. When the universe didn't hand her whatever she wanted, Lindsey simply took it, including Kate's longtime, heartbreak-level crush Nick. Without any consideration for her older sister.

Not much had changed since then. Lindsey still did Lindsey things: judging Kate for marrying a man with a kid, for not wanting kids of her own, for being a pathetic divorcee.

She looked down at the phone again.

Lindsey could stay on read.

With a dramatic flourish, the door swung open and Nikki Harper swept in, towing a roller bag behind her with an over-stuffed Goyard tote perched precariously on top.

Nikki was a walking contradiction of chaotic elegance. She was clad in a long black lace skirt, undoubtedly vintage couture, paired with a cropped band tee that probably belonged to her husband, and a Zara leather jacket Kate remembered was a sale rack score a few years ago. Her jet-black hair, with blunt bangs and rebellious purple streaks, was slightly wind-blown from her trek from Penn Station. She didn't bother removing her oversized sunglasses as she made her way over.

Nikki and Kate had been inseparable since they were thrown together as roommates at NYU freshman year. Nikki was the punk feminist crusader while Kate was preppy Abercrombie and New England modesty. The more Kate got to know Nikki, the more she reveled in her delightful unpredictability. She came to appreciate that Nikki had a way of never making her feel uncool, average, or unwanted. Today, she couldn't shake the feeling that she was all three.

Nikki spotted Kate and went straight in for a hug. She held tight as Kate breathed in deeply. It felt so good after all the drama of the day, tears started to well up in Kate's eyes.

"Ok, start from the beginning. I want to hear everything that happened," she declared, plopping down in the chair.

So Kate did, with Nikki listening intently, chiming in with "oh my god" and "holy shit" and "those assholes" as she recounted the many disasters of the day: her Botox fiasco, the shitty text from Lindsey, her emotional drive-by with Chris and losing her job.

"And that concludes my TED Talk on how to have the worst possible fucking day ever, question all your life decisions, and find yourself on the precipice of despair."

Nikki laughed. "Ok, I think we're being a *little* dramatic, and you know what that means coming from me. I can agree that today was not your day. It all sucks but if you've taught me anything, it's that we need a plan, right? Anything can be solved."

Kate sighed. "Yeah, maybe. I'm not so sure a plan or a vision board can solve this mess I'm in. I'm sorry you cancelled your meetings for my drama, both of us don't need to get fired today."

"Please. One, you didn't get fired, you were laid off. There's a huge difference. Good people get let go every day because of bullshit corporate chess and idiot executives making short-sighted decisions. Two, all of my meetings were with needy team members and schmooze-fests with execs that I'll see at dinner, anyway. I said I had an important networking opportunity come up with a Tik Tok influencer with two million followers. None of them know remotely enough about Tik Tok to ask me any questions."

"Well, thank you, Nik. It's been a really hard day." She looked down. Tears welling up again.

"Stop frowning! You're going to ruin your Botox. And you don't even have a Botox place to *go* to anymore."

Nikki always had a way of making her laugh. "That's true," Kate chuckled. "I can't imagine they want me to come back. That seems to be a recurring theme today."

"It's not that deep, boo. Everything happens for a reason. Maybe Chris *and* that lame-ass job were holding you back."

Kate arched an eyebrow. "Did you just quote a Peloton instructor and say 'everything happens for a reason' in the same breath?"

"At least I didn't say 'bless this mess'."

"Did I tell you I saw Cody Rigsby a few weeks ago?" Kate said, clapping her hands together in delight. Cody was Nikki's favorite instructor. When he was on *Dancing with the Stars*, Kate and Nikki voted for him like teenage girls trying to win Backstreet Boys tickets on the radio. "He was walking out of a taco shop in Brooklyn with some friends. He's so tall!"

"STOP IT RIGHT NOW. I'm so jealous! Did you talk to him!?"

"No, but Nik, he was *so* good looking! If I were still in college, I would have ignored all the signs and asked him out."

"You always thought those gorgeous gay boys were playing hard to get. It was kind of endearing. Remember Caleb from sophomore year?" Nikki teased.

"Oh my god, I *forgot* about him! He hadn't come out yet, and we tried hooking up. It was so awkward that we both just put our clothes back on in silence and never spoke again."

"Then we saw him in those pictures from Fire Island in a Speedo with his boyfriend!" Nikki was getting the giggles.

"He took one look at a vagina and thought, nope. That's a real quick no."

At this point, they were laughing so hard that the coffee shop patrons were taking notice.

"Not much has changed, I guess," Kate sighed as she pulled herself together. "Still trying to force doomed relationships and careers into working out, through sheer will and determination."

Nikki reached across the table to hold Kate's hand, seeing the laughter and light quickly fade from her eyes. She purposefully rested her fingers on Kate's bracelet, subtly encouraging Kate to remember what it symbolized and why Nikki had given it to her all those years ago.

"Kate. It's going to be ok. You know that, right? You're amazing. You've always *been* amazing. You shouldn't have to work so hard for everything. Boyfriends, jobs—they should have to earn *you*."

Kate felt the sting of tears again. This constant crying was becoming a real problem.

"Why am I like this?" Kate sighed, leaning back in her chair. "I keep wondering where I went wrong. I mean, some of this has to be my fault, right? I'm always planning, always trying to craft this picture-perfect life. Have I always been this way?"

Nikki tilted her head thoughtfully, her brows slightly furrowed as if she was chewing on something.

"You can disagree with *some* of that, you know..." Kate offered, filling the silence.

Nikki developed a slow, mischievous smile, her eyes lighting up with a familiar spark— the kind that usually meant she was about to suggest something outrageous like when she convinced Kate to go to Mardi Gras in 2013 and earn beaded necklaces on Bourbon Street "for the experience."

"I just... have an idea. You're going to love this." Nikki's grin widened.

Kate suddenly felt a little nervous. "Oh boy. What are you plotting?"

"I think you should take a sabbatical," Nikki declared.

Kate nearly choked on her coffee, laughing. "A sabbatical? Yeah, that's cute. Those are usually paid for by *employers*. And in case you've forgotten, I no longer have one of those."

"Didn't they give you severance, though? A decent package?"

Kate hesitated. "Well, yeah. Three weeks for every year, plus I can cash out my equity. But I should save that while I—"

"—take a sabbatical," Nikki cut in, her voice bubbling with excitement. "And spend the summer on The Cape."

Kate stared at her, letting that sink in. *The Cape? No. Not there.*

She instinctively touched the bracelet on her wrist again, tapping the silver bangle nervously. It had been over twenty years since she'd been there. And she didn't exactly part from that locale on good terms. Going back to a place with that kind of history felt like a terrible idea. Nikki continued, fully in the throes of her pitch.

"Think about it! Sun, ocean air, cute locals. You can slow down and get some clarity. What better place than the Cape to, you know, *find yourself* or whatever?"

Kate shook her head slowly. "You're insane."

"It was a million years ago. You're only remembering how it *ended*. But you're forgetting how *incredible* most of that summer was."

Predictably, Nikki knew exactly what Kate was thinking.

"For eight weeks, we had the time of our lives—busting our asses serving rich vacationers and then blowing our tips at The Squire that same night. Bonfires on the beach, dancing, singing at the top of our lungs…"

Kate couldn't help but smile. Those were great memories. She could see them playing out in her mind, could almost smell the mix of Stoli Raspberry and Sprite, mingled with the scent of the stale, salty air.

Nikki knew she had her right in the nostalgia zone. "Kate, I've never seen you so carefree, so alive and living in the moment. You were light-hearted, and you were happy. There was no plan—just you, being you."

"I was 22 years old, Nik. And blindly in love. It wasn't real life." Saying "in love" conjured up an image she hadn't thought about in many years. Of *him*.

"No, you were living your *best* life. You've been through a lot lately. Don't you think it's time to take a break? To find out who you are, without Chris? Without the job? Without fuck-ing *Debra*?"

Kate laughed at that. *Fucking Debra.*

"There's something magical about the Cape, don't you think?" The way Nikki said it, it was as if she was already on the sandy shores, a glass of wine in hand.

Kate wasn't sold yet. Not having a job or a new life plan was terrifying her. She should be spending her time off getting back on track. "Maybe you're romanticizing it because you have your own house there now, big shot."

Nikki scoffed, waving her hand. "Like you've even been there! Don't think I don't realize you've always made excuses—*lame* excuses by the way—not to visit. Besides, our house in Dennis is *not* exactly the retreat you'd be looking for. With my kids running around and Jay's family's lack of personal boundaries...that's not what I have in mind."

"Ok." Kate humored Nikki. "What vibe *did* you have in mind for this unemployed adventure of mine?"

But Kate already knew the answer. Nikki leaned forward, her voice dropping like she was about to share a secret.

"Maybe the universe is trying to tell you to reclaim what you lost that summer in 2002. Sometimes, to move forward, you need to go back. You need to embrace the Summer of Kate. In Chatham mother-effing Massachusetts."

Kate was unable to come up with a response. Nikki really expected her to blow through her severance, while unemployed, by going to a place she'd been actively avoiding for twenty years. This was a crazy idea—even for Nikki. Worse than the time she lured her to Tampa for a "beach getaway" that turned out to be a mission to seduce single Red Sox players at spring training.

Nikki took the silence as a signal to go in for the close.

"A little cottage by the water, fresh lobster rolls every afternoon, sunsets that make you forget why you were stressed in the first place. You could journal, take up painting... or just day-drink all that overpriced wine you like. Your only job would be to revel in your beauty and fabulousness. And find a hot, sexy tourist to take as a casual lover."

Kate laughed at the unhinged picture Nikki was painting. "Oh, is that all?"

"You've got the severance package. The drag of job hunting and interviewing will be right here waiting for you when you get back. Why not spend the summer living like the main character of your own rom-com?"

It was illogical and reckless to even consider this. Right?

Nikki smiled. "Maybe a little mystery, too? Who knows what—or who—you'll discover." Nikki paused for dramatic effect.

Kate was about to dig into the impracticality of the whole proposal when she heard a slow clap behind her. She turned to see four college-aged girls in front of iced matchas, grinning widely, clearly having overheard their entire conversation.

"YAS QUEEN! Your friend just *slayed* that pep talk," gushed a petite blonde in a crop top and flared jeans. "You totally have to go to Chatham after that! I don't know where that is, but it sounds dreamy. I'm *here* for the Summer of Kate!"

Her friends nodded vigorously, clapping in agreement.

Nikki gave a seated bow, and Kate nodded in their direction, amused. More clapping and squealing followed from the matcha girl gang.

Kate promised Nikki she'd think about it, mostly just to get her to drop it.

They slipped into easy conversation, the way they always did. Nikki pivoted to offering her wildly impractical career ideas—traveling masseuse? absolutely not—and Kate felt herself relaxing for the first time all day.

The idea of taking the summer off lingered in the back of her mind. There was something seductive about it.

But *Chatham*? Yes, it was beautiful. Magical, even. But it was also a vault of memories she'd spent years trying to lock away.

Later that night, back in her king-sized bed that felt entirely too big for one person, sleep remained elusive. She tossed and turned in the empty, cool sheets, her mind refusing to quiet. When sleep finally claimed her, it did so in a whirl-wind—her past crashing in like a storm, vivid and unrelent-ing.

The salty tang of the ocean filled her senses as she lay back in the truck bed, her body alive with the heat of the summer night.

The rhythmic music of the ocean echoed in her ears, mingling with the soft hum of his heavy breathing. She couldn't quite see his face, the moonlight catching only the edge of his jawline and the glint in his eyes. She wasn't sure who he was, yet she knew him.

His touch felt like something she had always known—like fire on her skin, daring her to let go of everything. His hands slid up her thighs as he hungrily kissed her, pressing his naked body on top of hers. He was hard against her, yearning to be inside her, teasing her by being so close. She wanted him there; she needed it. She was naked too, she realized. Her heart raced from his touch and the thrill of being so vulnerable out in the open.

"What if someone sees us?" she whispered, her breath hitching as his lips brushed the pulse point on her neck. He neared ever closer to being where she wanted him to be.

"It's only us," he murmured, his voice deep and smooth, like the ocean itself. " Let me take you, Kate. Let me be inside you. I need you, right now."

The wildness in his tone, the command in his words, sent a rush through her. She arched into him, her fingers digging into his shoulders as the night tightened around them and he plunged deep into her. The world beyond the two of them fell away—just the heat of his body, the salt on his lips, and the thunder of the waves matching his thrusts. She was untethered, unbound, giving in to a hunger that felt both unexpected and familiar.

The wind picked up, matching their frenzied movement. Her body tensed as she reached the peak, gasping his name, though she wasn't even sure she knew it. As the sensation crested a roar louder than the waves filled her ears.

A freezing torrent of water crashed over her, and the warmth of his body was ripped away. She flailed, clawed for the surface, for him. The moonlight above rippled and disappeared as she sank deeper, the salt stinging her eyes.

"Where are you?" she tried to scream, but the water swallowed her voice. Her limbs felt heavy, her lungs burned, and panic surged through her chest. She searched for him—his touch, his voice, anything—but he was gone. All that remained was the vast, endless sea pulling her under. And the faint melody of a song, just audible but there all along.

Anywhere you go. I'll follow you down...

Kate jolted awake, her body trembling and soaked in sweat. Her chest heaved as fragments of her dream clung to her—sultry, vivid, and unsettling. The heat lingered, mingling with the cool streaks of tears that traced down her flushed cheeks. She pressed a hand to her face, overwhelmed by the intensity, unsure which emotion—desire or despair—had shaken her most.

Chapter Four

2025

Kate stood in the middle of her bedroom, absently bopping to the beat of her 90s throwback playlist. Lately, her musical taste had taken a sharp turn. She now found herself drawn to angsty, sassy, melodramatic R&B tracks. And for that, there was no one better than Monica.

Despite spending $450 just yesterday to have her chestnut hair balayaged with golden blonde streaks—a bargain for New York—Kate had it piled into a messy top bun, with stray wisps clinging to her neck. Tonight called for comfort: black leggings and her ancient NYU sweatshirt, sleeves frayed with holes from years of wear. It was, she decided, the official uniform of her unemployment.

Her Pad Thai sat half-eaten in its original to-go container on her nightstand. It paired well with her half-packed suitcase sprawled open on the bed, clothes and bathing suits thrown around in every possible direction. She stared at it with mild bewilderment, glass of crisp Sancerre white in hand, wondering how in the world Nikki convinced her to spend an entire summer in Cape Cod.

Three weeks had passed since the layoff. Despite Nikki's constant pep talks about not rushing into "fix-it" mode, Kate jumped straight into action with a to-do list.

1. Update resume.
2. Revise a new "unemployed" budget.
3. Call parents and let them know what happened. Let them tell Lindsey.
4. Book Chatham Bars Inn.
5. Pack for the cape.
6. Create a new life plan with a perfect man and even more perfect job.

The only things left were the last two.

"This is impulsive and irresponsible," Kate muttered, reaching for a sundress only to toss it aside again.

Sydney sat cross-legged on the floor, scrolling through Instagram, wine in hand.

"Stop stressing," she piped up. "It'll be an adventure. And if anyone deserves a break, it's you. What is this song, by the way? Is this Whitney Houston or something?"

Kate laughed. "No, it's Monica. From when I was in middle school, I think."

"Hm, it's good. I'll have to add it to my running list. Hey, if you're not going to eat the rest of that Pad Thai, I'm starving."

"It's all yours. Must be nice to have your metabolism," Kate joked, passing over the cold takeout.

Sydney arrived earlier that afternoon for a girl's night with Kate before spending the rest of the weekend with Chris. She'd tried to come immediately after Kate told her about being laid off, but Kate insisted she finish her classes before semester break. When Sydney finally walked through the door, Kate embraced her tightly. She missed her stepdaughter more than she realized.

Sydney's perfectly manicured fingers scrolled through the feed on her phone, occasionally pausing to eat a forkful of noodles and sip her white wine. She somehow looked put together and almost glam in a pair of old boyfriend-cut jeans and a MassArt t-shirt, her blonde hair falling in soft waves. Petite and charismatic, Sydney was a thriving fashion design major but also a self-described book worm. She had the carefree spirit of young girl with the thoughtful wisdom of someone twice her age.

Sydney paused her scrolling and glanced up, her blue eyes sparkling mischievously.

"Also, just a minor suggestion. Even though the b-tox has given you the youthful face of a middle-schooler, maybe it's time to retire the khaki shorts and wear something a little more...current?" she suggested with an impish grin, motioning to what Kate was about to drop into the suitcase.

Kate gave Sydney a side-eye. "I'll have you know those shorts are perfectly acceptable if I pair them with a black body suit and my Hermès sandals. It's city chic."

Sydney shook her head. "Khaki shorts are never chic. But either way, you're not going to be in the city anymore. You don't want to look like Carrie Bradshaw stumbled into a clam bake. You need to think less Upper *East* Side, more upper *beach* side."

Kate sighed. "Now you're just making me feel... old. But thanks for using a TV reference from my era and not some Gossip Girl character I don't know."

"Gossip Girl came out when I was like four."

"Cool. Thanks."

Sydney sauntered over to the closet with confidence, rifling through the hangers until she triumphantly pulled out a long, white linen maxi dress. "This," she declared, holding it up like a prized possession, "has the Cape written all over it. Tousled beach waves, sun-kissed skin, gold hoops, and an Aperol Spritz in hand. Kate Walker, Goddess of the Cape!"

She twirled theatrically with the dress, making a playful flourish as if presenting it on a runway.

Kate chuckled, taking another sip of her wine, but the laugh felt more like a deflection. "The last time I was a 'beach goddess' was, like, 20 years ago. I'll try to channel that memory while I rummage through my decidedly 'uncool' closet."

Sydney raised an eyebrow, tossing the dress onto the bed with a curious tilt of her head.

"Beep, beep. Back up. Where were you 20 years ago? Did you have some hot, steamy summer fling when you were my age? Come on, you can't drop a line like that and not spill."

Kate's fingers hovered awkwardly over a pair of sandals as the remnants of her recent dream flittered on the outskirts of her memory. She hadn't meant to invite this conversation. The summer of 2002 felt like another life—an intoxicating blur of passion, reckless decisions, earth-shattering sex, heartbreak, and betrayal. She'd buried those memories far from the safe, stable life she'd carefully constructed.

"Nothing that dramatic," Kate finally said as she dropped the sandals in. "It was just a summer trip to the Cape with Nikki before my senior year. You know, the usual."

Sydney wasn't buying it. "Did something *happen* on the Cape? Is that why you don't want to go? Did you fall in love with a mysterious local boy, and when he tried to get too handsy, you accidentally killed him and fed him to the sharks?!"

"You listen to entirely too many true crime podcasts."

"You didn't say no."

Kate shook her head in amusement, but Sydney's curious gaze stayed on her. Kate fidgeted with her bracelet. Then she sighed in resignation, sinking onto the bed. She was going to have to give her something. Sydney would keep pressing until she got something satisfactorily juicy.

"I fell in love that summer for the first time. Head over heels, butterflies-in-your-stomach love. I thought I found my soulmate, but I was wrong."

Sydney's eyes widened, clearly hooked. "Wait, someone broke *your* heart? No way. I've seen pictures of you in your twenties—you were hot."

Kate scoffed, raising an eyebrow. "I guess I'll accept that very backhanded compliment."

Sydney backtracked. "No, that's not what I meant! You look amazing now, too, obviously. You know what I mean!"

"Thanks, but yeah. Tale as old as time. I was a stupid, naïve girl," Kate said, her voice softening. She didn't truly believe what happened to her was your garden variety summer romance. It felt different, at least to her. But it wasn't something she wanted to dive into with her stepdaughter.

"After that summer, I realized that taking risks wasn't for me. I started choosing more carefully. I looked for men who knew what they wanted. It's fun to go out of your comfort zone for a while, but it's not real. I think that's part of what drew me to your dad."

As soon as the words left her mouth, Kate immediately regretted mentioning Chris. Since January, she meticulously steered clear of any divorce talk or relationship dynamics with Sydney's dad. She and Chris agreed from the start: everything would be amicable for Sydney; their shared goal was making sure she felt loved and secure through the whole ordeal. But somehow, the words slipped out.

Sydney frowned and swirled her wine thoughtfully. "Yeah, but...that didn't make you happy either. So why is one kind of love better than the other?"

It was hard for her not to correct Sydney and tell her it was *him* who wasn't happy. But this was edging into territory Kate didn't want to be in.

"Your dad is wonderful. He's thoughtful, he's kind. I'll always love him. But maybe I never let myself freely love, you know? Because of that heartbreak. Sort of like you and Michael, right?"

Changing the subject to Sydney's first long-term boyfriend and real heartbreak navigated the conversation out of the dangerous waters she was wading into.

"Ugh, *Michael*." Sydney groaned, rolling her eyes. "I feel you. It's so hard to be vulnerable again after something like that. I'm *just* starting to put myself back out there, and it's been, what, 18 months? It's taken a lot of roommate therapy... and wine."

Kate nodded appreciatively as she sorted through her mismatched bikinis and tasteful one-pieces.

"Seriously, though," Sydney said, leaning back against the dresser. "I just want you—and Dad—to be happy. Even if it's not with each other."

Kate's heart swelled at the tenderness in Sydney's voice. The maturity of the comment hit her harder than expected. But before the moment could grow too emotional, Sydney lightened the mood by bringing it back to the matter at hand.

"So, I think you should shake things up. You are NOT old. You can still be wild and adventurous. At least for a summer."

Sydney stepped closer and nudged Kate, eyeing the one-piece bathing suit Kate had just pulled from the pile. "And *that* mom-suit does not look ready for an adventure, does it? Be honest with yourself."

Kate laughed, tossing the swimsuit aside with a dramatic flair. "Fine, fine, you're right. The one-pieces will stay behind." She grabbed two bikinis, holding them up as if they were her last stand. "These will have to do. What about you? You're interning this summer when you go back to Boston, right?"

Sydney's face lit up. "Yes! I'm interning for the designer I was telling you about; her company is called JJ Design. She's kind of blowing up in Boston, and a bunch of Hollywood 'it' girls have been buying her stuff in Nantucket and the Cape. It's super exciting. Two of my professors think she's the next big thing."

"That's so cool! It's going to be a great summer for you." Kate beamed. Sydney had always been the kind of girl who could take the world by storm—confident, driven, everything Kate hoped she'd be when she first met her at eight years old.

Sydney grinned and nodded toward Kate's still unfinished suitcase. "Alright, let's get back to you. Forget the whole awkward stepmom thing and the fact that you were married to my dad. What are you going to wear to catch the eye of some rugged Cape Cod lobsterman who'll sweep you off your feet?"

Kate let out a full laugh, shaking her head. "A lobsterman? Seriously? What, am I going back in time to the early 1900s?"

Sydney was undeterred. "Hey, don't knock it! If there are lobsters, there's gotta be lobstermen. And I'm willing to bet at least one of them is rugged, mysterious, and surprisingly good-looking—in a weathered, salty Yellowstone kind of way."

She rifled through Kate's pile of discarded clothes before pulling out a pair of cut-off denim shorts and a silk tank top. "Here, what about this? Sexy, but effortless. You can wear it to the beach, to dinner, or maybe to a bonfire where the lobsterman has cleaned up nicely and hands you a cold beer."

Kate smirked, taking the outfit. "This sounds like the plot of a cheesy Hallmark movie. And let me remind you, the

Cape isn't teeming with rugged seafarers. It's full of trust-fund mama's boys, lounging in their Lacoste polos, living off their parents' money. Or hedge fund finance bros in their forties who'd rather be dating someone *your* age."

"That is not main character energy, Kate," Sydney protested, crossing her arms. "You never know. Doesn't have to be Mr. Right. Could be Mr. Right now?"

"Sydney! I know what you're suggesting and it's giving me the ick!" Kate laughed, though she tucked the shorts and tank into the suitcase anyway. "Any guy I bump into will be when I'm tripping over a sand dune, knowing my luck. I should probably pack something more age-appropriate, too."

Sydney nodded sagely, as if imparting the wisdom of generations. "Definitely. A few flowy dresses will help you blend in with the old-money crowd. That's what I'd wear for patio day-drinking with an ocean view. And don't forget some cute sweaters for when it gets chilly at night."

The mention of day-drinking piqued her interest in a way that made her realize she might—just might—be looking forward to this summer after all. Day-drinking on a patio, gazing out at the ocean, with zero obligations? That was something she hadn't been able to do in... well, ever. Maybe unemployment had a few perks.

"Good call," Kate said, grabbing a cozy cardigan and tossing it onto the growing pile in the suitcase. "I think I can handle some daytime cocktails, preferably with a view. It's mandatory for a summer of 'finding myself,' right?"

"Exactly. Here's to you!" Sydney said, raising her glass in a mock toast.

Maybe Kate's life wasn't going according to the plan she'd carefully crafted over the years. But as she looked at Sydney, as they laughed and joked over wine, she started to wonder if maybe there was something to be said for throwing out the plan entirely. She was becoming less convinced that it did her any good in the end, anyway.

"Ok," Kate said, zipping up her suitcase with finality. "Looks like I'm doing this. A summer on the Cape. But if I come back with any crazy stories about beach bonfires with lobstermen, I'm holding you responsible."

Sydney grinned. "I'll be disappointed if you don't. Now, let's open another bottle of wine to celebrate. Nikki doesn't care if you're hungover, she'll pull over for you. Let's get the summer started now!"

Chapter Five

2025

K ate stepped out of her apartment building, squinting in
the early-morning sunlight, her head pounding lightly
from one too many glasses of wine. She quickly popped
down her oversized shades from atop her head and made a
silent prayer for the Advil to kick in. Late nights and wine reminded her she was no longer as young as the twenty-two-
year-old fast asleep, snoring in her bed.

The morning air was brisk for June and the quiet of Manhattan on a weekend morning was punctuated only by the
occasional honk and the hum of traffic in the distance. She
looked at her watch – 8:45 a.m. Nikki claimed she would be
there at 9:00 a.m. to pick her up, but Nikki was rarely on
time. Sometimes 30 minutes early, sometimes 45 minutes
late. Never on time. Kate had long ago accepted this as one
of Nikki's most annoying personality traits.

She glanced down the street impatiently. She just pulled her
phone out to check if Nikki had texted when she spotted

Chris walking up the block, carrying a brown paper bag in one hand and two coffees in the other.

What the hell...?

Chris looked a little startled when he saw her standing there.

"Oh, uh, hey...good morning," he said stammered, as if somehow confused about how he ended up outside their old apartment.

"Hi?" It came out as more of a question than a greeting. Information was processing at a snail's pace, even slower than usual for a hangover. Chris stood in front of her, for reasons unknown.

"Sorry," he said, looking down awkwardly. "Figured you'd still be asleep after last night with Syd. I was just going to leave this on your doorstep and text you both that it was there in case you needed it." He sheepishly held up the bag and a coffee tray.

Of course: classic, irritatingly thoughtful Chris. A fun little gut-punch reminder of what her life had once been like. She tucked a loose strand of hair behind her ear, trying to keep her expression neutral and her nausea at bay. "Well, I'm up," she said, forcing a tight smile. "We didn't go too crazy. Is that...Broad Nosh?"

Chris nodded. "Yep. Bagels and coffee. Hangover rescue kit. Sydney told me she was coming over, and I figured it might have been a late night."

Kate softened a bit. "That's nice of you," she said, though her guard was still up. "I was just waiting for Nikki. We're heading to the Cape today."

Chris shifted, looking momentarily surprised, but he smiled through it. "Oh. Vacation? Are you staying with Nikki and Jay?"

Kate was surprised Sydney hadn't mentioned her 'sabbatical' to him. She took a little pride in that. Girl code.

"Yeah, for the summer. Just need some space. Like a reset." She hesitated, not wanting it to sound too much like an 'Eat, Pray, Love' cliché. "I'm going to work on starting my own consulting business while I'm up there," she added. It was a little white lie. She *could* start her own business. Theoretically.

Chris's brow lifted in curiosity. "That's great. A fresh start, right?" His tone was careful. "I'm sorry you were let go, by the way. Syd told me; I hope that's ok. She was just worried. Debra should have fought harder to keep you. You were always too good for that place. Please—let me know if you need anything."

Kate's stomach tightened, but she forced a casual shrug. "I'm fine." Another white lie. Having a fully paid condo did make her expenses minimal. Plus, she had her savings even beyond the severance. Other things might not be fine, but she was financially stable. She didn't want to "need" anything else from him.

Come on, Nikki, please don't be late.

They exchanged a look, brief but charged with unspoken words. Sensing the tension, Chris chuckled, trying to lighten the moment. "Well, since I've already managed to come off as a total creeper, I could sneak upstairs and leave this on the counter like a bagel ninja. Sydney's probably still asleep?"

"Sure," Kate replied, relieved by the shift. "Yeah, she's out cold. Go ahead, you have the key."

Chris hesitated, his eyes lifting again to meet hers. "So—you're really going to the Cape for the *whole* summer?" He blinked, brow lifting. It was a clear break from what he expected of her—and that gave her a sense of quiet satisfaction.

"Yep, the whole summer," she confirmed, purposefully not sharing more.

Before Chris could ask any more questions, the low rumble of an engine cut through the morning quiet. Nikki rounded the corner in a black Audi convertible, top down despite the early chill, and expertly navigated into an open spot on the street.

Her eyebrows lifted in a half-surprised, half-amused expression. She stepped out, Chanel sunglasses perched on her head, her gaze flipping from Kate to Chris and back again.

"Well, now it's a party!" she ribbed with a smirk. "It would appear I am interrupting a meet-cute, but I think Kate's too smart to fall for that shit twice, so..."

Nikki's jabs always had a way of sounding casual and pointed at the same time, especially when defending Kate.

Chris expertly ignored the barb. He'd always gotten along well with Nikki. "Hey, Nik," he said, extending the bag and coffee tray. "Why don't you take these? I'll grab food with Sydney later. When sleeping beauty awakes from her wine-induced slumber."

Nikki grinned, snatching the coffees and bagel bag without hesitation or pleasantries. "I never turn down Broad Nosh. I'm glad you finally realized the world of finance is painfully boring. An Uber Eats side hustle is far more interesting."

"I'd appreciate a five-star review," Chris shot back.

"Not a chance," Nikki quipped.

The tightness in Kate's shoulders eased with Nikki there, bringing down the likelihood of another emotion-charged interaction with Chris.

"Anyway, thanks," Nikki said, grabbing the other coffee. "We've got to jet."

Chris nodded, his expression lingering with something unsaid. A few months ago, Kate would have pulled on that thread, wanting to know if it led to regret or possible reconciliation. But Nikki was right. It was time to go.

He turned to leave, walking in the opposite direction. Almost symbolically. "Safe travels," he called over his shoulder.

Nikki hopped back into the driver's seat, positioning the breakfast items and straightening her French-style drop waist midi tank dress. She peeled off her light-wash denim jacket adorned with colorful band patches, threw it into the back and shot Kate a sly smile. "So, is this what divorce looks like now? Bagel delivery on the weekend?"

Kate hoisted two weekender bags and an oversized suitcase into the backseat. "Better than the alternative, I guess. And really, Nikki? An Audi for a five-hour drive? Isn't that a little... extra?"

"Extra would've been the red Maserati," she said with a wink. "But someone beat me to it." She untied the floral Gucci scarf from her ponytail and draped it over her head like a vintage movie star—Grace Kelly, if Grace Kelly had a constellation of arm tattoos and a nose ring.

"Get in, chica," Nikki announced, reapplying her bright red lipstick. "The wind in your hair will do you some good."

Kate slid into the passenger seat, letting the cool leather soothe her hangover. She was thankful she opted for a comfortable t-shirt dress and Ferragamo flats. They pulled away and she slid her sunglasses back down, relaxing into the seat. The convertible purred back to life, and she closed her eyes for a moment as they pulled away from the curb.

Once they were cruising through the city streets, Kate took a sip of the latte Chris got her. Exactly, and annoyingly, just the way she liked it. "I salvaged what I could of your goopy bagel," Kate said, passing the warm, foil-wrapped mess to

Nikki as she navigated onto the highway, finally escaping the city.

"I want you to know," Nikki started while juggling the bagel, "While I'm looking forward to spending beach time with Jay and the girls, I will be popping in to see you. Day visits, night visits... I'm going to need a break from the family and will drive up to see what kind of trouble you're getting into in Chatham."

"Thank God," Kate shot back with a grin. "You can save me from drowning in a sea of Sperry-wearing middle-aged men." Kate leaned back as the Manhattan skyline slowly disappeared behind them.

"Make sure they're buying your drinks, babe," Nikki added. "You're unemployed."

"Oh, shit, you're right." Kate's voice dripped with mock seriousness as she glanced over at Nikki. "Turn the car around; this is a terrible idea."

"No, no, I'm kidding," Nikki chuckled. "By the way, didn't your Aunt Jan buy a vacation home in Chatham? Not that you don't deserve to stay in a five-star hotel for the summer, but why aren't you staying there?"

About a decade ago, Kate's wealthy Aunt Jan bought a charming little house in Chatham. At first, the whole family buzzed with the excitement of access to even a little piece of the famed Cape Cod summer. That excitement quickly faded when Aunt Jan began running the guest list like she was running the SoHo House. Kate decided early on to steer clear. Lindsey, of course, had no such qualms.

"Funny you should mention that. Her majesty of Wellesley did allow our family to stay in the house this year. In fact, the next two weeks. Guess who claimed them."

Nikki grimaced. "Oh, God. That's right! You mentioned she sent a passive aggressive text. Your sister did *not* factor into my summer fantasy for you." Nikki was thankfully impervious to Lindsey's calculated charm.

"I know," Kate sighed. "It's not ideal for my inner peace. But she's better when she's with Adam and the kids."

After the text, Kate's mom reached out to mitigate any hard feelings. She went on about Lindsey being more deserving of the house to "make memories" with the kids. The overt favoritism and excuse-making on behalf of her sister was standard for her mother. Per usual, Kate simply agreed and moved on because it wasn't worth the fight. It was always Lindsey's turn for everything.

"She's been texting and checking in more since everything happened," Kate added, more to convince herself.

"Sure. Or maybe she's just reveling in your misfortune. Isn't this the same Lindsey who stole your crush in high school? Who constantly tries to one-up you? She's basically Helen from *Bridesmaids*, right down to the annoyingly perfect hair and deep brown doe eyes. She is insufferable."

Where's the lie though, Kate thought. Lindsey was the popular, athletic, social butterfly. Kate was just "Lindsey's older sister"—studious, uncoordinated, forever orbiting the cool crowd. Everything came easy to Lindsey, though she worked hard to keep up appearances. Which made her competitive. And, let's be honest, a little manipulative. So yeah. Pretty much a Helen.

"Welp. Thanks for that pep talk, Nik," she said, sinking back into the seat.

Having Lindsey in the same small Cape town would most certainly complicate things. She could already predict the conversations—Lindsey would bring up Chris, with that slightly condescending, "How are you doing since...?" voice. She wasn't exactly subtle about her opinion that Kate let a "good catch" slip away despite knowing next to nothing about why things really ended. She hadn't even asked.

The East River faded behind them as the bustling cityscape gave way to the tree-lined roads of Connecticut. Quaint New England towns, dotted with Colonial-style houses and charming little shops, flashed past them like scenes from a postcard. As the wind whipped through the car, Kate inhaled slowly and felt some tension drift away. It was as if each passing mile was carrying her further from problems she could hit pause on for the next eight weeks.

Nikki reached for her phone and connected it to the car's Bluetooth, a sly grin spreading across her face.

"I made us a little something special for the ride," she announced. "Please sit back, relax, and prepare to be transported to 2002—a time when we ruled the Cape like a couple of overconfident twenty-somethings with bad highlights and questionable life plans."

Kate shot her a sideways glance, but before she could ask any questions, it was too late. The first track was already blasting through the speakers.

"Oh my god, I forgot about this song!" Kate squealed with delight, her eyes lighting up with recognition. "Michelle Branch! Yes!"

Nikki jumped right in, belting out the lyrics with gusto and Kate quickly joined in. "So lonely inside, so busy out there. And all you wanted was somebody who cay-ee-yay-airs." Getting the "cares" with all four syllables was important.

It was impossible to reconcile Nikki's love for bubblegum pop. But that was Nikki. As if on cue, the next song took a sharp turn. The acoustic guitar twangs and velvety sounds of Alanis Morrissette speaking nothing but the god's honest truth. Not even a hangover could stop Kate from belting out the chorus.

We'll fast forward to a few years later
And no one knows except the both of us
And I have honored your request for silence
And you've washed your hands clean of this

"Alanis knew what was *up*," Nikki declared.

"She was a prophet," Kate agreed solemnly. The lyrics of 'Hands Clean' made more sense today than they ever did in their early twenties.

Track after track pulsed out of the Audi's speakers. Missy Elliott rounded out by Justin Timberlake, each transporting Kate to a time tucked away in the back of her memories. Nikki half-twerked in her car seat and Kate did a full body rolls, her hands firmly in the air. Other drivers gawked from their vehicles at two grown women looking like they were auditioning for MTV's *The Grind*. Neither of them cared.

"When I hear some of these songs, I swear I can taste Smirnoff Ice in the back of my throat. I need Tums just thinking about it," Kate laughed, mimicking a gag reflex.

"I bet if you close your eyes," Nikki added with a mischievous smirk, "you can almost feel some guy trying to grind up behind you. Such a *magical* time."

"Seriously," Kate giggled. "It was like an X-rated dance floor gauntlet. The number of semis that we endured on the dance floor was obscene."

"I know, right?" Nikki shuddered dramatically. "But, damn, it was fun back then. Speaking of fun, though," she said, with a mischievous gleam in her eye. "I'm assuming it's been since, what, January since you've had any action? With an actual person, I mean. Are you *dying*?"

Kate laughed, shaking her head. "Wow, that was a hard pivot." Nikki was always the more brazen of the two when it came to talking about sex, and her curiosity was relentless.

"It's been a minute," Kate admitted, though she still carried the vivid imagery from that spicy yet dramatic dream she had weeks ago. "Honestly, I just haven't even thought about it. It's kind of hard to feel sexy when you're emotionally drained from your husband leaving you unexpectedly. Kind of a buzzkill."

"Haven't thought about it *yet,*" Nikki emphasized, grabbing hold of one word and ignoring the rest. "Look, most of the time, all I want to do is chill out in sweats, binge on Netflix, and avoid all human contact, including Jay. But you know, the second you feel like you *can't* get it, that's when you start wanting it more. Forbidden fruit syndrome or whatever."

Kate considered how it might feel to kiss someone for the first time again. The newness, the rapid build of tension, the thrill of anticipation--that pulse-rising moment where anything can happen. That rush where you're so ravenous for each other you don't care who's watching. A faint tingle rippled down her body as if some dormant part of her was beginning to stir. Maybe she was ready for something. She wasn't exactly sure what.

"Yeah," Kate said, exhaling slowly. "I'm sure I'll get there eventually."

"Well, you'd better," Nikki teased. "Because I was secretly hoping for a full-blown Bridgerton fantasy on the Cape, so don't let me down."

Kate grinned. "Oh, I'll keep my eyes peeled for men in pantaloons and puffy shirts, just for you."

"Good. And if you see one with a British accent, even better. I don't care if it's fake," Nikki said, laughing. "We're not here for authenticity. We're here for the fantasy."

Kate just shook her head, still smiling.

Before they knew it, they were zooming past Rhode Island and nearing the Massachusetts border. The air was starting to feel different—lighter, tinged with the faint saltiness of the ocean. They made a quick pit stop in Providence for Dunkin' iced coffee, snacks, and a bathroom break. Once back on the road, the Cape Cod signs began to pop up, and it was as if the playlist knew just how to keep the energy alive.

Kate's eyes widened. "Oh man! This is Yellow Card, right?"

"I should slap you for that. Jimmy Eat World!" Nikki corrected. "We danced to that song for a whole summer!"

"Speaking of, remember that bonfire on the beach? That guy from New Jersey—Mikey, or something like that? He pulled out his guitar and tried to play John Mayer for you?"

"How could I forget Jersey Mike? He was *so* determined to impress me—and he was terrible at the guitar." Nikki shook her head. "Honestly, that whole summer was one big montage of beach clichés. Clambakes, long bike rides, jumping off docks, eating way too much ice cream, getting sunburned because we refused to wear anything higher than SPF 8."

Kate winced knowingly. Over the years, they'd both come to view their disregard for proper skincare—and the benefits of daily SPF 50—as one of the biggest mistakes of their youth.

"And don't forget the time we tried sneaking onto that private beach," Nikki added. "We got caught by that cranky old lady in the gigantic sunhat. What was her name? She used to come into the restaurant all the time."

"Mrs. Winslow!" Kate chuckled. "That woman was relentless. She'd show up at the restaurant every Friday at exactly 5:00 p.m. to order three white zinfandels with no recollection of who we were. She's lucky we never spit in that cheap wine."

"Would've been an improvement."

Kate leaned back, a fond smile playing on her lips. "With the number of times she sent back her 'chicken-fried steak,' Matt would've looked the other way if we'd done it, for sure."

Kate almost didn't realize what she'd said, but then she saw Nikki's curious look out of the corner of her eye. Here she was, worried that Nikki would bring up Matt as road trip therapy. But nope. Kate was opening the door all by herself. Before she could shut it, a new song drifted through the speakers.

Kate recognized the opening guitar riff instantly, and her heart skipped a beat. Her fingers tightened around her iced coffee. It wasn't even a song from 2002. What was it doing on this playlist?

Nikki glanced sideways at Kate, then fixed her gaze back on the road.

Kate's voice came out softer, almost lost in the wind rushing through the car. "Did you really have to include *this* one?"

Nikki shifted in her seat, a quiet determination in her expression. "I just want you to find your light again. Maybe revisiting the past will help. For the length of a song?"

Kate didn't answer. The familiar notes tugged at the edges of her memory, drawing her back to that night. She closed her eyes, and it was as if she could see his face again, the way his gaze locked onto hers like she was the only girl in the crowded, noisy bar. That look made her feel so alive, so seen. The kind of intensity she hadn't felt in a long time.

And in that moment, she was transported back to 2002. Before the heartbreak, before the embarrassment. Before she realized she had misread everything.

Chapter Six

2002

"**I**'m over this song," Kate said, reaching over to hit the arrow button on the CD console.

"What? You're too cool for *What's Luv*?" Nikki protested, but with zero conviction. They had played that Fat Joe song to death—at every party, pregame, and road trip over the last four months.

Kate cruised down Massachusetts Route 3 in the silver Mazda she and Nikki had rented for the summer, the Sagamore Bridge rising ahead like a gateway to their upcoming summer adventure. They hadn't splurged for A/C—college budgeting priorities—so the windows were down, and the warm Cape breeze whipped their hair into tangles and knots.

Kate reached out to skip to the next track on the Summer 2002 mix CD Nikki had burned for the drive, the Sharpie-labeled jewel case wedged between the seats.

"Oh! Don't skip. I love this band," Nikki gushed, leaning over to crank the volume as a song Kate didn't recognize blasted through the speakers.

Fell in love with a girl
I fell in love once and almost completely

"It's The White Stripes," Nikki declared. "They're new and *so* fresh. The song is just getting radio play now, but I found it on LimeWire, like, months ago."

Of course she did. The punky chaotic song paired perfectly with Nikki's latest aesthetic: sexy skater-girl with a splash of Avril Lavigne and a hint of Mischa Barton. Kate tried to tell her it was far too hot for the low-rise jeans she was wearing, even though she paired it with a cropped white tank that showed off her belly button ring. But Nikki did exactly what she wanted, always.

Kate looked down at her own outfit—a short denim skirt and two layered pastel tanks, straight out of an Abercrombie catalog with a puka shell necklace poking out. She didn't mind that she dressed like every other girl their age. Standing out wasn't really her thing.

Nikki belted out the lyrics with surprising accuracy for a new single. She wondered how many times her roommate had already listened to this song. It was kind of weird. Catchy, though.

"We're making pretty good time," Nikki said, glancing at the clock on the dashboard. "I bet we'll be settled in before sunset and still have time to head out for a drink. Just don't forget we're not in New York—around here, things shut down early. The Squire closes at like, 1 a.m., and that's considered late for the Cape."

"Yeah, but you said there'll be bonfires and beach parties," Kate reminded her. "I don't want to miss anything. Remember, I'm a *local* this summer, not a vacationer!"

Nikki worked summers on the Cape for years at the same restaurant, *The Salty Anchor*. Her parents had a house in Harwich, just south of Chatham, and Kate joined her there for a week-long stay the last couple of summers. This year, Nikki's family offered for Kate to stay the entire summer as a guest. While interning in Boston or New York to pad her resume for senior year was the responsible choice, Nikki convinced Kate that it was their last real summer before adult life started. Responsible decisions could wait one more summer.

"My number one goal is to make enough money to go out and have fun our senior year. Drinking in New York is *so* expensive," Kate sighed.

She'd gotten into NYU on a scholarship, and while her parents helped a bit, it wasn't enough to cover overpriced cosmopolitans and cover charges. To survive—and thrive—in the city's club scene, she needed a paycheck.

"You just need to get better at pregaming," Nikki said matter-of-factly, digging through her Louis Vuitton monogram bag. She snagged the impossibly popular purse at a sample sale, refusing to settle for the knockoffs near Times Square. It was still more than Kate would *ever* spend on a bag. Her trusty Coach wristlet was chic enough.

"Do you think your friends will be back at the restaurant this season? I know a few of them, right?" Kate asked, trying to sound casual, though there was a dash of apprehension in her voice.

"Yeah, you definitely met some of the crew last summer," Nikki said, finally fishing out her silver Nokia cell phone. "I heard Matt's the general manager now. You didn't meet him—he was managing some place in New Hampshire the last couple of summers. He'll be making the schedule, so you'll need to turn the charm on."

Kate raised an eyebrow. "Interesting. Is he hot?"

Nikki paused, considering. "I mean... I guess? He's cute. Just not really my type."

It was an unusually vague and non-committal response from Nikki, which she found curious. She was inherently more interested now.

Kate slowed down as they reached the exit, the scent of salt-water and pine hanging in the air. "Well, I'd settle for having one make-out sesh with a cute older guy. This summer, I aspire to be more than Lindsey's less hot sister."

"Your sister is a skank," Nikki said, rolling her eyes and waving her hand dismissively like she was swatting away an annoying fly.

"That's a little harsh." Kate slowed down for a red light, a small smile tugging at her lips. There was always satisfaction in hearing Nikki be so blunt about Lindsey, even if she knew her sister was far from skanky.

"No, it's the truth," Nikki said, leaning back in her seat and no doubt texting some local guy she'd already hooked up with and fully intended to re-hook. "This is *our* summer, babe. Trust me—you'll be tossing cute guys back into the sea like a catch-and-release program until you find a good one."

Nikki glanced up from her phone with a raised eyebrow. "Just don't always go for the pretty guys, ok? Branch out a little. Your type has a *very* suspicious relationship with jazz hands."

Kate took her hand off the wheel to lightly shove Nikki. Mostly for being right.

"We do not *know* that Ben is gay. He's just super well put together. He said he was busy with finals and was going to text me to hang out when I get back."

"Kate. Come on."

"Fine," Kate laughed. "Maybe he was gay. And I guess there is no harm in trying a different approach this summer."

"That's the spirit! Let's get you some cash *and* some hot summer ass!" Nikki shot her a devilish grin.

"Ok, ok, Cash, check. Ass, check," Kate responded dutifully. She felt confident about accomplishing only one of those things.

The opening beat of No Doubt's 'Hey Baby' began pulsing through the speakers. The infectious song felt like the perfect anthem—an invitation for a summer of recklessness and reinvention. The Mazda hummed down the winding road as they neared the turn-off for Nikki's family's summer house.

With their road trip energy and the afternoon sun waning, they finally rolled up to the gray clapboard cottage with a whimsical sign that said "Harper" by the entryway.

While the Harpers called it a cottage, Kate and anyone reasonably minded would consider it a full-blown, five-bedroom, three-bathroom house. Even though the summer home had a cozy aesthetic and weathered with salt-streaked shutters, she suspected it cost a fortune. A tingly anticipation washed over her as she filled her chest with air. The salty breeze carried the scent of seaweed and driftwood, mingling with the thriving hydrangea bushes lining the walkway.

After lugging their suitcases up to the third-floor bedrooms they'd call home for the next eight weeks, Nikki wasted no time flinging clothes across her bed in search of her favorite NYU sweatshirt. By the time Nikki finally found her sweatshirt, Kate was already completely unpacked, her clothes stacked neatly in her dresser.

They made the short drive to Red River Beach just in time to catch the last streaks of the sunset. The sky was a vibrant blend of pink and orange, the colors reflecting on the water as the waves lapped gently against the shore.

Nikki took a long, deep breath, savoring the salty air, then let out a contented sigh as she popped open a bottle of wine and poured some into their plastic cups. "God, I love it here."

"It's perfect," Kate said, raising her cup with a smile.

There was something about this place—something that hummed just beneath the surface. She couldn't quite explain it, but it felt different. Charged. Like maybe this summer had something exciting in store.

"Let's make this a summer we never forget." She clinked her cup against Nikki's.

"Cheers to us."

* * *

That Monday afternoon, Kate stepped into The Salty Anchor. A few stragglers finished their late lunches, and the mid-afternoon lull hung over the restaurant like a warm blanket. The air smelled thick with fried seafood, mingled with a faint saltiness that wafted in from the nearby ocean. The carpets of the restaurant were old and worn, with faded blue-and-green patterns that soaked up decades of foot traffic. But there was a certain charm to the place.

It was nicer than a typical beach shack—white tablecloths and polished silverware gave it an air of casual elegance—but still had a relaxed ambiance, especially out on the patio, where diners could take in the ocean view.

A short, brunette hostess was bustling around the entrance and flashed a welcoming smile as soon as she spotted Kate.

Her hair was pulled back into a no-nonsense low bun, and she wore a simply navy wrap dress and ballet flats--an outfit made for a busy night at a restaurant.

"Hey! Kate, right? Nikki said you were joining us for the summer. I'm Natalie," she greeted her, giving Kate a quick hug. "No one at this place arrives on time, and here you are, 15 minutes early! Let's get you set up on paperwork before the dinner rush kicks in."

"Sounds great!" Kate said, immediately kicking herself for sounding too eager. If she was going to get along with Nikki's friends, she was going to need to be a little cooler than this.

Kate followed Natalie over to the bar area, introducing her to a bartender named Tara, who was cutting up fruit. Kate recognized her from last summer, though only vaguely. Tara was a seasoned bartender with short, fiery red hair, a nose piercing, forearm tattoos and a look that indicated you better have a good reason to be talking to her. Tara glanced over and gave Kate a casual nod before turning back to her limes, lemons and oranges.

After finishing the paperwork at the bar, Natalie led Kate through the swinging door to the kitchen, where the air was heavy with the smell of boiling lobster and sizzling butter. At the food prep station was a slender and graceful woman, moving with effortless elegance, even while assembling salads.

She turned and flashed a friendly smile full of perfectly white teeth, her skin golden tan against the casual simplicity of her white collared shirt and black pants. "Hey! I think we met briefly last summer at one of the bonfires. I'm Jessica." Her voice carried a friendly, easy tone. "We can work on these salads together. Then you can shadow me for the night."

Kate only had a fleeting memory of meeting Jessica, which surprised her, since she was strikingly beautiful. Her deep, expressive brown eyes were striking against her soft, blonde hair that was pulled into a low braid that cascaded over her shoulder. Even in something as plain as a work uniform, Jessica was stunning.

If any attractive men worked at this restaurant, Kate's chances would be slim—unless, of course, Jessica wasn't interested. Then, maybe she'd have a shot.

"Remind me, what kind of waitressing experience do you have?" Jessica asked as she led her to the main dining room.

"I worked at a diner for a few years in high school," Kate replied, keeping her tone upbeat. She wanted to make a good impression. "It was pretty fast-paced—no pagers, no heat lamps, just sprinting to get the food out before the eggs went cold."

"Sounds miserable," Jessica laughed, filling pitchers with ice and water. "On the bright side, our busy nights shouldn't phase you too much."

Kate felt like she'd passed a little test, and that was reassuring. As she helped Jessica get the restaurant ready for the dinner rush, she took in the bustling scene around her. The other waitstaff were chatting and laughing as they prepared for the shift, and Kate tried to commit their names to memory.

Kristen, a teacher from Boston in her late 20s, straightened a stack of menus while animatedly swapping classroom stories with a waitress Kate didn't know. Nate, a cute college sophomore from Penn State, wandered in with his eyes a little red and a faint scent of weed lingering in the air. He seemed to be a natural in the restaurant, setting up perfectly arranged tables despite being obviously stoned. Stacey and Allison—Jessica's friends and veterans of the summer crew—strolled in together late, still giggling about some party they'd been to over the weekend.

As the first wave of dinner guests started to trickle in, Kate quickly fell into an easy rhythm of reading specials, running food to Jessica's tables and refilling water. She was weaving her way out of the kitchen with a plate of crab cakes balanced expertly in one hand, already half-tuned out from the clatter of pans and shouted orders behind her. Just as she rounded the corner, the back office door swung open with zero warning—nearly slamming into her—and she staggered back a step, startled. She saw a person step out.

Not just a person. A man. A *stupidly* attractive man. The kind of attractive that comes at you in slow-motion, alongside a sexy song like Al Green's *Let's Get It On*.

He stepped into view—he had a medium build, but solid, like he knew his way around a gym. His posture was perfect, which gave him a subtle gracefulness. His dark hair was tousled, falling over his forehead in a way that was completely messy yet purposeful. And his eyes. *Those eyes.* Bright blue, glinting with something playful, something *knowing.*

His eyes found her then and a flicker of amusement passed across his face. He gave her a crooked half-smile like they were already sharing an inside joke. Kate's stomach did a traitorous somersault. She forgot about the crab cakes in her hand, nearly dumping them onto the floor.

She blinked, mentally slapped herself, and managed to hold the plate steady. By the time she gained composure, he was already gone, striding toward the dining room like he owned the place.

Which she was pretty sure he did, more or less. He hadn't said a word, but she knew it was Matt.

Kate silently cursed Nikki for not better preparing her. When she asked if he was hot, the answer should have been a resounding *yes.* Impossibly hot.

As often as she could without drawing suspicion, Kate stole glances from across the room, pretending to straighten menus while watching him glide through the dining area. He greeted regulars with easy charm and a warm, familiar smile, making each exchange feel personal. Even with new guests, there was a sincerity in his welcome that caught her off guard—like he actually meant it.

She had fully expected an ego to match the looks. Smugness, maybe a little swagger. But from her position as casual stalker across the room, she saw none of it. No posturing. No flash. Just a presence that pulled people in without trying.

But beneath that calm exterior, there was something else. An edge, maybe? His jaw would tighten when no one was watching, and he moved with a focused intensity that hinted at something deeper—something unresolved or complicated, as if he was hiding a tortured backstory or emotional baggage.

And then there was the way he observed people. Quick, sharp, assessing. Like he was always three steps ahead of everyone else in the room. Kate couldn't shake the thought that he might lock eyes with her and, without a word, cross the space between them and kiss her— hard, with purpose, with absolutely no warning.

The thought sent a shiver through her as she absently refilled the oyster cracker bin.

She knew she was being ridiculous. Building a fantasy out of broad shoulders, killer forearms, and unreadable blue eyes. But she could practically *feel* those forearms pinning her against the walk-in cooler and—

"Kate, you there?" Jessica's voice snapped her back to reality. "Table ten needs their check. And bring a few menus to the host stand on your way?"

Right. Cracker bin. Check. Menus. Not wall sex with the hot manager. Focus.

"Yep, on it," Kate said quickly, her cheeks flushing. She snatched the stack of menus piling up at the wait station and wiped them down with the fervor of someone pretending they hadn't just been fantasizing about their new boss.

She turned to head back toward the dining room—and promptly collided with a solid wall of human.

"Easy there, killer," said a deep voice, steadying her by the arms. It was *him*. Of course it was.

Matt's hands were firm but gentle, his touch sending a jolt up her spine. He smelled like aftershave and warm linen, with just a trace of something woodsy and unfairly distracting. When their eyes met, time stuttered for a beat.

"Appreciate the hustle," he said, a crooked smile teasing his lips, "but I should probably mention our insurance doesn't cover concussions."

"God, I'm so sorry," Kate said, trying to laugh as she attempted to remember how speech worked. "I'm Kate."

His eyes danced and his smile widened, gazing at her a moment longer than necessary.

"Nice to meet you, Kate," he said, his voice warm and dangerously easy to like. "You must be Nikki's friend from NYU. I'm lucky to have you here this summer."

Did he say "he" was lucky? Don't people usually say "we"? She was probably reading too much into it.

"Happy to be here. Looking forward to... constantly peeling butter packets from my shoes," she offered as a joke, instantly regretting everything about that sentence.

He raised a brow, clearly entertained by her apparent nervousness. "Well, that's good. Because Thursday is surf n' turf night. Your hair will smell like prime rib until Labor Day."

"Don't threaten me with a good time," she said, smiling, trying not to stare at his mouth. She was not nearly as good at flirting as her sister. Everything just sounded awkward.

Matt chuckled as he stepped back, releasing her arms but still watching her closely, like she was something intriguing. "It's going to be a fun summer. I can already see why you are friends with Nikki."

He glanced over her shoulder as Nikki entered, five minutes late for her bartending shift.

"Sorry, no autographs!" Nikki called out teasingly as she ducked behind the bar. Kate took the opportunity to make a quick exit and end the interaction on a high note before the conversation had a chance to get awkward again. She could feel Matt's gaze lingering as she walked away. Without even thinking, she straightened her posture.

Later, as the dinner rush finally eased and the clatter of dishes began to die down, Kate took refuge in the wait station, shoveling baked mac and cheese into her mouth like a veteran server. Nikki appeared beside her from out of nowhere.

"So," she began casually, "I saw you talking to Matt. You looked like you were about five seconds away from dragging him into the linen closet."

Kate choked a little on her pasta. "Jesus, Nik!" she hissed, glancing around. "Suggesting I want to fuck the boss is probably not the best way to make friends this summer."

Nikki smirked. "But you do, I can tell. Relax. Everyone's too busy praying for a cut shift to care. I'm not mad about it; he's not for me. You should go for him."

Kate pointed her fork accusingly. "*I'm* mad you didn't tell me he was *that* hot. It threw me off."

"Because you already seemed nervous about the job," Nikki said, unfazed. "Me telling you he was objectively good-looking would not have helped. Anyway, if you're fishing for info, he's about five years older than us, I think. Rumor has it he's single and—most importantly—not into guys."

Kate was a little embarrassed at how thrilled she was about this new information. "Ok," she said, stabbing another forkful of mac and cheese like it personally offended her. "It doesn't matter anyway since he's not going to be interested in me."

Not with someone as beautiful as Jessica at his fingertips. He could probably snag any waitress in this place. If he even dated at work, why would he pick her?

"Oh, please," Nikki said, crossing her arms and rolling her eyes in exasperation. Just then, Tara motioned for her to come back to the overcrowded bar. "We'll continue this later."

Kate waved Nikki off as she forked the last bite of mac and cheese into her mouth, cheeks still warm from the conversation. She didn't know why she was so captivated by a man she'd known for less than a full shift. It wasn't like hot guys were a rarity at NYU.

Matt felt…different somehow. Was he special? Ominous? She had no idea.

She tossed her fork into the bus bin, wiped her hands, and exhaled slowly. The dining room was quieter now, lit with the kind of low, golden glow that made everything feel cinematic—like anything could happen. Somewhere in the background, she heard Matt's voice, low and warm, laughing with a table of guests.

She didn't turn around. But she smiled.

It was technically her third day in Chatham.

But it felt like summer had just begun.

Chapter Seven

2025

See, my days are cold without you
But I'm hurting while I'm with you
And though my heart can't take no more
I keep on running back to you

Kate was lost in her 2002 memories until the familiar crooning of the next song, Ashanti's "Foolish," gently brought her back to the present.

The Audi gently veered off Route 6 as Nikki steered through South Harwich, past rows of little Cape Cod homes with weathered shake siding, perfectly white picket fences, and hydrangeas exploding in shades of pink, blue, and white. The scene was so quaint it felt like a postcard. When she was 22, Kate was too busy hustling summer cash and falling in love to truly appreciate the Cape's quiet beauty. Now, with years of chaotic city life behind her, the calm charm of the area hit a little differently.

The car remained devoid of conversation, with only music filling the silence. They drove by serene ponds surrounded by tall, waving grasses, clusters of pine trees, and occasional antique shops and corner stores. Kate inhaled deeply, letting the salty breeze whip through her hair and warm her skin. She exhaled slowly, releasing the warm memories that the previous song had resurfaced. She hadn't traveled down memory lane long enough to reach the painful ones.

Nikki, sensing her friend's reflection, drove in companionable silence, waiting patiently for Kate to speak first.

"Nik? Can I ask you an important question?" Kate asked, leaning toward her friend.

Nikki glanced over cautiously. "Of course… but first, I'm sorry for putting that song on the playlist. It wasn't even from 2002," Nikki grimaced, her words pouring out in a guilty rush. "I just thought—"

"Do you think you could text one of your old exes so that I can get laid and just get it out of my system…?" Kate interrupted. Her face was a mask of seriousness as she waited for Nikki's reaction. "I mean, if Seth is still hanging around, I feel like I could see myself in the backseat of a Honda Civic with a spoiler."

"Kate!" Nikki's eyes widened in shock before she burst out laughing. "Oh my god! You were so quiet for like, so long, I thought you were having emotional PTSD!"

"It was five minutes, tops," Kate chuckled.

"I *totally* forgot about Seth. He was one thousand percent the bottom of the barrel that summer. I had questionable taste back in the day."

"I prefer to see it as you never settled for ordinary."

"Well, I'm going to assume you weren't being serious, but if you were, I have a few calls I could make to help you get your groove back. Either way, I can tell you one thing. If Seth is still hanging around the Cape, it sure as shit not going to be hanging out *here*."

Nikki slowed the car as they turned onto Shore Road, where the beach came into view on the left, and the grand facade of the Chatham Bars Inn emerged to their right. Kate's breath caught; the inn was even more enchanting than she remembered. The main building, with its stately grey shingles and white balconies, seemed to beckon guests toward a world of New England charm and luxury. A crisp brick walkway led up to the entrance, and a stately wooden sign hinted at the five-star experience inside. Kate could practically hear the clink of champagne glasses and feel the evening ocean breeze on the wide veranda where wicker chairs awaited anyone wanting to soak up the view. She noticed an array of pristine white Adirondack chairs placed perfectly to watch the sunset with a glass of cabernet franc or perhaps have a quiet morning cappuccino.

"Wow," exhaled softly, craning her neck to take it all in as they rounded Seacliff Street. "I'd forgotten how stunning this place is." Her anxiety about the exorbitant cost of the stay gave way to an eagerness to explore what awaited her here.

"I'm already regretting not booking to stay with you, even for the weekend," Nikki sighed as she eyed the veranda. "I could just see myself in head-to-toe J. Crew, dirty martini in hand, judging people with imaginary friends named Beverly and Chad. Saying something like 'good help is *so hard* to find these days.'"

"You're *so* right," Kate added in a haughty faux accent. "And, oh dear, did you see that horrid woman with the black hair and black nails? Simply scandalous! Are they just letting *devil worshipers* in here now?" Kate winked at her friend, poking holes in the idea that Nikki could simply blend in with upper-crust New England society.

"Oh please, the only thing that talks at a place like this is money," Nikki admonished with an eye roll. "You'd be surprised what you can get away with if people think you have money."

Nikki pulled the car up to the inn's bustling portico, lined with perfectly trimmed boxwood hedges, wooden benches and hundreds more bright pink hydrangeas. Guests in crisp, designer resort wear milled about, their sunglasses gleaming and hair sun-kissed and meticulously kept. The valets were busy attending to the polished luxury vehicles pulling up with families and couples eagerly unloading their luggage. They stood behind a towering black Rivian SUV with a young, well-dressed family of four arriving for what seemed like the entire summer, based on the sheer number of bags and suitcases.

Lingering near the entrance was a mid-fifties statuesque platinum blonde woman whose bright orange Hermès bag gleamed in the sunlight as if it were on display in a museum. Nikki sighed dreamily.

"Look at that *Birkin*," she swooned. "In iconic amber, too. I think I might be turned on right now."

"Keep it in your pants," Kate laughed as she collected her belongings. She felt oddly eager to begin her so-called summer of transformation—despite having no real blueprint. No step-by-step plan for self-discovery, no clue what needed fixing, or even where to start. Was she supposed to just wander around waiting for the universe to drop meaning in her lap? That wasn't in her comfort zone, but she was willing to try.

"Ok, babe. While I *am* bummed to miss the parade of luxury goods and entitled rich people, Jay and the girls are waiting for me," Nikki pouted with exaggerated sadness as two attendants unloaded Kate's bags.

"Don't worry, I'll capture every fashion triumph, faux pas, and quasi-celebrity sighting while I sip overpriced French rose and slurp oysters like a Park Avenue housewife," Kate declared, draping her hand dramatically across her forehead like she might faint from the burden.

"I know you're being facetious, but that sounds like the *perfect* afternoon. Keep your eyes peeled for cute guys to flirt with. And for the love of everything, do *not* wear that tankini I know you packed. PROMISE."

Kate held up a solemn pinky. "Pinky-swear. Even though the tankini is very convenient and tasteful." They linked pinkies, Kate giving a look of utmost seriousness. "And thank you for the ride. And the playlist, even with the off-theme song. I love you."

"Love you too, lady. Now get moving—those poolside cocktails aren't going to drink themselves!"

A sharply dressed bellhop named Ian waited patiently as Kate unbuckled her seatbelt and leaned over to give Nikki a quick kiss on the cheek and a hug. He extended a white-gloved hand to help her out of the car as she smoothed her cotton dress, trying to erase any evidence of a long car ride.

"Oh! Almost forgot—I booked you a 60-minute 'Aroma Journey' massage for tomorrow at 10 a.m.!" Nikki announced with a grin. "It's in one of those cute little outdoor cabanas. And don't even say I didn't have to. I wanted to."

Kate tilted her head in affectionate disapproval and placed her hand on her hip. "Nikki, that was far too generous. But thank you."

She knew Nikki could splurge like that without thinking about it. Usually, Kate could too, but she was trying to make smarter financial choices as an unemployed single woman, which is exactly why Nikki booked it.

"I promise I'll enjoy every second," Kate said, blowing a kiss to her friend as Nikki waved and drove off.

Inside, the lobby of the Chatham Bars Inn greeted her with timeless elegance and charm. Polished hardwood floors and rich oriental carpets anchored the space, creaking gently and pleasantly as she entered. The grand decor belonged to the 1920s, a preservation of a Gatsby era gone by.

"Welcome to the Chatham Bars Inn, Miss," Ian said warmly as he wheeled her bags alongside her. He was quite tall and stately, with a calm poise that suggested he'd been a part of the staff for many years. "Is this your first time staying with us?"

"Yes, as a guest," Kate replied, smiling. "I've been here for drinks and dinner, but it's been... maybe twenty years?"

"Well then, welcome back! The weather should be perfect this week, and it sounds like you have a massage booked—so you're off to a strong start. May I bring you a glass of champagne while you check in?"

"That sounds wonderful, thank you."

While she waited in the short line at reception for Ian to return, Kate took in the luxury of the lobby. It was brimming with nautical accents, brass fixtures, large-framed paintings, model sailboats, and one handsome grandfather clock. An expansive sitting area to her right featured a large fireplace, likely cozy in cooler months. The scent of fresh-cut flowers mingled with the faint salty tang of sea air drifting through the open French doors to the veranda, where guests lounged in wicker chairs, enjoying late afternoon drinks.

Large windows framed views of the rolling lawn and the ocean beyond, filling the lobby with a soft, warm light. Light jazz music floated through the air from the live pianist at the nearby Sacred Cod restaurant. She made a mental note to visit for dinner.

She glanced toward the front desk, admiring the craftsmanship of the dark wood counters topped with cool marble. Staff members behind the desks wore perfectly tailored uniforms and exuded warm professionalism. Overhead, an intricately coffered ceiling reflected light from a grand chandelier, casting a glow of vintage glamour. Kate wondered if her room would dazzle like the main building, even though she didn't splurge for the ocean view.

She was so caught up in the scenery that she missed Ian's return, his white-gloved hand holding out an impeccably clear champagne flute, two-thirds full of golden bubbly. *If I oversaw the wine at a place like this*, she mused, *I'd go with something California chic. Like Domaine Carneros or Schramsberg. Elegant, a little unexpected.*

"Ma'am," Ian said, nodding and smiling as he handed her the glass. "I believe Diana is ready to check you in. I'll wait here and escort you to your room with your bags."

"Ms. Walker, I presume?" an older woman at the front desk greeted her, flashing a knowing smile. She sported a navy blazer, coiffed hair and large pearl earrings. Kate wasn't exactly sure how Diana knew who she was before she passed over any identification. It must've been some sort of Devil Wears Prada situation where the staff had a morning meeting with the photos and descriptions of all the guests checking in that day.

"Yes, that's me," Kate replied, sliding her ID and credit card across the marble and taking a small sip of her welcome drink. She was delighted to discover that they had, in fact, selected a Napa region sparkling wine. It tasted like crisp pear and grapefruit with hints of vanilla and honey, finished with floral undertones and a distinctly rich quality.

"Mmm," she sighed to herself. "Mumm Napa was a *perfect* choice."

Diana looked up with a smile of surprise. "Wow... well done! You've got quite the palate! How did you know it was Mumm Napa?"

Kate blushed, realizing she'd spoken aloud. "Oh...I just love wine, I guess," she replied with a sheepish grin.

If she was going to be a tourist, she might as well make the most of it. She took a quick selfie with the wine to send to Sydney.

"Oh! I have good news, Miss Walker. We have a note to up-grade your room to an ocean view for the *entire* stay!" Diana beamed, looking thrilled to deliver the news.

Ugh, Nikki! Too much! Kate thought, equal parts uncomfortable and excited for an upgraded room at such a swanky place. She was going to need to sternly tell her best friend to stop buying her things. She might not be working, but she wasn't exactly poor.

Diana handed over the keys with a smile. "Enjoy your stay, Ms. Walker. And do let us know if we can assist with anything else."

Kate offered a polite thank you and followed Ian as he guided her through the bustling lobby and up to her suite. On the second floor, he opened the door to what would be her new home for the next eight weeks.

The room was everything she was hoping for: bright, elegantly decorated with seaside touches, and perfectly inviting. Blue throw pillows and a neatly folded cashmere blanket accented a cozy queen-sized bed with pristine white bedding. A quaint writing desk sat by the window while French doors opened onto a spacious balcony that framed a stunning view of wispy bluffs and the deep blue ocean, dotted with whitecaps and sailboats.

Housekeeping thoughtfully left the doors open, allowing a gentle sea breeze to drift in, bringing with it hints of dune grass and the fragrance of fresh lilies arranged on a small dining table. In the distance, Kate could hear the soft sounds of seagulls and waves crashing against the shore.

After Ian disappeared, she stepped onto the balcony with her wine, closing her eyes to savor the warm sun on her face. It felt like a pocket of peace—a tranquility she hadn't felt since the year began.

Cheers to me, leaving the past behind, and to starting anew, she thought, lifting her glass in a private toast. Any embarrassment over the pity upgrade vanished. The suite was perfect.

Deciding to embrace spontaneity right away, Kate set aside the usual ritual of unpacking. She swapped her travel clothes for a sleek navy bikini, hesitating only a moment over a one-piece before deciding that "Cape Kate" had more confidence. Besides, one-pieces were notoriously inconvenient when cocktails and bathrooms were involved. That's why they invented the tankini, which she just pinky-swore she wouldn't wear.

After tossing sunblock, sunglasses, her new Emily Henry novel and a water bottle into her new YSL raffia beach tote, she snapped a quick selfie on the balcony to send to Nikki.

> Thanks for the YSL tote recco – she's gorgeous. Headed to the pool. Can't BELIEVE you upgraded me to this amazing room. No more surprises! It's too much! XOXO

With a smile, she slipped her phone into her bag, vowing to leave it untouched for the rest of the afternoon.

Another warm breeze drifted through the open window, carrying the unmistakable scent of fried seafood—crispy clams, maybe, or battered cod—from the poolside snack bar. It was a sensory cocktail that was oddly comforting.

But she realized it was more than a smell—it was a memory, dancing at the edges of her mind. For the first time in weeks, she felt light, even hopeful. But alongside that glimmer of optimism was something else. A quiet, insistent tug from the past.

Chapter Eight

2002

It had only been a couple of weeks, but Kate built up enough skill to handle a small section on her own. The familiar rhythm of a restaurant returned to her, like muscle memory. Similarly, Nikki moved behind the bar like a steampunk ballerina, gracefully stacking glassware, pouring beers, and filling ice buckets.

Kate managed to make casual small talk with Matt every chance she could. She found herself calculating where he'd be in the restaurant so that she could navigate close by. If she saw him go into the walk-in cooler, she'd coincidentally need more cocktail sauce. If he were in the wait station, she'd realize it was time to start another pot of coffee.

On the surface, it was a simple workplace banter that helped pass the time between dinner rushes and table flips. But underneath their quick exchanges, there was a flirtatious undertone she was pretty sure she wasn't imagining.

Kate was halfway through folding the third stack of dinner napkins into tidy fan shapes when Matt strolled up.

"You look like you're in the middle of a Martha Stewart fever dream," he laughed.

She purposefully didn't look up, trying to remain coy and just out of reach. "Just because the air smells like clams and fryer oil doesn't mean I can't inject a little dignity into this operation."

He smirked. "I bring plenty of dignity, I'll have you know."

She gave an exaggerated eyeroll, refolding a crooked fan. "I'm pretty sure you showed pre-shift in a Red Sox tee that was inside out."

"It *was* inside out," he agreed. "Dries faster that way. I flipped my kayak before work."

Kate paused, looking up from her napkin menagerie. "You kayaked *before work*?"

"A little pre-shift paddle clears the mind. Plus, I think I saw a Great White fin."

She blinked. "That's not... relaxing. That's a sign to stay on land. Normal people drink coffee and read the paper."

"See, that's why I need someone grounded in my life. Some-one to keep me safe from apex predators."

Kate opened her mouth to respond, but nothing clever arrived. He was *definitely* flirting with her. All the coolness she had been able to muster was dissipating quickly, so she picked up another napkin and refolded it more aggressively than necessary.

Matt stepped back, clearly pleased with himself. "Anyway, carry on, Napkin Overlord."

He sauntered off, leaving her staring at a pile of fabric triangles and wondering why her face suddenly felt five degrees warmer.

Matt wasn't the preppy, well-polished guy she usually went for. Yes, he was smart and witty. And he laughed freely. But there was a mysterious intensity that danced at the edge of his conversations and in his blue eyes. Despite what he just said, it's obvious he thrived on adventure and spontaneity. He probably dated girls who climbed mountains, camped, and went on road trips with no hotel reservations.

Kate was not that girl.

Yet. She'd catch him glancing over at her when he thought she wasn't looking. He leaned in closer than necessary whenever they spoke. And when he placed his hand on her back as he handed her the menus, the warm, unexpected touch felt purposeful and thrilling. She had to remind herself to keep her composure when he was near—it would be mortifying to let out a sigh. Or worse, a moan.

That night, the rush hit at 6 p.m. sharp, crashing over the restaurant like a tidal wave of drawn butter and medium rares. After hours of slinging lobster tails and dodging rogue ramekins of horseradish sauce, Kate collapsed onto a barstool, limbs jelly and apron covered in unidentified stains.

She'd survived her first surf n' turf night—and as it turned out, one of the few perks of the job (aside from character building) was a free post-shift drink or two. Tonight was her initiation into staff drinks, and she intended to take full advantage.

Matt slid behind the bar with an ease that suggested he'd done it a thousand times, his movements smooth and assured. Kate reminded herself not to come across as too flirty. She needed to be cool and ambivalent to his charm. Most guys liked a chase, so if she played this with precision, she might be able to keep him interested.

All of that focus nearly when out the window when he shrugged off his dress shirt and revealed a fitted white undershirt that clung to his body. His chest was broad and sculpted in a way that suggested he kayaked a lot more than he let on. As he reached for a bottle of tequila, every visible muscle flexed.

"You can't hate free drinks," Nikki sighed happily, sliding into the stool next to her with the satisfied flop of someone officially off-duty. "God, it's so nice to be on this side of the bar."

Kate nodded absently, still laser-focused on Matt, who was now expertly shaking a cocktail shaker, the muscles in his arms rippling in a way that made her momentarily forget how to speak. She imagined herself running her hands over that chest—purely as a scientific inquiry, of course. To research the male physique. This would be *important* research.

Without even looking, Nikki whispered "Whatever fantasy you're having right now, I hope he's making you cum."

"You are insufferable," Kate retorted quickly, shoving her laughing friend as Matt approached them.

"Nikki, Kate. It was a hell of a night. What can I make for you? Anything you want, as long as it's not top shelf or frozen."

Nikki's lower lip jutted out in a cheeky pout. "But I want a Ketel One martini. Up, and extra, extra dirty? Only a *prude* would say no to extra dirty..."

With an exaggerated sigh and a side-eye, Matt looked at her as if she was asking him to perform a miracle. "If anyone asks, it's well," he said, grabbing the Ketel One.

"It's cute that you think anyone here would believe I'm drinking well vodka," Nikki shot back with a smile.

"And what about you, Katie?" he asked as he grabbed a cocktail shaker.

Katie? The unexpected nickname caught her off guard. But she didn't correct him. Nikki stifled a giggle and nudged Kate under the bar with her foot.

"A cosmopolitan?" Kate suggested, arching a brow.

"Carrie Bradshaw! Is that you?" Matt gasped in mock surprise, his tone dripping with flirtation. "All the way from the big city to grace our humble bar?"

"So what you're saying is," she said, leaning in slightly, "you don't know how to make one. Should I teach you?"

He locked eyes with her, grinning. "One Ketel One Cosmo, coming right up. Anything you want, I can make it happen."

A slow shiver worked its way down her spine at the way he said it—casual, sure, but laced with heat.

"Careful. A promise like that could get you in trouble."

He leaned in just a fraction, eyes sparkling. "I like a little trouble."

She laughed—a little too quickly. She could feel Nikki's eyes roll beside her, but she kept her commentary to herself.

As he moved behind the bar, his hands were confident, his rhythm practiced and smooth—every shake of the cocktail shaker a little too hypnotic. The bottle flip wasn't flashy, but it was fluid, sensual even, like his body just... knew what to do. Kate tried not to imagine what else he might be good at with that kind of control.

By the time he placed the martini glass in front of her, she was already several fantasies deep. Their fingers brushed as she took it—just a blink of contact, but it sent a bolt of heat buzzing through her, shooting straight down to her pelvis.

Before Kate could thank him, Jessica slid onto the last available barstool, effortlessly gorgeous and irritatingly unbothered. She was the final server to clock out but somehow looked like she'd just stepped out of a Neutrogena commercial rather than survived a soul-crushing dinner rush.

Matt smiled at her. "Jess—glass of pinot?"

"Yes, please, boss," she purred, tucking a golden strand of hair behind her ear like it was choreographed. Then she went back to counting her tips, her perfectly manicured fingers flicking through bills with quiet superiority. She definitely cleaned house, tip-wise.

Kate sipped her Cosmo and tried not to glare. It wasn't jealousy, exactly. More like... a keen awareness that she was trying to play in a league where Jessica existed. And Jessica didn't sweat. She glowed. Her mascara didn't smudge. She probably permanently smelled like Bath and Body Works Sun-Ripened Raspberry.

Kate, on the other hand, smelled like garlic and lobster juice.

She snapped herself out of the downward spiral and aimed for casual curiosity. "So, Matt," she said, forcing a light tone, "if you're an English major, how'd you end up managing restaurants?"

Matt looked up mid-pour, amused. "Ah, the existential résumé question," he said. "I'm not totally sure what I want to be when I grow up. I thought I'd teach. But... life detoured. Turns out managing restaurants pays actual bills, gives me time for my hobbies, and I'm halfway decent at it. Plus," he added, raising a brow, "people are fascinating. Especially in hospitality."

Kate laughed. "Ah, so you're collecting *material*. Got it. Just promise if I ever end up in your novel, you'll change my name."

He met her gaze with a slow, deliberate smile. "What makes you think you haven't already?"

Her brain scrambled for something clever to say, but rather than risk blurting out something awkward, she lifted her glass in a silent touché, hoping the gesture looked cool. Sometimes, silence was sexier than a witty response. At least, she hoped.

"What about you?" he asked, eyes steady on hers. "You strike me as someone who's got it all mapped out. What's the grand plan after graduation?"

Kate twirled the stem of her martini glass, buying a second. "I mean... I wouldn't say *all* mapped out," she said with a self-deprecating laugh. "I've always been good at school. Organized. I like people. I took one of those high school career quizzes and it spit out 'marketing'—so I guess I took the hint. It's practical. And I'm really good at executing a plan."

As soon as the words left her mouth, she worried she sounded boring. Like a walking cover letter. She resisted the urge to apologize for being Type A.

But Matt didn't look bored. In fact, he looked genuinely engaged. "Yeah," he said, his voice low and warm. "I get that about you."

Then—suddenly—he leaned in. Close. Closer than necessary. His face hovered just inches from hers, eyes locked on her like he was about to say something important... or kiss her.

Holy shit. What is happening?

She was sure he could hear the pounding in her chest. Or maybe she was imagining it. Either way, she didn't move. Not yet.

His voice dropped, low and conspiratorial like he was letting her in on something just for her.

"If it fits into that master plan of yours... you should come see my band Saturday night. We're usually at The Squire, but this weekend it's a backyard gig on Dune Drive. Low-key. If you're out in time, swing by with Nikki."

Kate blinked, trying to remember how to breathe and ignoring the wholly unprofessional visions flashing in her mind. She took a slow, deliberate sip of her Cosmo. Be cool. No big deal.

Of course he was in a band. He was the emotionally unavailable, devastatingly hot frontman type. He probably had a list of one-night stands a mile long. It should have been a red flag. It really should've.

But damn if it wasn't also stupidly attractive.

"What kind of music do you play?" she asked, keeping her tone light.

"Little bit of everything—classic rock, some alternative. A few originals," he answered, his eyes gleaming as if he was reading her thoughts. "I'm sorry to say, though, we don't play anything off of Usher's new album." He feigned a look of disappointment.

"You don't know what I listen to," she countered. She *did* love Usher. He didn't seem like the type. "I like the Red Hot Chili Peppers. And The White Stripes," she protested, trying to bolster her credibility (thanks Nikki). "And Pearl Jam, when I'm in the mood."

He nodded with approval. "Well, we might just have something for you."

Kate felt a pulse of satisfaction, pleased at the glint of interest in his eye. "Well, I'll pencil it into my schedule for Saturday," she said.

"What are we penciling in?" Nikki's voice broke in as she reapproached the bar after making her social rounds with the rest of the staff. "What are you committing us to?"

"Matt's playing at a house party on Saturday," she said casually, casting a quick glance toward him as he turned to pour another glass of wine. "I said we'd consider it. It could be fun."

"Kind of sounded to me like you *committed* to going," Nikki pushed back, raising her eyebrows.

"I mean, we don't have to go," Kate said defensively. "There are plenty of other things to do."

Nikki gave her a sly nudge. "No way, *Katie*. We're *definitely* going."

Kate glanced back at Matt, catching him mid-conversation with a couple of servers. Their eyes locked across the bar. He didn't pause his words, didn't even smile—but she knew he saw her. Felt it.

A quiet current passed between them.

At that moment she tapped Nikki to quietly slip out, trying desperately to maintain the illusion that she wasn't chasing him.

She was one hundred, thousand percent chasing him.

Chapter Nine

2025

Kate was chasing the last bits of afternoon sunlight before sunset. At least at this time of day, she could find a decent lounge chair by the popular Chatham Bars Inn pool.

As she crossed the street and descended the peony-lined steps to the Inn's pool, she could hear the lively sounds of chatter mingling with light, contemporary pop music. The rhythmic clapping of the pool water blended seamlessly with the faint roar of ocean waves just beyond. Elegant white cabanas bordered the lagoon-inspired pool, their curtains catching the breeze. Plush blue loungers surrounded the water, occupied by guests in wide-brimmed hats and chic designer cover-ups, sipping iced cocktails under the late afternoon sun.

Kate scanned the area for a quiet spot where she wouldn't be intruding on families or honeymooning couples. Thankfully, at this hour, most had left to get ready for dinner, and she found a shaded chair beside a large umbrella. Settling in, she slathered a generous layer of SPF 50 over her fair skin, then reclined, feeling the cozy warmth on her face as she cracked open her latest beach read.

Just as she was getting into the first chapter, an eager young server approached, clad in a standard Polo-inspired uniform, her strawberry blonde ponytail bouncing as she smiled. "Good afternoon! I'm Lauren. Can I get you something to drink or snack on? Perhaps a glass of rosé or an order of lobster nachos?"

"An Aperol spritz would be perfect," Kate replied. Though they sounded divine, it was a little too close to dinner for lobster nachos.

Lauren reappeared a few minutes later with a picture-perfect Aperol spritz—vibrant sunset hues of orange and red swirling in a large wine glass, a fresh orange slice perched on the rim. Kate took a long, refreshing sip, tasting the bright notes of orange zest, the subtle herbal undertones, and the crisp sparkle of quality Italian prosecco. The bittersweet flavor cooled her throat and she leaned back in her chair. *This is heaven.*

Before she was able to open her book, her watch buzzed with a text message. She had kept her word not to be glued to her phone, but she forgot about the distractions of her Apple watch. She sometimes missed the days where all she had was a clunky Nokia phone that could only call people and send analog texts. Unplugging nowadays was nearly impossible

She glanced at her watch. It was Lindsey.

When do you arrive? Should we plan to go for a run together?

She scoffed and shook her head. The last time she'd run was a 5K six years ago when their aunt roped the whole family into a charity race. Lindsey had matched her pace the entire time, headphones in, pretending they were doing it together—until the last half mile, when she took off in a dramatic sprint to beat Kate to the finish line. Classic Lindsey.

She'd have to make plans to see her sister eventually. But not today, and it definitely wouldn't be running.

She cleared the message.

Chris would've liked it here, she thought absently. He always loved New England summers. They'd explored many of the oceanside towns in driving distance of the city, and it's the one time where they planned together. They'd hit up dollar oyster happy hours and walk around with ice creams, taking in the warm summer nights together. Thinking about all of their trips and memories brought on a sharp pang of sadness.

No thinking about Chris. She cut off the thoughts before they could swell into anything heavier.

Should I start consulting? I could consult. No, no, no, Kate—stop. She didn't want to spiral into job stress, which would inevitably lead her down a rabbit hole of LinkedIn searches, resume tweaks, and mild existential dread. Not exactly how she wanted to kick off her self-healing summer.

Ok, so what *did* she want to think about? Being alone with her thoughts was never her strong suit. Her mind always needed to fixate on something. She picked up her book.

Three chapters and one empty glass later, she paused to look around for Lauren. Or maybe it was Sophia. With no server in sight, she tied her white sarong around her waist and decided to wander over to the poolside bar herself. Maybe she'd give in to the lobster nachos after all.

The polished wood of the bar gleamed in the late sun and the entire area smelled of sunscreen and coconut. As Kate leaned in to catch the bartender's eye, she felt a presence just behind her—uncomfortably close, even though the bar wasn't crowded.

Some people have no concept of personal space, she thought, rolling her eyes with quiet exasperation. Nevertheless, she was surprised. This was New England, where people usually kept their distance.

Then, without warning, two strong hands settled lightly on her hips. A warm breath tickled her ear as a low voice whispered, "Hello, beautiful."

Her heart thudded, and she spun around, ready to put this presumptuous guy in his place—until she saw him. Dark hair, piercing blue eyes, and a tanned, chiseled chest that seemed almost too perfect to be real.

It can't be.

The empty glass slipped from her hand, hitting the floor with a sharp crack, shattering at her feet.

Chapter Ten

2002

Kate tightened her grip on the Mazda's steering wheel, her jaw dropping as shock settled over her like the fine layer of sand on the car floor.

Is this a joke?

Matt said this was a house party. It was a *sprawling estate* party. The kind that came with a private path to the beach, balconies for days, and a circular driveway studded with gleaming luxury cars like they were on display at a dealership.

Kate suddenly felt her chest tighten. These were not the plastic-solo-cup crowds of NYU parties or even your average Manhattan nightclub. She felt distinctly underdressed and out of her league. When Matt said his band was playing a house party, this was not at all what she pictured. Did he run in these crowds?

"Chillax, it's just a house," Nikki said, reading Kate's expression. Her tone was breezy, dismissive, as though arriving at a

$3 million home was a typical Saturday. "Trust me, no one will be checking bank accounts or clothing tags."

As they parked and exited the car, Kate felt a little exposed, tugging at her top to make sure everything stayed in place. Nikki had personally styled Kate's look that evening, and she was wearing low-rise bootcut True Religion jeans and one of Nikki's low-cut black lace tops that tied underneath the bra line and flared open to expose her entire midsection.

"I look like I'm auditioning for a Ja Rule music video," Kate muttered. Would Matt think she looked hot? Or like a city girl trying too hard? She should have just worn her trusty denim skirt and a tank top.

Nikki narrowed her eyes, hands on her hips like a stylist about to make a declaration. "You're wearing jeans and a going-out top. I'm pretty sure Lindsay Lohan wore this exact outfit."

"Well, in that case," she shot back, rolling her eyes. She appreciated Nikki's attempt at a pep talk, but she felt a little...skanky.

"That's the spirit!" Nikki replied, ignoring the sarcasm. In contrast, Nikki was wearing camouflage capri pants tied at the calves and a white ribbed tank that said "Boy Beater" across the breasts. She looked sexy and cool. And way more confident than Kate.

They made their way toward an expansive porch lined with elegant potted plants and fairy lights draped across the railings that cast a warm glow. The scene felt straight out of a movie.

The party was in full swing, the lawn teeming with people in their twenties, all mingling beneath the glow of tiki torches. Everywhere Kate looked, there were clusters of guests laughing, talking, and sipping cocktails (from actual glasses) as caterers threaded through the crowd, offering drinks, beers, wine and shots on silver trays. Near the beach, a bonfire crackled, casting fiery light over the waves. The band was getting ready to play on a pavilion that overlooked the water.

"This is... a lot," Kate murmured. The sign over the sitting room mantle seemed to suggest it was Brad's 25th birthday. Whoever Brad was. Probably a douche, if she had to guess.

Nikki gave her an encouraging nudge as they edged past a group of laughing partygoers. "You'll be fine," she said, her tone equal parts reassurance and command.

"Have fun, don't let your drink out of your sight, and don't even *think* about sneaking out early," Nikki added. Then her grin turned wicked. "Unless, of course, Colin Farrell is here. Then all bets are off."

Ah yes. The Farrell Clause. New, but already binding.

Nikki had cycled through a dozen celebrity crushes since Kate knew her, but her Colin Farrell obsession was intense. The wild part was at *this* party in *this* zip code, there was a non-zero chance he could walk through the door.

Kate gave her a half-hearted "aye-aye." Nikki pushed her toward the kitchen, where she quickly located the liquor and made them each a strong Cape Codder with quick, practiced motions. The band started playing as Kate and Nikki made their way to the pavilion, drinks in hand. Matt, guitar in hand, led the band in the first song, "You Wreck Me" by Tom Petty.

Kate took in the sight of Matt on stage. If he was attractive while managing the restaurant, up there—with a guitar slung over his shoulder and a mic in hand—he was downright hypnotic. He looked completely at home in the spotlight. His voice was gritty and soulful, rough around the edges in a way that made the body come alive. His dark hair was artfully disheveled, like he'd just rolled out of bed, and the snug white t-shirt clung to his lean, defined frame. Over the shirt, an open plaid flannel hung loosely, giving him a rugged, almost grunge rockstar look.

She couldn't look away, goosebumps prickling up her arms as he gripped the microphone with an intensity that was nearly sensual. His jeans rode low on his hips, just enough to be suggestive, and she wondered what it would feel like to have him pull her close with that same passion. Kate had never experienced such a sudden, visceral pull to someone before. Her body was in the driver's seat, her brain in the back seat merely along for the ride.

The drink was starting to kick in and her limbs relaxed. As the band transitioned into a Red Hot Chili Peppers cover, Kate found herself swaying with the music. The makeshift dance floor near the pavilion was packed, and she and Nikki slipped right into the rhythm, laughing and bumping shoulders as they danced. The buzz of alcohol and the party's electric energy flowed through her veins.

Kate's gaze kept drifting back to the stage. His mouth at the mic, the veins in his forearms as he strummed the guitar. At some point, a quiet certainty settled in that was boldly unlike her: *I'm not leaving this party without kissing him.*

What had started as a simmering curiosity had erupted into a full-blown, aching need. She needed to feel his hands on her. Not in her overactive imagination—the exact weight of them on her waist. The press of his body, feverish and hard with desire, when he finally pulled her in. And if he used his mouth in bed the way he did on stage—gravel-rough, laced with just enough danger to make you want to beg—just the thought had her thighs pressing together.

By the time she snapped out of her fantasy, two other girls had stationed themselves at the edge of the stage, clearly having similar thoughts. She wasn't the only one circling the flame.

Each one subtly—or not so subtly—was vying for Matt's attention. One petite yet busty blonde was twirling a strand of hair around her finger, swaying her hips and giving Marilyn Monroe eyes. The slender brunette next to her, whose jeans were criminally low, was dancing with her arms up and ensuring that she was very visible to the lead singer. They were both undeniably beautiful and confident, exuding the promise of a good time. She couldn't be sure if Matt was flirting with them, but every other male in proximity had taken notice.

Kate shrank. She hated competing for attention—hated how small it made her feel. She wasn't Lindsey Walker. Lindsey was the girl who could walk into any party, lock eyes with the cutest guy in the room, and somehow *know* she'd be the one going home with him. It had always been that way.

Even back in college, when Tyler Musto had spent an entire night talking to Kate—laughing at her jokes, refilling her drink, leaning in like she was the only girl in the room—none of it mattered once Lindsey arrived for the weekend. All it took was a smile and a toss of her hair, and Tyler was suddenly hers.

Kate's initial insecurity prickled back to life, and she turned to look for Nikki. But she had already wandered off—most likely tracking down Ryan, her seasonal friend-with-benefits. *Nikki, where the hell are you?*

In the absence of a better plan, Kate kept drinking and tried not to look awkward or alone, should Matt see her and realize she wasn't quite as cool as she'd let on. Thankfully, it seemed like the band was taking a break and a DJ set up to spin some club music.

Her bullishness about kissing him tonight seemed girlishly naïve now. This was just a party, not a special night of romance. Kate navigated through the crowd to console her bruised ego with another drink but stopped short when she overheard two girls loudly gossiping over the music, just inside the next room. She hung back for a beat and could see it was two young bus girls from The Salty Anchor. She planned to find another route to the kitchen, but the topic of conversation quickly gave her pause.

"I really don't get why Matt is flirting with the new girl," one of the girls shouted to her friend.

"She seems boring and uptight," the other girl responded, rolling her eyes and sipping on what looked like an appletini. "He could have any waitress in the place. That wouldn't be my pick."

Kate's chest tightened. They were talking about her. Her face turned beet red. God, they were absolutely right. Kate knew better than to think she had a chance with someone like Matt. She wasn't cool like Nikki or hot like Lindsey.

Fuck this, I'm out. She turned to leave, but Nikki appeared out of nowhere, blocking her path.

"No – don't even," Nikki said, her tone fierce. She clearly overheard them, too. "They're just jealous little mean girls. Why would you care what they think? They can't even legally *drink* yet, for Christ's sake."

Kate gave a half-hearted shrug as she tried to move past Nikki, but her best friend was like an ox when she wanted to be.

"They're probably right, Nikki. He's gorgeous and in a band—what am I even doing here? Girls like me don't end up with guys like that. Not for real. There are at least three girls here tonight who look like Abercrombie models."

Like Jessica.

"Do you think Matt would be shamelessly flirting with you for the past two weeks if he wasn't interested?" Nikki asked, locking eyes with her.

Maybe. She'd seen it before—hot guys who flirted because they could, not because they meant it. They craved the validation.

"Kate, come on. You're smart. You're sexy—yes, I said it. And despite what you tell yourself, you're a total badass. You think just anyone can rock a 4.0 on a scholarship and still shut down the dance floor on weekends?" Nikki leaned in. "That takes brains, hustle, and moxie. So... are you going to sit here and spiral? Or are we going to show these Cape Cod amateurs how we party—New York style?"

Kate hesitated. Every instinct told her to play it safe. That's what she did—she made smart choices, stayed in control, avoided unnecessary risk. It was practically a core personality trait. And honestly? It had served her well so far.

But here she was, standing in a mansion she had no business being in, in a top she'd second-guessed three times, watching a guy she maybe liked—but didn't actually *know*—captivate a room full of women who probably *didn't* overthink everything like she did.

Nikki was still watching her. Waiting. With a look that screamed, *come on, let's go.*

Kate's mind was still churning with uncertainty. What if she misread his flirtations? What if she made a move and he laughed—or worse, pitied her?

A server strolled by carrying a tray of obnoxious "Happy Birthday Brad" birthday cake shots. Kate didn't think—just reached out, grabbed one, and knocked it back.

It burned. A little too sweet, a little too fake—just like Brad, probably. But it worked. She felt a defiance rise, subtle but insistent, somewhere in her chest

Nikki raised her brows in approval.

"Fuck those little underage assholes," Kate muttered, wiping her mouth.

Nikki grinned wide. "Let's show them how to *really* party."

Nikki grinned and ran up to the DJ. They were both aware that most DJs didn't take requests from random partygoers. But this one looked like he'd say yes to anything Nikki wanted.

Moments later, Nikki reappeared, seized Kate's hand, and lifted it triumphantly like she'd just won a title match. "Let's go," she declared, leading her onto the dance floor.

Right on cue, the lights dropped and the opening beat of Nelly's *Hot in Herre* blasted through the speakers. The crowd let out a collective cheer. The song was brand new, but of course, NYC girls like Kate and Nikki had been dancing to it for weeks.

Kate felt the pulse of the bass in her chest as Nikki tossed her hair and started to move.

The snare drum's backbeat pulsed through the party and into their bodies like a second heartbeat. Nikki dipped low, one hand trailing seductively down her thigh, hips moving in slow, deliberate circles like she was daring the room to keep up. Beside her, Kate arched into a sultry grind, her movements fluid and teasing. They danced with that effortless intimacy only college girls seemed to master—close enough to draw stares, far enough to claim deniability. Their bodies moved in sync, a teasing choreography of glances, sways, and fleeting touches. It was a practiced art: dancing for themselves, for each other, and for whoever might be watching.

Even the Cape Cod crowd wasn't immune to the primal pull of a good grind. The dance floor filled quickly because it was never a bad time to get a little inappropriate in someone else's living room.

For the first time that night, Kate didn't feel out of place in her outfit. Her hips dropped low just as someone hollered from the sidelines, "Get it, New York!"

If Matt was busy charming his fan club, so be it. She was having fun. She was in the moment. And if her thighs were sore tomorrow? Worth it.

Seemingly at the mere thought of him, Matt appeared on the frays of the dance floor. His eyes were unmistakably fixed on her as he took a swig from a bottle of beer. There was an undeniable spark in his expression, a mix of amusement and desire that sent a rush through her. Throwing caution to the wind, Kate held his gaze and winked at him, feeling a thrill of confidence wash over her. There were other girls around her, dancing just as provocatively. But his eyes were on her.

Matt clearly wasn't *un*interested. In fact, he seemed quite focused on her.

After a few more songs, Kate was breathless and flushed from dancing. She made her way to the edge of the dance floor, noticing that Matt disappeared again in their constant game of cat and mouse. She grabbed a beer in an attempt to cool off as the band started their second set. Not wanting to get out there too quickly, she found Brad and wished him a happy birthday. He was exactly what she imagined: popped collar, frosted tips and all.

Her anticipation was simmering; her body hummed with impatience, waiting for Matt to finish the set. She was going to find him. And she would not leave until she had her moment.

Finally, around 12:30 a.m., the band wrapped up, but the party showed no signs of slowing. Just as "What's Luv" reared its ugly head again, stoner Nate from the restaurant appeared out of nowhere, spiritedly pulling her back onto the dance floor.

"Let's go, New York! Let's see some more of those moves!" he laughed. She put two and two together and realized *he* had been the one shouting from the dance floor. Before she could decide whether to give him one dance or feign a bathroom break, she felt a hand on her waist and someone approached closely from behind.

"Oh, sorry dude." Matt's hand lingered on her waist. "I need to grab Kate for something." It felt like lightning.

Somehow, after a full set on stage, Matt didn't look sweaty or tired. Up close, she could see a soft dusting of stubble along his jaw. What was it about a five o'clock shadow that made men instantly ten times more attractive?

Nate shrugged, looking as though he didn't quite believe Matt's excuse. He also didn't seem particularly interested in protesting. He spotted Jessica and Allison on the dance floor and shimmied his way over to them.

"Thanks for the save," Kate said. Matt grabbed her hand and led her away from the crowd toward the glowing warmth of the bonfire. She tried not to dwell on how natural her hand felt in his—firm and warm, his grip both protective and possessive.

"I'm pretty sure if I had waited another song, there would have been six more guys in my way," he said, his voice low and unreadable.

She caught the barest hint of a smirk at the corner of his mouth, but his eyes were harder to read—dark, steady, and almost too calm, like he wasn't going to give anything away unless he wanted to. Kate felt a sense of triumph anyway. He almost seemed jealous.

"Please," she shot back. "I could say the same thing about your groupies in the front row. Girls go crazy for a lead singer."

Matt chuckled, shrugging as his hand remained wrapped around hers. "They're at every party. Trust me, I'm not interested." His tone was light, but the way he was looking at her—intense and unwavering—hinted at something else.

They wove their way through the crowd, the party growing more chaotic and lively the later it got. Laughter and music pulsed in the crisp night air, mingling with the rhythmic crash of waves just beyond the glow of the bonfire, casting flickering light over groups huddled in the sand and dancing silhouettes that moved in and out of the shadows. A salty breeze blew in from the ocean, carrying the scent of seaweed and smoke, while the muffled thud of a distant bass beat vibrated through the sand beneath their feet.

She resisted the urge to ask what kind of girl he *was* interested in, not wanting to ruin whatever was happening here by being too forward. But she ached to know.

"You guys were good tonight," she offered. "Maybe not *Usher good*. But still impressive."

"High praise," he replied, his grin widening. "By the way, we're working on something I think you'll like. Right in the '90s genre."

She nodded with a small smile, though her stomach fluttered with mild panic. The idea of him learning a song just for her was both flattering and terrifying—especially since she may have oversold her knowledge of '90s rock by, well, a lot.

He stopped short, and she nearly collided with him. The sudden proximity stole her breath—not just from surprise but from the clean, magnetic scent of his cologne. It clung to the air between them, crisp citrus layered over something warm and woodsy. A shiver traced down her spine. Before she could get lost in the sensory overload of standing so close to him, he turned slightly and asked, "Need a drink?"

Kate wasn't sure she trusted herself with another drink—her usual inhibitions were already teetering on a dangerous edge. But she was ready to say yes to anything he asked. "Yeah, that'd be great."

A middle-aged caterer shuffled by, offering up a tray of mysterious drinks with the dead-eyed expression of someone who'd absolutely had enough of rich twenty-somethings. Matt lifted two drinks with a nod and handed one to Kate.

"I can't say I've ever been to a house party where they hand-passed drinks all night long," she noted casually. "You have some high-class friends."

He laughed, the sound low and warm. "That couldn't be further from the truth, I'm afraid. Brad's more of an acquaintance than a friend. His family has another monstrous house on Lake Winnipesaukee, and he used to show up at the restaurant I managed a couple of nights a week. After hours, he and his buddies would come see me play at this little dive bar nearby."

She took a slow sip of the drink, its vibrant blue hue unmistakably Hpnotiq, almost unnervingly matching the shade of his eyes.

"Anyway, when I told him I was moving back down here, he practically begged me to play his birthday party. Pretty sure he was hammered at the time, but hey, a gig's a gig. So, here I am," he said with a crooked grin, raising his glass. "I'm the hired help."

Kate's eyes gleamed with a mix of amusement and mischief. "Oh, I see. So, is the 'hired help' package all-inclusive, or just the music? Any VIP perks?"

He turned to face her, his eyes burning with a new intensity as he tilted his head slightly, studying her. In a single smooth movement, he pulled her close, his hand pressing gently against the small of her back while the other slid behind her neck, fingers running up through her hair as he gently drew her face closer to his. She felt paralyzed with anticipation, the thrum of the party dissolving into a hazy blur of heat and music.

Was he really going to kiss her, right here? Now?

As he pulled her closer, the roughness of his cheek as it grazed hers, their skin barely touching. Their bodies were so close she could feel the heat radiating off him, and she inhaled deeply, the intoxicating scent of him filling her senses. A shudder of longing rippled through her, spreading like wildfire from her core, her pulse quickening. The tension between them thickened, every second stretching longer, unbearable. *God, kiss me,* she thought, the desperate plea nearly escaping her lips. *Right now. Please.*

Matt leaned in, his breath warm against her ear, his voice low and edged with a teasing roughness that made her pulse skip.

"Anything you want."

He released her smoothly, breaking the embrace with a casual ease that left Kate momentarily stunned, her heart still racing. Without a word, he gestured toward a bench closer to the fire, its worn surface framed by a couple of folded blankets. She hesitated, trying to make sense of the tension that still hung between them—strong, undeniable, and yet, *unresolved.*

What the hell just happened? she wondered, following him toward the warmth of the fire. He was leading her on, playing with her. Part of her hated it—because damn it, she *needed* the release and why wouldn't he just kiss her already? But another part of her was in too deep to turn back.

The night was now brisk, a cool ocean breeze cutting through the party. Despite the heat that still simmered beneath her skin, she welcomed the fire's warmth against the chill. Her outfit—perfectly chosen for making an impression and grinding on the dance floor— proved less practical now that the sun dipped below the horizon, leaving her bare arms and stomach exposed to the crisp night air. She pulled one of the blankets around her shoulders, its rough texture a comforting contrast against her skin, and sank onto the bench, grateful for its proximity to the crackling flames.

Matt tossed a nearby log into the fire, the wood hitting the glowing coals with a satisfying crackle that sent a spray of sparks spiraling up into the night. As he settled onto the bench, he swung one leg over to straddle it, facing her with an easy, fluid motion that seemed so effortless. Everything about him exuded a sexy confidence, from the way he moved to the faint smirk that played on his lips.

Kate's heart was still thudding in her chest from the almost kiss.

"So," he said, taking a sip of his drink. "Tell me how you learned to dance like that. Was it like *Dirty Dancing*—did some guy pull you into a sweaty underground club in New York?"

She laughed at the completely unexpected question. If he was running some sort of game on her, she might not care. He was genuinely funny and charming. "Something like that. I'm surprised you know that movie."

"I'm a man with many interests and hobbies," he said, leaning in. "The big city must be full of dull, unenlightened men who can't appreciate a well-done chick flick."

She sighed at the unfortunate accuracy of that statement. "I'm not sure the locale matters, to be honest. I'm surrounded by men, boys really, who only know about sports, the stock market, or how to gamify dating. I'm not against a good time, but it gets exhausting when men so clearly don't know what they want—either in life or in love. I guess I don't have it all figured out either, but at least I have some semblance of an idea."

She hadn't meant to, but her response had come out far too serious for his light, flirty comment. Already kicking herself, she quickly pivoted. Letting the blanket slip from her shoulders, she revealed the curve of her chest and the flat of her stomach, making sure he noticed.

This was still a game, and she wasn't about to take a loss tonight.

"Speaking of," she teased, her hand brushing lightly over his chest, "how old are you exactly? Please tell me you're not actually a senior in high school."

Matt's hand slid over hers, still resting on his chest. "Hold up. Don't change the subject, Katie," he said, his eyes locking with hers. "Here's what I think. You haven't met someone who knows what to do with a woman." His voice dropped, a challenge in his tone. "Maybe you've been expecting a boy to do a man's job."

It was almost unbearable, the way his gaze held hers. She could almost hear the tension crackling between them, the magnetic pull that made her want to lean forward, close the inches separating their lips. He reached over, lightly trailing his fingers along her arm. She was sure he was going to kiss her. Finally.

Just as she began to lean forward, familiar voices intruded. Jessica, Allison, and Nate ambled up, beers in hand and tipsy laughter spilling into the night.

"Anyone need another beer?" Jessica asked as she approached the fire, offering up a couple of Coronas.

Just inside the circle of firelight, the flames caught her blondish waves, which were artfully wind-swept and soft. She wore a pale blue halter top that set off her tan and low-slung white cargo pants, the kind that somehow made her look both casual and put together. She was smiling—warm enough and polite—but it didn't quite reach her eyes. Something lurked beneath the surface. Not anger exactly, not even open jealousy. It was more complex than that. A sharpness behind the gaze. A sadness, maybe.

The interruption sliced through the moment like a cold breeze. Matt straightened up, his leg swinging back over the bench as he turned to face his friends. Whatever unspoken possibility lingered between them vanished.

Kate felt like it was time to do the same. At this point, maybe the universe was trying to tell her something.

"I'm going to find Nikki and head out, actually. Too many shots, I'm pretty wasted," she lied. It was an easily accepted excuse, particularly when everyone else was too drunk to know any better. She felt Matt's eyes on her.

Jessica offered a strained smile, a contrast to her giggling and drunken compadres. "How responsible," she said evenly.

The comment stung in a way Kate wasn't expecting. It landed like "goody two-shoes," and amplified the feeling that she was out of place at this party and with these people. Her body tightened, and she glanced toward the darkened edges of the bonfire's glow, her mind set on finding Nikki and getting out of there. *Where the fuck is she?*

With perfect timing, Jessica pointed just past the fire. "Your girl's over there," she said with a smirk. "But don't think she's ready to leave anytime soon."

Kate followed Jessica's gaze, squinting into the shadows beyond the fire. There was Nikki, sprawled on a beach blanket, straddling the DJ. Their bodies tangled together, making out like there was no one else around, and it was clear they had no plans to stop.

Kate exhaled sharply, an impatient sigh slipping past her lips. The tension burning inside her had shifted—still hot but now laced with frustration. She didn't want to ditch her friend or break some unspoken college-girl code by leaving solo, but she was reaching her limit. All these almosts—almost kisses, almost touches, almost something—were starting to feel less like a slow burn and more like a tease with no payoff.

If he wanted her—*really* wanted her—he was going to have to stop circling and make a move. Because as fired up as she was, she wasn't about to beg for it. She did have some pride.

"I'll take you home," Matt's voice broke through her thoughts.

She glanced at him in surprise. Leaving didn't seem to be on his agenda until now. But there he was, already standing up.

Without missing a beat, he said, "See you guys tomorrow," with just enough finality to make it clear there'd be no protests. Jessica looked slightly startled but recovered quickly. He started walking toward the driveway.

Kate gave a small wave to the group and sped up to catch Matt, her heart thumping as she pulled her phone from her clutch.

Matt is bringing me home. Enjoy the DJ. Be safe!

The night air brushed her skin and she shivered, both from the temperature drop and the renewed anticipation.

If something was going to happen with Matt, it would happen now.

No more excuses. No more interruptions.

Just the two of them.

Chapter Eleven

2025

The two of them stood there at the pool bar, frozen for what seemed like minutes but was likely only ten seconds.

How could it be him?

The man was still touching her as she faced him, his hands now on her arms after her hasty turnabout. The contact felt electric and familiar, yet also strange and awkward.

He jerked back like he'd been burned, pulling his hands to his chest and stepping carefully away from the shattered glass at their feet. His expression shifted fast: shock, recognition, then pure embarrassment.

"Oh god—don't move, I'll grab someone to clean this up. I'm so sorry! I thought you were someone else. Jesus Christ. *I'm sorry,*" he stammered, panic visible in his eyes.

"Matt?" she whispered, her brow furrowing as disbelief and recognition battled for control.

No…not it wasn't Matt. Not exactly?

The man before her was stunningly similar but younger. Much younger than Matt would be now. He had the same warm eyes, except they were velvety brown, not blue. And very similar tousled hair, but wavier. His skin was tanned, and his open white linen shirt revealed a tight torso and visible abs underneath. That kind of athletic body was likely the result of a very disciplined fitness routine, probably involving long-distance running or swimming. More importantly, he was in his mid-twenties, not mid-forties.

"Sorry, I missed that…? Do we…know each other?" His panic turned into curiosity.

"Oh, um… no," Kate said, feeling a wave of secondhand embarrassment crash over her. She couldn't believe she'd just mistaken this hot, probably-still-taking-midterms guy for *him.*

Kate cleared her throat and forced a small smile. "But hey, word of advice—if you keep greeting women like that, you're going to spend your summer with a couple of black eyes and a reputation. Maybe both."

Mystery man laughed and nodded his head. "Fair enough."

"I really am sorry," he offered with an apologetic smile. His voice was smooth, confident, but kind. "I thought you were my friend, back for the summer. You look just like her from behind. Totally my bad."

My bad? Kate almost laughed out loud. *How old is he?*

The more she looked at him, the more she realized she had been manufacturing what she wanted to see. There were some remarkable similarities, and she felt drawn to him, but this was not Matt.

"It's ok," she finally replied, with a small smile as she composed herself and stood up a little straighter. "You just startled me. You remind me of someone I used to know."

He laughed softly, and the sound was so rich it practically sparkled in the humid air. "You were sort of looking at me like I was Marty McFly telling you I came from the future."

Her lips parted in surprise at such a throwback reference, and then she laughed. *More like the past*, she thought to herself with amusement. She had to remind herself that despite whatever feeling just zinged through her, he was not going to be part of her summer adventures.

"Ok, well. I appreciate your 80s movie acumen, well done. But we're good, just a mix-up. I can grab a waiter to help clean this up. I'm the one who dropped it."

He tilted his head, not moving. He seemed to be studying her with amused eyes. "Let me buy you a drink or something to make it up to you?"

Wait, is he flirting with me? It's certainly what it felt like, but that seemed highly unlikely. He was just being nice.

"Oh, I see. Is this your go-to move?" Kate asked, raising a brow. "Just sneak up behind women and hope they're flat-tered instead of filing a restraining order? What if I were married?"

Her tone was light, teasing. She couldn't help it—flirting felt like muscle memory coming back to the surface.

He lifted both hands in mock surrender. "Honest mistake. But for the record, I never offer to buy a beautiful woman a drink without checking for a wedding ring. I'm not an amateur."

She rolled her eyes but couldn't stop the slow smile tugging at her lips. "Does that line work on the college girls?"

She meant it as a jab, but he just grinned wider—those dangerous, bedroom eyes making it suddenly hard to think straight. He had that easy charm some men were born with, the kind that didn't require effort or rehearsal. He must have a dozen girlfriends.

What was even happening right now? Who *was* she? She'd been in Chatham all of *one* day and she was flirting with a guy who was—God, please let him be at least twenty-one—very possibly young enough to still be in college.

"I don't know," he said, gaze lingering just a second longer than polite. "You tell me."

Then, with zero warning: "I like your swimsuit, by the way. Is it Ferragamo?"

Kate blinked. "It is," she said, thrown for the second time in as many minutes. "I'm surprised you know that."

He paused a beat and smiled. "I just appreciate nice things." The words were casual—but the way he said them made it feel like anything but.

Before she could process, a melodic voice called from behind him. "Hey, Aiden! Is that you?"

So, this mystery man's name is Aiden. He turned, his smile broadening as he greeted a young woman, petite and brunette in a flowing maxi dress. She looked bubbly and girl-next-door cute. They appeared to be good friends judging by their goofy grins and sibling-like embrace. Aiden turned to face Kate.

"This is proof that I wasn't making it up. This is Anna, we've been friends since we were ten. Anna looks like you from behind." He winked at Kate, and she blushed yet again. The resemblance was there, but being mistaken for Anna felt like a generous compliment.

"I'm Kate," she said, reaching out her hand, feeling like she was caught in a strange dream. She was just here for a simple drink refill ten minutes ago.

"Kate," Aiden repeated thoughtfully. "That suits you."

"Nice to meet you, Kate!" Anna said warmly, reaching out her hand, ignoring what likely came across as a weird comment without any context. Kate noticed the way Anna's eyes passed between them, assessing. If Anna had any claims to Aiden, she didn't show it. Instead, she gave him a playful nudge. "Are you working tonight?"

"Hmm," he said, glancing down at his watch. "Yep, in fifteen minutes. I'm going to head over there now to make Kate a drink after I grab Stefan to clean this up – watch your step."

Of course. He *worked* here. That made more sense—his friendliness, his attention. He was just being charming for the guests, like any good bartender. Kate bet he was a huge hit with women her age. He must make a fortune in tips.

"I'll see you at the bonfire next weekend, yeah? Gotta run to meet the girls for champers and oysters. Ciao!" Anna said, excusing herself as she flitted away, leaving Aiden and Kate alone again.

"Come on, there's a seat here with your name on it." He motioned to the bar, which had started to fill up with former happy hour patrons now donning breezy shirts and summer dresses. He caught the eye of Stefan, motioning for him to help with the remnants of their chaotic encounter.

Kate knew she should walk away, chalk the whole encounter up to summer air and Aperol-fueled misunderstandings. A cute, harmless moment, nothing more. But for some reason, she didn't. Something in her told her to stay and see what happened next.

Aiden slipped behind the bar and casually buttoned up his linen shirt, covering the sun-kissed skin and toned torso that had been staring her in the face only moments ago.

Kate studied the drink menu with the focus of someone weighing a life-altering decision—rather than choosing between wine or tequila to distract her from being into this vaguely familiar, stupidly attractive boy-man.

"What can I get you?" he asked, eyes glinting with just enough mischief. "It's on me. And for the record—I don't usually hold onto strangers and whisper in their ear... unless I'm invited."

Now all she could think about was his hands on her waist, whispering into her ear and kissing her neck. She had to snap out of it—she was acting like a teenager with a crush. Maybe the six-month dry spell was affecting her more than she realized.

"Just an Aperol spritz, please," she managed. At least she didn't say Sex on the Beach. At this point she didn't quite trust what would come out of her mouth. He winked and began pouring prosecco into a fresh glass.

"So...do you work here every summer? Are you on break from school?"

Aiden looked up and gave her a mischievous grin. "Kate, are you trying to figure out how old I am?"

"No," she said quickly, flustered. "I just figured..."

"It's ok," he interrupted, handing her the drink. "I'm twenty-two. I graduated college this past spring."

"Well, with the Back to the Future reference, I was actually guessing you were *older* than me, with a really good plastic surgeon."

He shrugged, his grin impish. "Maybe I am thirty. You'll never know."

Cute that he thinks I'm thirty. That's a win, if nothing else.

Kate took a sip of her drink, fighting a smile. Two spritzes later, she was perched at the bar, half-reading and half-chatting with Aiden between his customers. She stopped scolding herself for ditching her quiet dinner plan at the Sacred Cod. Despite her initial hesitation, she was actually enjoying herself—and maybe feeling a little risqué hanging out with the young bartender. Sabbatical Kate was settling in for the summer. Nikki would be proud.

Aiden moved with effortless grace, flipping bottles and pouring drinks like a pro. She tried not to stare at his arms or the way he ran his hands through his hair when he was reading the drink tickets.

She couldn't help but imagine how good it would feel to take him back to her room, just for one night—let him take control, ravish her. He probably could go all night. The thought made her ache in ways she hadn't in far too long. *Get a grip, Kate.*

She'd clearly had too much to drink, and the bubbles were starting to go to her head. How long had she let this go on? Two hours? Yeah, humiliation was setting in.

"Oh, I need to check emails...and um...grab some dinner before I get too tipsy," she said, cringing inwardly.

"Wait," he said, his fingers lingering on hers. "What are you doing tomorrow night? I'm off, and I'd be a terrible local if I didn't introduce you to the best lobster roll on the Cape. Want to grab dinner?"

Her stomach did a flip. *Was he asking her out?*

"Oh, um... I'm not sure what my plans are," she hedged. Whatever older woman complex he had, she was confident he'd change his mind when he learned she was 44 years old.

He smiled, unfazed. "Well, when you figure it out, you know where to find me. I'll be around."

She slipped her hand away, gave him a tentative smile and walked as casually as she could back to her room given the interaction and the spritzes. Back in her room, Kate called Nikki immediately.

"Question. Asking for a friend. What is the official age gap before you have to register as a cougar?"

Chapter Twelve

2002

"Need some help getting in, tiger?" Matt teased as Kate eyed the towering cab of his blue pickup truck. She had not really pictured him as a truck guy.

"Uh, no. I've got it," she said, trying to sound breezy as she hoisted herself up. But the gravel driveway made the motion awkward, and her balance wavered.

His hands slipped around her waist—strong, sure, and confident. He lifted her like she weighed nothing, his grip firm but careful, fingers pressing into the thin fabric of her lace shirt as he guided her into the passenger seat. A pulse of heat bloomed low in her belly. She tried not to react, but every nerve was keenly aware of where he'd touched her, how close he'd been. How good it felt to be handled by him.

She sank into the leather seat, heart thudding in her chest. Whatever he was thinking, whatever he might do next, she had no idea. It was exhilarating.

As they pulled out of Brad's driveway, the soft purr of the engine filled the air, mingling with the faint crash of waves in the distance. The silence between them was charged, like the moment before a match strikes.

She stole another glance at him, noting the way his forearm flexed on the steering wheel, the way his jaw tensed and relaxed like he was thinking about something he wasn't saying.

Matt glanced at her then, his expression filled with curiosity.

"So," he started, breaking the silence, "why did you *actually* want to leave the party?"

She hesitated, no longer convinced she was pulling off her little white lie about having too much to drink. "I just figured I should call it a night." That wasn't *untrue*.

He raised an eyebrow and glanced over at her. "You didn't seem drunk to me," he replied softly. "More...distracted. Like something was bothering you."

Kate had an unsettling feeling that he could read her like a book. "What do you mean?" she asked tentatively.

"Well," he said, watching her carefully, "My sense is you're a bit of a people pleaser. You say what you think people want to hear instead of what you're actually feeling."

Kate tensed up at the accusation. Was that true? Was she a people pleaser?

Perhaps it wasn't far off. It was easier for Kate growing up to be the easy child. Similarly, it was less stressful to just let Lindsey get what she wanted. Now that she thought about it, in most of her friend groups, she was the one who shouldered all the planning, the organizing, for everyone. The caretaker.

She looked away for a moment, watching the quaint little cape houses blur by as they wound down the residential streets. It was unsettling to be seen so clearly by someone she didn't know very well. But there was no edge to his voice. No smirk or satisfaction in calling her out.

She nodded, almost to herself. "Yeah. You're not wrong."

It wasn't the kind of thing she admitted out loud. But it felt like maybe she didn't have to hide it right now. As they pulled up to the empty driveway of Nikki's family beach house, the porch light sputtered over the darkened windows. Kate felt unusually compelled to be truthful.

"Whatever this is between us," she gestured between them, "it's sitting right there, I can feel it. But then nothing happens. It's like whatever I'm doing is not enough to hold your attention. Or maybe you just like to flirt. But to be honest, I'm so tired of chasing unavailable men. Then the bus girls at the party called me a goody two shoes that you'd never be interested in, and with girls like Jessica around, no one stands a chance—anyway, it's not important. I have no business being attracted to you."

Her cheeks flushed, realizing just how much truth she had shared out loud. Mortified, flustered, and her hand already on the door handle, she jumped out of the truck as quickly as she could without falling, which would have made things ten times worse.

"So yeah...thanks for the ride home," she muttered as she turned toward the house. Before she could walk away, Matt had already rounded the truck.

"Wait." His steps were purposeful and smooth as he deftly made his way to where she was standing. He stopped in front of her, his eyes searching hers, something raw and urgent simmering behind the softness. Moonlight carved shadows across his face, but she could still see everything: the question in his expression, the heat behind it, the hesitation in his breath.

She braced herself for the pity hug or some awkward platitude about how she was a "great girl." She'd played her cards fast and loose and come across as a pathetic girl with a crush on her boss. She felt so stupid.

He was close enough that she could see the muscles in his jaw tighten, the glint of frustration in his eyes—but not at her. At himself.

"You think I'm not into you?" His voice was low, disbelieving. "You really think I could spend five minutes around you and not feel something?" He gave a short, incredulous laugh. "Kate, I've been trying to keep it together since the second I saw you."

She opened her mouth, but nothing came out.

He continued, his voice gentler now. "You have no idea what it's been like. Being around you, trying to act like an upstanding guy, when all I've wanted to do is—" He stopped himself, running a hand through his hair.

She didn't move. Didn't speak. But she held his gaze, and that was enough. Something unspoken passed between them, electric and inevitable. It was all the permission he needed.

He closed the gap, giving her every chance to back away — but she didn't. His hand found her hip, warm and steady, and then the other, bracketing her waist. The pressure was firm, grounding, but not demanding.

She wasn't sure she was taking in oxygen.

Then, gently he backed her up against the truck, his body pressing against hers with urgent need. She felt his chest rise against hers, the pounding of his heart echoing her own, the heat of him almost too much. Her hands slid up his arms, needing to touch something, to hold on.

Without a word, he kissed her—deeply, fierce and raw, as if all the pressure building up over the past week was pouring out in this one moment. It was unlike anything she'd ever experienced. His lips moved hungrily over hers, and heat coursed through her, her body arching desperately against him.

She completely submitted to him as she wrapped her arms around his waist, pulling him even harder toward her. Every single moment of tension released as they devoured each other.

"You are so fucking beautiful," he murmured, his voice rough with need. "I've wanted to do this all night."

"What took you so long?" she purred into his ear as she kissed the nape of his neck.

She tilted her head back with a soft gasp, the cool night air brushing her skin in sharp contrast to the searing warmth of his lips. Each kiss was slow, deliberate, like he wanted to memorize the taste of her.

She could feel him—hard, insistent—pressing between her legs, and it nearly unraveled her. Every nerve sparked to life, need pulsing through her in waves. The denim between them was both a frustration and a tease, heightening the tension as her hips shifted instinctively against his.

He paused, pulling back just enough to look at her, his breath uneven. His eyes searched hers, not for permission—he already had that—but for connection, confirmation that she was right there with him. She was. God, she was.

He reached down to unbutton her jeans, sliding his hand to where she wanted him most. The touch of his fingers sent a shockwave of pleasure through her, and she moaned softly, unable to hold back. It felt incredible—better than she'd imagined—and her body arched into his hand, her breaths quickening.

Yet, even as she let herself sink into the moment, doubt crept in.

It's going to take me too long, she thought as she continued to writhe in rhythm with his touch. But was already in her head. *I'm not going to be able to finish, and he's going to think I don't like it.*

The anxious thoughts crowded her mind, threatening to ruin everything. She hated to do it, but she panicked. She let out a louder moan, eager to show him how good it felt, rocking her hips against his hand. She forced her escalation to a crescendo, coaxing her body to tremble with release. She clung to him, her nails digging into his shoulders. He smelled sweaty and salty, his body throbbing with need and desire.

As he pulled his hand away gently, she lifted his t-shirt over his torso, revealing tight abs and a tuft of hair just above his beltline. She moved her hands across him, and up and down his jeans as he tilted his head back and groaned in pleasure. He was rock hard, turned on from having pleasured her, which made her want him more. Just as she reached for his belt, headlights flashed behind them. She froze.

"Fuck," she whispered as the lights grew closer. She knew it was Nikki's car. They reluctantly pulled away from each other, trying to smooth their clothes and regain some semblance of composure. Matt leaned in, his breath hot against her neck as he whispered, "To be continued." He pulled her in for another hard kiss before peeling away.

Nikki emerged from the car, a sly grin spreading across her face.

"Oh *hey*, Matt," she nodded at him, her tone dripping with amusement. "I can go back to the party if you need more time?"

"I was just heading out," he said, glancing at Kate with a secret smile before hopping back into his truck. "Just to warn you, she's 'drunk' and 'tired,'" he added before closing the door. Kate savored the intimacy of his inside joke.

As the truck rumbled down the street, Nikki turned to Kate, her eyebrows raised. "So... did you guys fuck or what?"

Kate let out a giddy sigh, her face still flushed. "Not exactly," she said, her voice breathless. "But you might have come home a *little* too soon."

Nikki grinned as they headed inside, bounding up the stairs to her room. "You better spill every last detail," she demanded. "I want to hear all about it."

Kate felt a mix of exhilaration and disbelief as she recounted the entire night, play-by-play to her best friend.

Even as she spoke, every place he'd touched her still tingled with heat, like sparks left smoldering on her skin.

Chapter Thirteen

2025

A dozen new freckles surfaced on Kate's skin from the smoldering summer sun. She smoothed on more sunblock and adjusted her glasses as she reclined on the pool chair, trying to look relaxed amid the mid-morning buzz at Chatham Bars Inn. The sky was impossibly blue, and the gentle splash of ocean waves nearby was soothing.

Or it *would* have been soothing if she weren't so concerned with looking put together, just in case she ran into Aiden. Which she hadn't. She was more disappointed than she cared to admit, even to herself.

That morning, Kate picked her sexiest bikini—a brightly colored Agua Bendita triangle top combo she'd bought five years ago for a trip to Cabo (and never quite got the courage to wear). She told herself it was just practical to wear it at least once—but even she didn't buy that. Not with the way she'd triple-checked her reflection before heading to the pool.

It had been years since she'd felt this flustered about a man noticing her. She supposed she *could* call him a man now, given she knew he was twenty-two years old and no longer in college.

She tried to focus on reading her book and not people-watching. Or watching for him. The air smelled like a cornucopia of different coconut- and cocoa butter-scented sunblocks. The occasional splash and kids' laughter gave the perfect cover for her wandering thoughts.

Her phone buzzed on the table beside her.

Are you free tonight?

Lindsey. Again. Her sister rarely texted this much unless she needed something.

Kate squinted at the screen with suspicion. It wouldn't be money—Lindsey had married a well-off and surprisingly kind man. In finance, of course. When that viral TikTok video came out about young girls looking for a six-foot-five' man in finance with blue eyes, at least six people had sent it to her with just the word "Lindsey" and a crying laughing face emoji.

Babysitting, maybe? That was probably it. While she adored her six-year-old niece Addison and eight-year-old nephew Bryson, she wasn't about to be cast as aunt nanny her first week here.

Sorry, not free tonight.

She flipped the phone facedown to keep it from overheating, but it buzzed again. Persistent.

But this time, it wasn't Lindsey.

> Have you banged the bartender yet?

Kate laughed under her breath. Nikki.

> I haven't seen him! Stop. He doesn't want to bang me. I could be his mother.

> Maybe he has an Oedipus complex

> That's not a selling point Nik lol

> You don't need to marry the dude

> I'm aware. He probably has like six summer girlfriends who aren't old enough to rent a car.

> Maybe, but I know what you're doing. Don't self-deprecate. You're attractive. You have charisma. Not all girls do. You're scared.

Kate sighed. She did have some self-worth, despite the current state of her life. She wasn't *scared*. She just knew what humiliation felt like. And drama. Specifically, when it came to summer flings.

> I'm not scared, I'm realistic. He's not actually interested in me.

You remember Schitt's Creek? That episode where David says -- I like the wine and not the label.

Pretty sure that conversation was about being pansexual

Yes, I KNOW that. I'm saying he likes the wine. Isn't wine better when it's aged???

You have a point there

Kate was mid-chuckle when a shadow crossed her body. She looked up—and there she was. Black vintage swimsuit, sleeves of tattoos, oversized dramatic sun hat.

"I always have a point," Nikki said, grinning triumphantly.

Kate sat straight up, shielding her eyes with one hand. "Nikki?!"

"Mrs. Robinson, is that you?" Nikki asked with a smirk as she tossed her massive tote bag onto the lounge chair like she was making an entrance at Cannes. "Did you really think I *wasn't* going to check out the sexy bartender who is trying to seduce you? In fact, I'm here to make sure he does."

Kate laughed, hugging her tightly. "Hi. I'm happy to see you. And I *told* you I haven't even seen him since I got here. Don't embarrass me if he shows up."

"Oh, honey," Nikki said, pulling a comically large tumbler from her bag. "With that little 'fuck me' bikini you're wearing? He'll be here. That suit is basically a beacon for every available penis in a ten-mile radius."

"And unavailable," she added, scanning the pool like a cougar in Gucci shades.

Kate rolled her eyes. "It's not that scandalous. I appreciate you pumping me up, though."

"Something is going to pump you up in that, my friend," she said without missing a beat, casually flipping through the pool drink menu. "Now I really do need that bartender, so I get us started on a bottle of bubbles."

As if on cue, Aiden sauntered into the pool area like summer itself had sent a gift to the ladies of the Chatham Bars Inn. Without the haze of bar lighting or the blur of Aperol Spritzes, Kate could really see Aiden. His dark hair was messier than before, and she couldn't tell if he styled it that way or he just rolled out of bed. And that *smile.*

He moved through the pool crowd like a local celebrity, offering nods and hellos, his presence generating a gravitational pull. Women turned their heads. Men checked their own posture. Aiden barely noticed, heading straight for the lifeguard stand.

"He's a lifeguard, too?" Kate muttered under her breath, blinking like she'd hallucinated the whole thing.

And then—God help her—came the shirt removal; one smooth, cinematic peel that seemed to move in slow motion. He must have practiced that at least a hundred times to get that so perfectly. Kate inhaled sharply and ducked behind Nikki like she was avoiding sniper fire.

"Sweet mother of torso," Nikki whispered, sliding her sunglasses down her nose. "Is that him? If you don't bang him, I will personally volunteer as tribute."

"Nikki!" she whisper-yelled with a giggle. "What about Jay?"

"Jay *who*?"

Kate exhaled. "He is criminally hot. But I still think it's weird how much he looks like Matt."

Nikki squinted. "Mmm... maybe? You might be projecting. Or manifesting. I haven't seen that douche canoe for twenty years, so my memory is foggy."

"Fair. Let's not talk about him."

"Exactly. Let's focus on that young Adonis slathering sunscreen all over his tight body." Nikki fanned herself with a drink menu for dramatic effect.

Kate shook her head, but she couldn't stop staring. "A hot guy showing up on day one of my magical healing summer feels suspicious. Like someone scripted it."

"Nope," Nikki quickly corrected her. "It's karmic justice. The universe finally got tired of messing with you. You need to, and I mean this literally, embrace that absurdly perfect man body. Look at him. He's hot *and* he cares about his skin."

"Yeah, he's dreamy," Kate sighed. "Or maybe all young guys look dreamy when you're over forty."

"Kate! I don't want to hear another word about how young he is. He's a man, he's well over 18 and from what you've told me, he's charming. If he acted like a boy, you wouldn't even be *considering* this."

"I'm not considering this. And twenty-two is not that much older than 18."

"Don't get me started on the double standard about women dating younger guys."

Kate was about to protest when Aiden spotted them. He gave a little wave, hopped off his chair with ease and started to make his way over.

"Oh no, he's coming over. Please behave Nikki!" Kate was mildly panicked.

"I would never misbehave," Nikki said, putting on her most innocent expression. That made Kate panic more.

Aiden approached, standing in front of them with those full-frontal abs and a hint of amusement. "Good morning, ladies."

"It *is* a good morning," Nikki said with a grin that Kate recognized as pure mischief. She was too far away to pinch.

"So, do you work every job here?" Kate teased to ease her own anxiety. "What's next, bellhop?"

"Just the jobs where I might run into you," Aiden said smoothly with a wink. He turned to Nikki and reached out his hand. "Nice to meet you. I'm Aiden."

"Nikki," she said, holding out her hand with exaggerated formality. "Visiting for the day. Lucky me."

"I told you we'd run into each other," Aiden said to Kate, his grin widening. "It's serendipity."

"Maybe," Kate shrugged casually. "It's not so unusual to be at the pool."

"Well, since lobster rolls clearly aren't your thing," Aiden said, locking eyes with Kate, "there's a bonfire on the beach tonight. Super low-key—just a few of us hanging out. You should both come."

"She's not actually—" Kate began, but Nikki cut her off.

"We'd love to," Nikki interrupted with a broad smile.

"Great! It starts around nine when the sun goes down." He turned to leave, then looked back grinning at Nikki. "By the way, watch that Dior hat. It's windy today, and I don't want to have to rescue it."

Kate stared after him, unable to look away. His retreating figure was an Olympic-level display of perfection. *Seriously, who made this man?*

Nikki let out a slow whistle. "That ass should be illegal. It's honestly rude. Are we absolutely sure he's not gay?"

Kate laughed, shaking her head. "Pretty sure. Although, he does know way more about Dior than I do."

Kate squinted at Nikki like she was trying to solve a riddle. "Wait, what about your kids? Don't you have to go home tonight?"

"Oh, please," Nikki replied, waving her off. "I told Jay I might stay over. Someone needs to make sure you don't retreat into the safety of your tortoise shell. Now, the real question: what are you going to wear?"

Kate groaned and buried her face in her hands. "God, I don't know. Are we seriously doing this? It's going to be all twenty-somethings and then us—two fully grown adults lurking in the background like suburban cougars looking for prey."

Nikki grabbed her by the shoulders. "Kate, listen to me. He's clearly into you. Just be yourself and let that sweet-assed boy unleash all that 20-year-old enthusiasm on your body. Or at least let him get to second base."

Kate snorted, trying to hide her grin. "I feel like your advice is biased by wanting to live vicariously."

"Maybe a little," Nikki winked. "But that doesn't mean it's wrong. You trust me, right? This will be good for you. You need to move on from Chris."

Kate hesitated at the sudden sentiment. Chris's words to her the night he ended their marriage echoed in her head—how there was no spark, no passion between them. He'd claimed it was mutual, that they'd both let things fizzle. But deep down, she carried the weight of it. It was her fault. She was the one who unknowingly traded passion for comfortable friendship. She'd designed them a safe life, steady and reliable, but in doing so, had she made it lifeless too? The thought still tightened her chest and sat heavy in her heart.

Nikki was right. It was time to dig out the woman she used to be—not all at once, maybe. Just enough to remember how it felt to be vibrant again.

"I think I have a few things Sydney made me pack," Kate said finally.

"Oh, please tell me we're throwing it back to college ho days?!" Nikki clapped her hands. "Do you have a going-out top?!"

Kate laughed, shaking her head. The rest of the day passed in a blur of sunbathing, reminiscing, and wine, with Kate sneaking glances at the lifeguard who, to her growing delight, kept glancing back.

Maybe it was the lingering buzz from the Perrier Jouët—but as she reclined beside Nikki, who'd slipped into a lazy mid-afternoon nap, Kate's mind began to drift.

She pictured Aiden's body—sun-warmed and impossibly perfect—hovering over her, his mouth grazing the sensitive spot just beneath her ear. His hands pinning hers above her head, his weight deliciously grounding her. The cool slide of her swimsuit bottoms being moved aside, the heat of him pressing against her, then inside her, in one smooth, hungry motion.

Her breath hitched at the sheer clarity of it, every nerve suddenly awake. She shifted slightly on the lounge chair, hyperaware of the tingling ache between her legs.

Two things were clear. One, she needed to get a hold of herself. This was a luxury resort, not the set of a softcore porn. Two, she still had some passion within her, after all.

Tonight was going to be interesting.

Chapter Fourteen

2002

Avril Lavigne's "Complicated" blared for the second time that hour in near-distortion levels through the boombox in Kate and Nikki's room. Kate stood barefoot on the hardwood floor, carefully flat-ironing strands of her hair and releasing wafts of Herbal Essences into the steamy air. Despite being tired of the song, she mouthed along to the lyrics.

She almost didn't hear the faint buzz of her red Nokia vibrating against the top of the antique wooden nightstand.

1 New Message.

She dropped the flat iron onto the vanity and snatched the phone.

Leaving early. Meet me @ Lighthouse Beach.

Her stomach flipped. Kate sank onto her bed, grinning at the tiny glowing green screen like it had just handed her a lottery ticket. She stared at his name a second longer before tossing the phone beside her, heart fluttering.

After that steamy night outside Nikki's house, she braced herself for the worst—no call, or worse—Matt pretending nothing had happened. Guys liked to do that for some reason.

But to her surprise and delight, he had called the very next day. They'd talked for hours, their conversation weaving through childhood memories, favorite movies, and the bands they still dreamed of seeing live. Kate confessed she loved the Gin Blossoms (even though they hadn't put anything out in ages). Matt revealed he cried like a baby reading *Where the Red Fern Grows*.

They'd agreed to keep whatever this was between them under wraps at work. It wasn't ideal—red flags danced in the corners of her mind—but he *was* technically the boss. For now, she decided, a secret romance was ok.

Unfortunately, Kate found it more challenging to be around Matt at work than she'd anticipated. Each time he brushed past her, a simple touch of his hand or a glance in her direction made her pulse skip like a scratched CD. His eyes would catch hers with a glint of mischief. Her mind kept drifting back to what they'd done outside Nikki's house.

No one really seemed to notice, which was good. Natalie, Allison and Stacey scattered around in their own little worlds and Nate shamelessly flirted with her between taking orders and serving food.

It was Jessica, though, who seemed to have picked up on a change, her gaze lingering just a bit longer whenever Kate and Matt crossed paths. Jessica was friendly enough the first night Kate trained, but since that party, her warmth had cooled. There was stiffness in her interactions now, something Kate couldn't quite pin down. If there was tension, maybe Jessica was interested in Matt, too. Kate resolved to be extra nice to Jessica—charming, helpful, the picture of camaraderie—leaving no room for her to harbor any dislike.

Be there in 20 min

She looked at her watch. Kate didn't have nearly enough time to get ready for her first real date with Matt. She quickly chose a short floral summer dress, the chiffon soft and flowing over her sun-kissed skin. The dress was both girlish and subtly seductive, with a plunging neckline that hinted at her curves without being too obvious. With her highlighted hair already straight, she spritzed herself with just a hint of body spray and hopped into the car.

Hot and stuffy, she immediately rolled down the windows and cursed herself, again, for not splurging for A/C. She popped in her summer mix into the CD player looking for some inspiration.

Gravitating to sultry hip hop or anything featuring Ja Rule, she skipped forward until she landed on "Down 4 U" with Ashanti and cranked the volume, letting the music carry her to the beach.

The sun dipped lower on the horizon, painting the sky in vivid shades of orange, pink, and deep red. As Kate pulled up, she spotted Matt leaning casually against his truck, the evening light casting a warm glow over him. He wore a pair of well-worn Levi's and a faded Dropkick Murphy's concert t-shirt—a band she'd have to ask about later. Anticipating a cooler night, he layered a gray zip-up hoodie over the shirt, and wore flip-flops, his laid-back look fitting seamlessly with the beach setting.

In one hand, he held a beach bag slung over his shoulder, and in the other, a bottle of wine. When Kate stepped out of the car, the crunch of gravel under her feet, Matt's face brightened instantly, his eyes locking onto hers with a mix of excitement and something softer—like relief that she had decided to come.

"Hey, Katie," he said without taking his eyes off her as she approached.

"Hey," she said, feeling suddenly shy under his gaze.

"Everything ok?" He asked, seemingly aware of her nervousness.

"Yeah, I'm good." That didn't sound convincing. "It's just I didn't have a chance to grab dinner, so I hope there's food involved. Or some oysters we can dig up."

"I wouldn't make you forage for your dinner," he replied with a warm smile, reaching for her hand. "We're having a picnic."

His touch made her feel almost giddy as he led her down the beach. They found a secluded spot away from the few lingering beachgoers and laid out a blanket. The air was still warm, and Matt brought an impressive spread of cheese, crackers, grapes, almonds, prosciutto, and even a couple of actual wine glasses.

"You look pretty," he said, his voice soft as he leaned in to kiss her on the cheek. It was gentle and sweet. "And you smell... surprisingly good."

Kate laughed, swatting him lightly. "What, were you expecting me to smell like?"

He chuckled as he opened the wine. "Well, since you worked this afternoon, my money was on fried shrimp."

"Well, that's fair. Instead, you get Love Spell. And fried shrimp."

"Delicious and refreshing. Guess you really can have it all," he sighed mockingly, holding his hand over his heart.

They settled in, sharing snacks and small talk, the conversation drifting lazily like the waves. As the stars began to emerge, Kate felt a shiver run through her. Matt reached into the bag, pulling out another blanket and wrapping it around them both.

"So. Tell me more about your family," he said, pulling her close.

Kate hesitated for a moment, because she really didn't love talking about her family. But Matt didn't seem to ask questions to be polite, he really wanted to know her. And he listened intently, asking surprisingly insightful questions. She had not met one guy like this in almost four years in New York.

"Well…it was kind of chaotic growing up," she admitted. "My dad has worked in IT for one company for 30 years, but my mom was all over the place—new job every year, constantly changing plans, directions and hobbies. Because of that, our finances were erratic and we'd either be taking a big trip to Disney or on food stamps. My dad is very introverted, and my mom was in charge. He didn't step in when he really should have."

She paused, looking down at her hands. "The unpredictability was hard for me."

"I can't imagine how hard that is for a kid," he said softly as they both looked up at the night sky. "It explains why you are so focused on trying to control and adapt to your surroundings. There is safety for you in being able to influence the future. Must be tough to let that go and embrace the present. Not knowing what will happen is scary. But it can also be invigorating, too."

She stared thoughtfully at the waves rolling forward and back into the darkening sea. And for once, she let silence hang there for a moment without trying to fill it immediately.

"Are you sure you don't want to be a psychologist?" she asked finally, with a small smile, hoping to deflect the conversation away from her.

"And you said you had a sister, right? Leslie? Were you both close?" he continued, expertly avoiding her deflection.

"Lindsey," Kate sighed heavily. "We were never close, except maybe when we were young. As we got older, she was good at everything where I needed to try twice as hard. She was popular, she was athletic, she was pretty. And she always seemed to want whatever I had, just because she could have it. Caused a lot of issues between us in high school."

She wished she hadn't brought Lindsey up. Even when she wasn't there, she was ruining Kate's special moments. Matt listened quietly, putting his arm around her as if to shield her from the memories.

"I get it," he said after a moment. "It's not quite the same experience, but my brothers were kind of like that, too. One's a surgeon, the other's a helicopter pilot in the Coast Guard. I always felt like the odd man out, the stereotypical middle sibling. They were always so driven, while I just..." He shrugged. "I never knew what I wanted, except to be happy. Music makes me happy and being around people makes me happy. I've always loved kids. Which is why I'm thinking of becoming a teacher."

That was the first time he'd mentioned wanting to become a teacher. As soon as he said it, she could see it so clearly. He'd be a great teacher. He was kind, charming and a great listener. Kids would love him.

"For what it's worth," Kate replied thoughtfully. "I don't know your brothers, but I'm not sure all of us overachievers are all that happy. I suppose we are usually searching for something that it looks like you've already found."

He smiled at her, gentle and inviting. "You know, you're pretty amazing, Katie."

She smiled back at him, feeling warm all over.

"Why do you call me Katie, by the way? No one else calls me that."

"I like that no one else calls you that," he grinned. "But if you don't like it, I can stop."

"No...I like it," she said. In that moment, with the sound of the waves and the warmth of his embrace, Kate felt almost euphoric.

"Can I ask you something, a little out of the blue?" Matt said, his tone thoughtful.

"Sure," she replied, tilting her head up to meet his eyes.

"Did you actually have an orgasm the other night?"

She tensed up immediately. This was not even in the *realm* of questions she expected getting. She considered continuing with the white lie, as she always had with other men. But there was something about the way that Matt saw her and the connection she felt to him. Even a white lie just felt...wrong.

"No..." she said quietly, feeling a surge of vulnerability.

"I didn't think so," he said, his voice calm and understanding.

Kate blinked, still stunned that he'd even asked, much less noticed.

"It's not that it didn't feel *amazing*," she explained quickly. "It's just... I always feel pressure to show I'm enjoying it, and I guess it takes me longer. I don't know, it's probably just a me problem."

She bit her lip, deciding whether to open herself up even more.

"I've actually never had one with any of the guys I've been with."

Matt looked deep in her eyes. She thought she might cry—she felt very exposed.

He touched her cheek tenderly, his fingers grazing her skin. "I'm glad you told me," he said softly.

He leaned in closer, his breath warm on her face. "We'll work on that."

Her heart swelled at his words. No guy had ever asked her this before or cared enough to wonder. She had become an absolute expert at faking it over the years. She was confident that not one of her partners knew. She hadn't meant to lie, necessarily. But she didn't feel it was worth vocalizing. Bruised egos certainly do not make for better sex or better relationships.

And here Matt was, not only attentive enough to know she was faking, but smart enough to ask her at a time when she didn't feel compelled to save face.

He was unlike anyone she'd ever met.

The intensity of her desire for him came on quickly. She leaned in toward him, resting her hand on his stubbly cheek. The moonlight danced on his crystal blue eyes, which remained locked on her, filled with longing and lust.

He kissed her then, slowly laying her back on the blanket, his hands moving with deliberate tenderness over her body. Each kiss felt like a spark, igniting every nerve. The rest of the world faded away on the quiet beach.

Matt's touch was achingly slow as he kissed gently down her chest, and she arched up to meet him, craving more. He pinned her wrists gently above her head and trailed kisses down her stomach, inching ever closer to her thighs.

With a quick fluid motion, he pulled the blanket over them to shield their bodies from the view of any possible lingering beach walkers. She appreciated the discreteness – this kind of risqué activity was not something she'd ever done before, and she was pretty sure they could get arrested for public indecency. But for once, she didn't care. She didn't want him to stop.

Her pulse quickened as he moved lower, lifting her dress and brushing his lips over her inner thigh. The sensation sent a shudder through her, but an undercurrent of anxiety threatened to rise—what if she couldn't relax? What if she over thought it and ruined the moment? The thought of him going down on her turned her on immensely, but she wasn't feeling confident. She was going to disappoint and embarrass him.

Sensing her hesitation, Matt returned to her, his eyes meeting hers with reassuring calm.

"Relax, Kate," he whispered. "I'm going to take my time. I'll stay here all night if that's what it takes."

And then, with a gentle touch of his tongue, he resumed. As promised, there was no rush, just a slow build of pressure that grew steadily, deliciously, until she couldn't hold back.

"There," she said, finding a voice she didn't know she had. "*Right there, don't stop,*" she moaned. When the climax came, it was real and unrestrained, washing over her in waves of bliss.

This time, he didn't have to ask. He knew.

He made his way slowly back up her body, kissing her navel lovingly. She lay there in the quiet moonlight, feeling alive, but also overwhelmed with unexpected emotion. As he kissed his way up her body, he made eye contact with her, checking in to make sure she was still ok. She returned his gaze confirming her desire for what she knew was coming next. This was so much more than she expected. While she was not a virgin, this experience felt more like becoming a woman than any other she'd ever had.

He gently pulled her dress down while adeptly keeping them covered in the blanket, exposing her bare breasts for the first time. She moaned lightly and pressed into him, and she could tell he was enjoying this as much as she was. He sat up, pulling off his shirt, his tight chest and body driving her wild with yearning. She grabbed his hips as he leaned down to kiss her neck with barely restrained hunger. She unbuttoned his jeans, impatient to take everything else off him. She could not wait any longer to feel him inside her.

In a moment of confidence, Kate stopped him, only long enough to push him onto his back and position herself on top of his now naked, perfectly toned body. He became more aroused, and she positioned herself so he couldn't hold back. The blanket had already been cast aside. At this point, she didn't care, it was worth whatever trouble they might get into.

Their passion was reaching a fever pitch, but it was the unmistakable adoration in his eyes that truly made her heart surrender. As she leaned down to kiss him and he was finally inside of her, she knew this wasn't just a fling. She could feel it as deeply in her soul as she felt him in her body.

They collapsed into each other, making love until the stars faded from the sky.

Chapter Fifteen

2025

The stars were scattered across the night sky like glitter on velvet, casting a quiet shimmer over the dark, eerily still ocean. As Kate and Nikki pulled into the dusty beach lot, she was surprised to find it packed with cars—far more than she'd expected for what was supposed to be a low-key bonfire.

The warm and salty summer air carried whispers of the ocean and laughter from the beach. The fire on the beach glowed bright against the inky sky, its embers dancing upward like fireflies. Dozens of people milled about, illuminated by the golden light—some tossing a football in the dark, others clustered in groups, their red solo cups highlighted by the fire's glow.

Kate adjusted her loose beach waves in the mirror, which had taken quite a lot of effort to look effortless. Her white eyelet peasant top and high-waisted cutoff jean shorts felt casual enough for a bonfire while still being cute, and her new green leather sandals added a subtle touch of class to what

Nikki described as a "very Vineyard Vines" ensemble. Nikki, on the other hand, opted for leopard print jeans and black tank top. The contrast between her outrageous confidence and the beach's relaxed vibe was almost comical.

"You look like a young Jen Aniston, I LOVE it," Nikki cooed.

"None of these people here are going to be old enough to even know who she is," Kate muttered anxiously.

"First of all, they all watch *Friends* reruns; it's a whole thing," Nikki retorted matter-of-factly. She scanned the crowd like a hawk spotting prey as they approached the party.

"Look over there," she said, pointing at a couple standing off to the side. "See those two? Definitely in their late thirties. I hereby forbid you to make any references to age gaps tonight. Got it?"

Kate gave a lighthearted scoff. "Fine, but don't say I didn't warn you when we end up hung over tomorrow from losing at beer pong."

"Your memory must be failing you in your old age, because, as you'll recall, I *never* lose at beer pong."

Just then, a warm hand landed on both their shoulders. Kate turned, her breath catching as she met Aiden's gaze.

"Hey, ladies," he said, his smile easy and disarming. "I'm not sure anyone brought the beer pong table, but I could probably rustle one up. I'm really glad you came."

He was looking at her when he said that last part—intently, like he was speaking directly to her and her alone. Aiden wore a loosely buttoned collared shirt and his relaxed jeans hung low on his hips. He radiated sex appeal and charm. At the same time, she could tell he was checking her out, and the way he looked at her body, Kate felt flushed.

Nikki, not one to keep her opinions to herself, raised her eyebrows and let out a quiet, approving hum that Kate prayed only she could hear. Thankfully, Nikki spotted someone across the fire.

"Oh my god, is that Marco?" she exclaimed. "Oh, I know him from fashion week! I forgot he and his boyfriend rent a house over here. Excuse me, Aiden, I must go say hi to my people. Come find me later. Or don't." She winked at Kate.

As Nikki strutted away, Kate turned back to Aiden and shrugged. "That was about as subtle as Nikki can manage."

He grinned. "She's great, I like her. So, do you want to check out the fire and grab a beer or a wine?"

"Sure," she nodded. He grabbed her hand as he led her further down the beach, which took her by surprise. She had to admit, it felt nice.

"I'm kind of impressed," Kate said, trying to distract herself from the fact he was holding her hand. "I assumed it would be all beer and High Noons."

Aiden laughed, "Usually, you're right. But I thought you might like wine, so I brought a bottle just in case."

Her eyebrows shot up. "You brought wine to a bonfire for me?"

"I may have," he said teasingly.

She was surprised and impressed at his thoughtfulness. *For his age,* she added. Nikki couldn't yell at her for thinking it.

As they walked toward the fire, she caught him glancing at her sandals. "Are those the Hermès Oran sandals? It's a nice pop of color, I like them," he said casually.

Her laughter bubbled out, unrestrained. "Ok, how do you know that! What guy knows Hermès?!"

He smiled. "My mom's a fashion designer. I've picked things up over the years. And I just finished my degree in design and business, so I've been doing some part-time designing for her."

Kate blinked. This was a lot of new information. "Wait, you design for her? What kind of things?"

"Mostly casual wear and graphic tees, but she's been pushing me to try more. To explore my artistry." He paused, his gaze thoughtful. "Her business is doing well, and she wants me to join full-time. Not sure it's what I want to do for the rest of my life, though. But I'll figure it out."

Kate's perception shifted. Aiden wasn't just a hot guy to flirt with, he was clearly smart, driven, and creative. She realized how shallow her initial assumptions had been.

As they reached the circle of coolers half-buried in sand and surrounded by tipsy twenty-somethings cracking beers and passing bottles, he reached into one like it was a treasure chest and pulled out a chilled white. With a dramatic flourish, he held it up. "Sancerre work for you?"

Kate let out a startled laugh, her brows lifting as he uncorked the bottle and casually poured it into a solo cup like they were at a vineyard tasting. Sancerre. At a beach bonfire. It was one of her favorites—and about five rungs above what she'd expected. "You're ridiculous," she said, taking the cup. "And full of surprises."

He grinned, handing her the drink with mock ceremony. "I'm flexing muscles I don't usually have to. I don't usually have to work this hard to get noticed."

He said it with a smirk and a dash of mischief, but there was truth in that statement. Aiden was clearly used to being pursued, not doing the chasing. And with those dark, smoldering eyes and that maddeningly perfect body, Kate couldn't blame anyone.

The thing was, she wasn't *trying* to play hard to get. She was just stuck in a tug-of-war between her practical, almost-divorced adult brain and the teenage girl in her head screaming, *he's hot—just kiss him already.* Her internal chaos only seemed to make him more intrigued.

"Well, it must be *exhausting* having girls throw themselves at you all day," she said, her voice laced with mock sympathy and a teasing glint in her eye. "Sorry to be so difficult."

A slow, satisfied smile tugged at his lips. "I like a challenge," he said, stepping closer. The space between them evaporated until their bodies brushed—barely—but enough to set her nerves on high alert.

He leaned in, his lips grazing the shell of her ear, his voice a quiet tease. "And the night is still young."

And so are you, she thought. And confident in the way only a guy his age could be. Still, the thrill of having him whisper in her ear hit like a rush of champagne bubbles, light and dizzying.

"Touché," she managed to mumble, her breath catching as his cheek brushed hers, the moment thick with possibility. She thought he might kiss her. She wasn't sure if she wanted that or not, despite an almost animalistic pull toward his body.

He pulled away as smoothly as he leaned in. Almost tenderly, he tucked a strand of hair behind her ear, his fingers grazing her temple, lingering there for a moment. His eyes met hers with an earnestness that had not been there before.

"You have incredible eyes," he said softly. "They actually sparkle when you smile."

He was turning on the charm—smooth, practiced—but damn if he didn't make it feel effortless.

"Does that line usually work on girls your age?" She tilted her head with a smirk.

Aiden grinned, unbothered. "Most of the time," he said with a wink. "But I mean it. You have beautiful eyes. And your aura has this glow...it's sexy."

Her aura? She almost laughed out loud. But it was kind of cute.

Suddenly, she was hyper aware of the laughter and chatter drifting around them, of the warmth radiating off his body, of how very *close* they were. Nothing had happened—not really—but standing this close to a man she had no business flirting with felt just rebellious enough. She took a measured step back and lifted her wine glass to her lips, trying to cool the heat crawling up her neck.

It was then that Kate's eye caught a familiar silhouette just beyond the fire. Wide-leg linen pants swayed gracefully as the wearer shifted, the cropped top accentuating a slender, statuesque figure. Long, dark hair cascaded like silk, tumbling over her shoulders as she threw her head back in a laugh that rang out, unmistakable to Kate. She didn't have to see her face to know—it was Lindsey. And for the life of her, Kate couldn't imagine what reason her sister would be doing there. Lindsey was the absolute worst person to encounter while chatting up a much younger man. Her pulse quickened. She needed an excuse to disappear, and fast.

"It's a little too warm by the fire, isn't it?" she said, hoping he'd pick up on the hint.

He looked thoughtfully at her, temporarily surprised by the pivot. "Yeah, you're right," he said, his lips curling into a mischievous grin. "Time for a swim!"

Before she could protest, he scooped her up in a fireman's carry, her glass of wine tipping precariously as she squealed in surprise.

"Aiden! Don't you dare throw me in!" she shouted between peals of laughter. She really didn't want to be salty and sticky for the rest of the night. Then again, that would be better than an impromptu visit with her sister. What was she even *doing* here anyway?

Before she could think too hard about it, they were almost at the water's edge. She was bracing herself when his foot caught on the corner of an unoccupied beach blanket. They toppled over in a heap, wine splashing everywhere as they both erupted into uncontrollable laughter.

They lay there, side-by-side in the moonlight, their breath mingling with the ocean breeze. Kate turned her head to look at him, her chest rising and falling as she tried to catch her breath. His easy smile softened as his gaze settled on her, his eyes tracing the contours of her face.

She was losing the will to resist his charm. What was so bad about a harmless make out?

But then, as she lay on the blanket, a vague sense of déjà vu hit her. This place, this moment, felt familiar, like a memory tugging at the edges of her consciousness.

Before she could untangle the feeling, Aiden shifted closer, cupping her face gently. His touch was tender, his eyes searching hers. "Would it be ok if I kissed you?" he asked, his voice barely above a whisper, his face just inches from hers.

Kate's heart was hammering in her chest. She nodded.

He leaned in, cradling her face in his hands as his lips met hers. The kiss was hungry yet fluid, gentle yet charged. She let herself fall into it, matching his intensity as his body hovered over hers, his hands moving to frame her face. His lips trailed to her neck, and she melted under his touch, his fingers tangling in her hair.

As he kissed her with raw unfiltered desire, a switch flipped in her chest, it all came rushing back—the salt-tinged air, the soft hush of the waves, the curve of the shoreline bathed in moonlight.

This wasn't just any beach. It was *that* beach. This very spot.

She'd laid here once before—years ago, dizzy with love and wide-eyed with sexual awakening. With Matt.

Before everything fell apart.

Before she learned how fragile love could be when it's held too tightly.

Before she learned the cost of letting someone all the way in.

The air thickened, her breath catching as the memory wrapped around her like sea mist—sudden and disorienting.

For a moment, she wasn't sure which version of herself she was—a grown woman kissing a beautiful stranger under the stars, or the girl who once believed she found her soulmate.

Two timelines, two hearts, two versions of Kate... pulled together in the undertow.

Chapter Sixteen

2002

For possibly the first time in her life, Kate was letting herself drift in the current.

Her world was spinning—warm, wild, and entirely consumed by Matt.

She was completely and utterly in love.

It hadn't happened all at once. But after that night on the beach, she let go of her reservations and allowed herself to feel everything. To be present, to be in the moment.

What started as a summer crush had bloomed into something that felt impossibly bigger. Realer. A rhythm formed between them quickly, like they'd known each other forever.

On lazy afternoons they both had off, they rode bikes down the winding trails of the Cape, racing each other until they were breathless and sweat-drenched. They'd stop at tiny roadside stands for soft serve ice cream and sit under shady trees, legs tangled, watching cars crawl past.

"You eat ice cream like a five-year-old," Matt teased one afternoon, reaching out to wipe a chocolate sprinkle off her chin with his thumb.

Kate smirked, licking the cone slowly just to mess with him. "You say that like it's a bad thing. Most five-year-olds I've met are objectively happy."

He laughed and then kissed her. His lips tasted like chocolate vanilla swirl.

He was so much funnier than she'd expected. He had a dry, observational humor that caught her off guard and made her laugh more than she had with any other guy she'd dated. He quoted her favorite movies—*Say Anything*, *The Princess Bride*, even *Reality Bites*—sometimes just to make her smile.

"You realize you're just Lloyd Dobler with better hair," she told him once.

"And better taste in women," he shot back with a wink.

After work, they'd meet at some pre-decided place—usually the parking lot at Forest Beach or Pleasant Street Beach—and walk hand-in-hand to the water. The moon would cast silver streaks across the water, the tide whispering secrets as they talked about everything and nothing.

"I've never met a 21-year-old who can name a favorite Italian wine region," Matt said, watching her swirl the Chianti as they walked along the shoreline, waves lapping at their feet. He'd started keeping real wine glasses in the console of the truck after her dissertation on how plastic cups ruined wine.

Kate laughed. "After I ordered that first cosmopolitan—it shouldn't have been *that* shocking. And I've been known to drink Miller Lite or Smirnoff Ice. I can't always afford the good stuff on a college girl budget."

He grinned. "Well, I have good news for you. Some of the college kids at work were raving about this new Trader Joe's wine that goes for $1.99 a bottle. I'm not sure that Wine Spectator has rated it yet, I'm afraid."

Kate mock-gasped. "Excuse me, sir, you're talking to someone who once carried the inner bladder of a box of white zin in her purse for pre-gaming. I respect a wine for every occasion."

He looked her over, sincerely. "You know, when you get passionate about something, it's kind of irresistible."

Whether it was the wine or the kiss, she felt warm all over.

When they weren't drinking wine in the late-night hours, they sometimes joined bonfires with the guys from his band, all non-restaurant people. Matt would bring his guitar and disappear into acoustic covers, his voice blending with the surf and firelight. Kate would sit cross-legged in the sand, mesmerized.

After hearing one of the band's original songs, something that sounded like O.A.R. or jam band adjacent, she turned to one of the girlfriends beside her and whispered, "How are they not booking more gigs? They're so good." It was evident how talented Matt was, and it made her even more drawn to him.

The girl shrugged as she sang along to the tune, clearly an original fan. "I don't really think they care that much about making it or being famous, to be honest." Kate was comforted by that answer.

The summer days seemed to fly by with Matt. They never had a plan, and for the first time in her life, that felt exhilarating. One day they were boogie-boarding the Nauset Beach waves like carefree kids, her hair tangled with salt water and seaweed. The next, they were sipping wine and slurping oysters at the Chatham Bars Inn like they were wealthy honeymooners.

"You know this is kind of absurd, right?" Kate said, sipping her prosecco as they sank into oversized Adirondack chairs. The Atlantic stretched out before them, shimmering in the late-afternoon sun like something out of a Nancy Meyers movie. "We can't afford to even breathe the air here. They're going to realize we can't trace our lineage to the Kennedys and have us escorted out."

Matt leaned over and pressed a kiss to her bare shoulder, his lips warm against her sun-dappled skin. "Absurd is totally underrated," he murmured.

She laughed, the bubbles in her glass matching the lightness in her chest. "Tell that to my credit card."

He clinked his glass gently against hers. "I say we drink pros-ecco until someone physically drags us out."

And honestly, with him, the absurd didn't feel reckless or ridiculous. It felt magical. Like they were living inside a secret dream—one where the rules didn't apply.

They spent the majority of nights at his small, beach-town apartment, its slanted ceilings and creaky floors becoming a kind of sanctuary. They made love often—sometimes with gentle, unspoken affection, other times with the wild aban-don of people discovering each other for the first time.

With Matt, she felt seen. Sexy. Brave.

"You're so damn beautiful when you're just... you," he whis-pered once, fingers trailing down her bare back. "You don't have to try."

No one had ever said that to her before.

They'd lie tangled in sheets, talking about life—what they wanted, what they feared. The future hovered around them like fog, close but intentionally unspoken. They never de-fined what they were or how long it might last—afraid that putting it into words would burst the delicate bubble they'd built around themselves.

* * *

It was one of the last Thursday nights of the summer, and everyone at The Salty Anchor was heading to The Squire to watch Matt's band play after work. Kate was genuinely excited to see him perform on stage again, and she used that excitement to help her get through the shift.

Strangely, the restaurant—where they'd first met and fallen into rhythm—was now the one place Kate felt out of sync with Matt. She initially agreed that it made sense to keep their relationship discreet, but as the summer wore on and they became more serious, she began to question whether it was necessary to keep it a secret. Matt was very adamant about keeping things under the radar, and she was starting to feel a little hurt that he didn't want to acknowledge their relationship. Nikki was the only person who knew.

She and Nikki were among the first to cashout, stealing one of the only bathrooms to transform from tired restaurant staff into party-ready twenty-somethings.

"Is everyone coming tonight?" Kate asked, reapplying a light layer of mascara. She tucked a loose strand behind her ear and gave herself one last look in the mirror. The ripped Express jeans and strapless olive top that fluttered at the hem felt sexy and casual. She hoped she looked sexy enough to be the lead singer's girlfriend.

"I think so. Well, maybe not Jessica since she's been sick with a stomach bug or whatever," Nikki replied as she dug around her make-up bag for her purple eyeliner.

Kate's body stiffened. The weirdness with Matt was always worse when Jessica was there. Normally relaxed and charming, he became visibly awkward around her. And Jessica, who managed to be friendly with just about everyone else, had turned cool and unreadable with Kate. She told herself not to read into it, but the unease prickled at her anyway, like something unspoken was quietly simmering under the surface. She made a mental note to buy Jessica a drink, if she was there. One last attempt to connect.

"Ugh. I still smell like food, and I look like trash," Nikki complained.

She did not. She was somehow pulling off a brunette Gwen Stefani look—tight black crop top, low-rise baggy jeans, and red hoop earrings. She looked great.

"You look perfect, per usual." She was telling the truth, but she also didn't need Nikki rethinking her outfit. Matt had already left, and she wanted to get there as soon as possible.

"You seem jittery," Nikki said, pivoting her attention away from her outfit and directly to Kate, hand on hip. "Everything all good with Matt? Still floating around on cloud nine?"

"I'm good. I'm just excited to see him tonight on stage," she said leaning against the wall. She relished any opportunity to talk about Matt with the only other person who knew they were a couple. "I know I've probably said this a hundred times, but—"

"Tell me again," Nikki said as she moved to gather her clothes and cosmetics. "I never get tired of hearing about Cape Cod's resident heartthrob."

Kate grinned. "He's just... different. Like, I don't have to perform with him. I'm not editing myself, you know? We'll just sit there—on his crappy couch with our coffee, the breeze coming in from the window—and I feel like I'm exactly where I'm supposed to be."

Nikki paused and lifted her head, a knowing glint in her eye. "So. when are you telling him you're in love with him?"

Kate hesitated. "I haven't said it yet. But...yeah. I think I am."

There was a beat, and then Kate added, barely above a whisper, "I'm even thinking about staying. Maybe taking a year off. Just... seeing where this goes."

Nikki didn't blink. Didn't tease. She unexpectedly wrapped her arms around Kate, and said, "I'm proud of you. For once, you're not overthinking everything. You're letting yourself be happy. That's big."

* * *

The Squire was already packed when they arrived, buzzing with vacationers and locals, heat rising from too many bodies packed under lazy ceiling fans. Twinkle lights strung above the patio cast a golden haze over the crowd, where people danced, shouted, and swayed with the music. The night smelled of sweat, salt, and beer.

They wove through the crush of bodies, dodging a clumsy makeout and narrowly avoiding a flying beer as a guy threw an arm around his buddy. Nikki waved at someone she recognized near the bar.

"Vodka lemonades?" Kate shouted over the noise.

"Perfect," Nikki agreed.

As Kate ordered, she spotted Matt tuning his guitar and felt a rush of excitement. A warm, wild summer night, her best friend at her side, and music about to fill the air—what could be better?

When Matt launched into "American Girl," the crowd surged toward the dance floor like someone had thrown a switch. Kate barely managed to pay for the drinks before Nikki grabbed her arm, pulling her—cocktails and all—into the mass of swaying bodies. The beat thumped through the speakers, hot and alive, carrying the night with it.

Kate let herself move with the music, her body loosening, a grin spreading across her face. Matt's voice rang out, warm and raspy, threading perfectly through the band's jangly guitars. When she spotted him on stage, eyes closed and completely in his element, her breath caught.

His gaze swept the crowd and landed on her. A quick wink. That familiar, delicious jolt zipped up her spine. She bit her lip, smiling, and twirled back into the crush of dancers. There it was again—that electric pull between them, undeniable even across a packed room.

As the song ended, the dance floor thinned, and Kate spotted more coworkers drifting in. Jessica and Stacey hovered near the bar. Determined to make one final attempt, Kate turned to Nikki. "Be right back," she said.

Nikki nodded. "I'm going to hit the bathroom."

Kate squeezed through the heat and press of bodies, skin glistening under the bar lights. She reached Jessica, tapped her on the shoulder, and leaned in. "Hey!"

Jessica turned, managing a tight smile. "Hi."

The band took a break, and with the music gone, the lull amplified the tension. Kate pressed on. "Let me buy you a drink? I know you've had a shitty couple of weeks."

Jessica shook her head no, barely making eye contact. "I'm good. I appreciate you covering my shift the other day, though. Thanks."

"No problem, sucks to be sick. Was it food poisoning?"

"Yeah. Food poisoning." Jessica's reply was flat, her eyes already scanning the room.

Ok, Kate thought. Time of death on this friendship attempt: officially called.

Kate turned and made her way to the bar, trying to shake the encounter. The buzz of voices and clinking glasses filled the space, along with the low hum of the band tuning up for the next set. She leaned against the bar and ordered another vodka lemonade. Whatever weirdness Jessica was carrying around was her business, Kate was done trying.

She looked back and spotted Matt weaving through the crowd. Her pulse quickened. It had been electric watching him on stage, but now she wanted to touch him, kiss him.

Before she could move toward him, Jessica slipped effortlessly into Matt's path. "I love when you play that one," she said, her tone light but laced with something... familiar.

The move caught Kate off guard. But she knew Matt was heading for her. She looked forward to Jessica's face when he leaned in to kiss her. Casually, she rested an elbow on the bar and let her fingertips trace the rim of her glass, her expression relaxed, composed, quietly confident.

Matt caught her eye and smiled—but there was hesitation in it. Jessica was still planted between them, and instead of walking past her, he reached out and gave her shoulder a quick squeeze.

"It's a great song. Thanks for coming," he said.

Then, without even glancing at Kate, he turned to Nate, who was requesting a Green Day cover.

Kate's stomach dropped.

He wasn't coming to her. In fact, he'd just given more of a greeting—affection, even—to Jessica than to the person who had been in his bed this morning.

What the hell just happened?

A flush crept up her neck as her mind scrambled for an explanation.

Determined not to spiral over a single misread moment, she grabbed her drink and headed toward him. She didn't need him to come to her. She wasn't that girl—clingy, insecure. If he was going to keep playing music in public, she'd need thicker skin anyway.

She threaded through the crowd, catching the end of a conversation about the next few songs in their set. She slid beside him, waiting for a beat—just long enough for him to notice her. Maybe he'd pull her in, drop an arm around her waist, offer some kind of affectionate hello.

But he didn't.

He kept talking, eyes never landing on her. She hovered, uncertain. He had to see her. He was standing *right* there.

Tentatively, she reached out, resting a hand lightly on the small of his back—a subtle signal, nothing overt, just a reminder she was there.

It was only a slight move, almost undetectable to anyone around them, but he edged away from her hand.

And he edged away.

The movement was slight. Barely perceptible. But it was deliberate.

Something in her fractured.

The noise of the bar receded, replaced by a tidal wave of confusion and hurt. Her heart pounded in her ears, her throat tightening.

God, had she really just told Nikki she might stay on the Cape? That she was willing to hit pause on her life—*for this?* For someone who couldn't even acknowledge her in public?

So that's what this is, she thought bitterly. *A secret summer fling.* Fun when we're alone, forgettable when we're not. Not girlfriend-worthy when Jessica's in the room.

"Fuck this," she muttered as she pushed her way through toward the exit, ready to leave the whole group—Matt included—behind.

This was more than she could handle. She didn't care if she was running away. The man who she knew in her heart that she loved seemingly didn't feel the same way. She needed to leave before she broke down in tears from the hurt and heart-crushing disappointment. She could feel the tears welling up in her eyes.

She quickly sped up toward the door and away from her feelings.

Chapter Seventeen

2025

We need to slow down, the words echoed in her mind, even as her lips and body betrayed her resolve.

As Aiden's mouth explored hers, everything felt too familiar. The briny air, the crash of waves just beyond the dunes—Matt had kissed her here, too. For a second, Aiden's breath felt like Matt's. Her body was reacting as it remembered things her heart hadn't let go of.

Kate pulled back slightly, her forehead resting against his. "Hey," she whispered, her voice barely audible over the murmur of the waves. "Can we... maybe slow this down a little?"

She met his gaze, his velvety brown eyes soft and questioning. "I'm not usually this... impulsive. You're sweet. And *unbelievably* hot, but..." She trailed off, searching for the right words.

"But you've got some stuff to unpack," Aiden said gently. His voice was calm, unbothered. "It's cool. I get it. No pressure."

He gave her a half-smile, the kind that said he was mature enough not to take it personally.

She nodded, grateful for his patience. "Yeah. I have this history with Chatham that keeps creeping back. I'm not even sure if it's good or bad, but it's... there." She gestured vaguely as though the memories were floating around them, carried on the ocean breeze.

"Do you want to go back to the fire? Get some space?"

Kate shook her head, a small smile tugging at her lips. "No, I'm ok to sit here for a bit."

She leaned against him, and he slid an arm around her shoulders. The warmth of his body against hers was grounding, comforting. For a moment, she closed her eyes, letting herself simply feel: the gritty texture of the sandy beach blanket beneath her, the cool ocean breeze on her face, the lingering tension of a passionate summer kiss.

"So," Aiden said, breaking the silence with contemplation. "You've been here before. And some young college asshole did you dirty?"

Kate sighed wistfully but with a slight chuckle at the end. "It was a long time ago, but being here brings me back. It's like it was yesterday. Who I was before I had everything all planned out. Before I started working, got married and stopped taking any risks. Not for nothing, but he didn't seem like an asshole at the time."

Aiden tilted his head, feigning consideration. "I'm going to assume he was either an asshole or an idiot. You seem like a catch to me."

Amazing, she thought. Had she known being a completely unavailable head case was attractive to hot guys, she would've let her life go to shit years ago. She could have had a much easier time dating.

"I'm not so sure I'm a catch. I thought this guy was different, maybe even my soulmate. I loved other men of course. But not like that."

She stopped herself, aware that she was oversharing, yet again. *What is wrong with me lately*, she scolded herself. Despite his confidence, he was still so young—had probably never even had his heart broken yet.

"So," she said, changing the subject, "What are your parents like?"

Stellar. That was even worse than oversharing about her past love life. His parents were probably her age. What a stupid question.

He was thoughtful for a moment like he was deciding if he should continue turning on the charm or answer honestly.

"They split up when I was maybe two years old. My arrival was not planned, and they were young. They're fine now; they get along ok. My mom remarried and I have a pretty great stepdad. My dad is great too – he never really settled down again but he's a chill guy."

Kate nodded silently. She'd always envied people whose family dynamics were less fraught. "Any siblings?" she asked.

"Nah," he said. "Only child."

A cool breeze rippled through the air, and Kate shivered, realizing how late it had grown. The laughter and crackle of the fire in the distance was muted, as if the world were wrapped in a soft haze. She absently twisted the small gold bead on her bracelet.

"I've always liked those," Aiden said, nodding toward the bracelet. "They're very Cape Cod. Seems very...you."

Kate glanced down at the bracelet, her fingers stilling as the memory surfaced. It had been an extravagant gift for a college student, but Nikki had brushed off her protests, saying, *I love you. And no matter what any guy does, that's never going to change.*

The warmth of the memory mingled with the coolness of the night, but before Aiden could ask anything that might steer them toward conversations she *definitely* didn't want to have, Kate sat up briskly.

"I think I'll go find Nikki," she said with a decisive smile, brushing sand from her hands.

"Sure, ok. Let's head back," he said, helping her up.

"Could we... try this again, maybe? Another time?" she asked, breaking the silence. She couldn't believe her own daring, her honesty. Cape Kate, indeed.

"I'm not sure what *this* is, exactly, "she continued, "but I'm open to exploring it. There is one thing I need to tell you, though."

"We can go as slow as you want." His fingers trailed lightly down her arm as he spoke, sending shivers through her. "And tell me anything. I want to learn more about you."

Her face flushed. She thought about downplaying her confession but then realized she had nothing to lose by being honest.

"I wasn't just being coy when I said I'm going through a lot. I'm in the middle of getting divorced. I have a stepdaughter who is your age. I live in Manhattan. I used to work in marketing, but I got laid off. Which brought me here for the summer until I can figure out what the hell to do with my life. And I'm not exactly sure how old you think I am. But I'm 44. Sorry. That was like...six things."

She braced herself for the awkward silence she was sure would follow. But Aiden didn't flinch. Instead, he pulled her into a firm, steady hug. It was unexpected—but warm. Kind. When he finally let go, his hands lingered briefly on her shoulders, his eyes locked on hers.

"I can't imagine how hard that's been," he said, his voice low and sincere. "Sounds like it's been a hell of a year. I'm really sorry."

His kindness caught her off guard, tightening her throat. She blinked fast, willing the heat behind her eyes to disappear.

"So... wait. You don't care that I'm, like, twice your age?" she asked, her voice catching, thrown by how unfazed he seemed.

Aiden tilted his head and smiled—slow, easy, just this side of cocky. "Should I care...?"

"I... guess not."

"Good," he murmured, stepping closer, his breath grazing her ear. "Because I'm pretty sure there's no expiration date on beautiful women. Shall we?"

He offered his arm like a gentleman in a teen movie, and she let out a laugh before slipping hers into his. Their bare feet moved in sync over the cool sand, the hiss of the ocean and the crackle of the bonfire weaving together in the air thick with salt and smoke.

Kate glanced around, scanning the firelight for Nikki, but Nikki found them first.

She emerged from the shadows, windblown and flushed, a Solo cup clutched tight in one hand and a look on her face that Kate couldn't quite read.

"Hey, you two," Nikki said, her voice a touch too bright as she hurried toward them, her cup sloshing precariously. "This has been *so* fun. Really great vibes. But I need my beauty rest, naturally. Mind if I borrow Kate for a quick exit?"

Kate frowned slightly, her radar pinging. Nikki never bailed on a party this early, and she certainly didn't look like she hadn't been enjoying herself. Something was off. Their eyes met, and in an instant, they had an entire conversation without saying a word.

Oh, shit. Kate's heart raced as the realization hit her. They needed to go. Fast. Quietly.

She turned to Aiden, unsure what sort of goodbye she should offer after this roller coaster night, but before she could sort it out, an all-too-familiar voice sliced through the night.

"I *thought* that was you."

The tone was syrupy sweet and laced with the sharp edge of a few cocktails. Kate's body tensed as Lindsey approached from the right, moving with practiced poise. She was beach-glam perfection: sun-kissed skin, impossibly long legs, and dark, glossy hair cascading in perfectly curled waves down her back.

"I knew when I saw Nikki it must be you," Lindsey cooed, sporting a smug smile.

The air was dense with tension, the kind that had always flared between Kate and Lindsey like static before a storm. Nikki shifted uneasily beside her, fingers drumming on her Solo cup, eyes darting between the sisters like she was bracing for impact. Aiden glanced between them, brows drawn slightly in confusion.

Kate's heart thudded as Lindsey's eyes settled on Aiden—and stayed there just a second too long.

"Oh wow," Lindsey said, voice bright with mock astonishment and razor-thin condescension. "That was fast. Is he even old enough to drink, Kate? I mean, good for you. I didn't know you had it in you."

Lindsey didn't mean one word of that. Kate felt anxiety washing over her. She didn't want to engage with her sister. Could she make a break for the car with Nikki? It wasn't far.

How do I get out of this??

"You seem like a catch," Lindsey said, flashing Aiden a grin. "Not sure what spell my sister cast, but let me save you some heartache, Romeo—there's a pack of girls over there more your speed. Kate's a little lost these days, and you're way too young and attractive to be lugging around that kind of baggage." She laughed lightly, as if she'd just made a clever joke.

Kate caught Aiden's expression—confused but calm. He hadn't said a word, he didn't try to come to her rescue. He didn't know who Lindsey was but seemed to pick up on the fact that this was complicated. With a barely-there nod, he stepped back, giving Kate space.

It was a small gesture of kindness and maturity, but a strong spark of defiance grew in her chest. Why was she about to treat someone who'd done nothing but be kind, funny, respectful—like a secret she had to hide? She knew *exactly* what that felt like. And it sucked.

Kate straightened her shoulders, her tone cool but edged like glass. "You'll have to excuse my sister—she never quite mastered basic manners." She turned to Aiden, her voice lifting just enough for effect. "Lindsey, this is Aiden. He's charming, kind and he made me feel good—which, frankly, I really need right now."

Aiden gave a slight wave, his mouth curved in amusement.

Kate kept going, the words rising fast now, too long held in. "And yes, he's young. But I'm a single, grown-ass woman. So, I'm not going to feel bad about this. At all."

She stepped slightly closer, her eyes locked on Lindsey's. "You've spent your entire life being self-involved and trying to one-up me. Here's a radical idea: worry about your own re-lationships. Oh wait. Where *is* your husband tonight? Or are you just as lousy at being a wife as you are at being a sister?"

The silence that followed was instant and absolute. Even the waves seemed to hesitate.

Lindsey's mouth opened, then closed again, as if a retort had started to form but got lost. To Kate's surprise, her expres-sion shifted—less smug than usual, more...unsteady. She al-most looked hurt.

But that couldn't be right. Lindsey didn't *get* hurt. She in-flicted pain on other people, namely, Kate.

Nikki stood slack-jawed beside her, eyes wide in disbelief. She looked as stunned as Lindsey—maybe more. Kate had expected a fist bump or at least an approving glance. But Nikki's silence said something else: *Maybe that was too far.*

Before anyone could say another word, Nikki snapped into motion. "Okay," she said briskly, cutting through the tension like a blade. "That's enough family drama for one night. Time to go."

She turned sharply and started toward the car. Kate hesitated only a second before following, her adrenaline ebbing into a slow, sick churn. Aiden trailed behind, glancing once over his shoulder at Lindsey, who hadn't moved.

It had taken twenty-five years, but Kate had finally put her sister in her place.

It didn't feel like she expected it would. It felt kind of...awful.

The Audi convertible remained parked right where they left it, top down in the moonlight. Nikki climbed behind the wheel and let out a long sigh as she started the engine. Aiden followed Kate over to the passenger side.

"I'm sorry about...all that," she said quietly. "My sister doesn't exactly bring out the best in me."

Aiden gave a small wince. "Well. On the plus side, it was kind of having a front seat to a *Real Housewives* reunion. Minus the wine throwing."

She let out a weak laugh and shrugged. "If we'd have stayed longer, you might have gotten that, too."

"Seemed like you had a lot to get off your chest," he added, more gently this time. "Are you okay?"

Kate stared out at the dark road ahead, a lump rising in her throat. "I honestly don't know. I really should get going, Aiden."

He nodded, but didn't move. "We're all going to The Squire tomorrow night—live music, decent drinks. You and Nikki should come."

That was unexpected. She was surprised he wasn't running for the hills.

"Unless" he said reading her mind, "you think there are other dramatic encounters or relatives lurking around town? What's the opposite of a meet-cute?"

She smiled. "Let me get back to you on that."

Kate glanced at Nikki, who was busy checking her phone but clearly listening. She was waiting for her friend to give an indication of whether they should accept the invite. But Nikki was letting her work this one out on her own.

If she was feeling weird about the beach, she couldn't imagine what memories would be dredged up at The Squire.

"Sure," she said impulsively. "That sounds fun."

Aiden leaned in closer, pressing a light kiss to her cheek, the gesture loaded with sensuality. "Goodnight, Kate."

* * *

The drive back to the inn was short—but just long enough for more shame to settle in. Kate stared out the window, her stomach tight, replaying every word she'd hurled at Lindsey.

"So..." Nikki ventured carefully, eyes on the road. "How are you feeling about that?"

Kate exhaled. "Pretty awful."

Nikki nodded. "Yeah. That was... a lot to unload. And in front of Aiden."

Kate turned toward her. "Do you think I went too far?"

Nikki didn't answer right away. She waited—if anyone would be honest, it was Nikki.

"You know I'm no fan of your sister. She's a narcissist who's been a crap friend to you for years. But you've also avoided calling her out your whole life. She's probably clueless you've even got an issue with her."

Kate blinked back the sting in her eyes, her gaze fixed on the road. That was the worst part—Lindsey probably *was* clueless. And maybe her therapist, if she had one, would've said the same thing: don't repress it for 20 years and then blow it all up in one go.

"So yeah," Nikki continued gently, "calling her a lousy wife and sister in your first real confrontation was a little harsh."

"Maybe I'm the bad sister," Kate murmured, voice tight.

That thought had never once occurred to her—until tonight. She avoided her sister instead of trying to work on the relationship. Resented her silently. Fixing things would take a lot of time and effort, and it would be messy. And yes—she didn't like confrontation. She kept herself busy to avoid it at all costs. Maybe this wasn't just about Lindsey. Maybe this was a pattern.

Nikki shrugged. "Well, let's not get carried away here—she *does* deserve some hard truths. For all we know, no one's ever told her she's a bitch."

Kate gave a watery laugh. "Well. She probably knows now."

"Oh yeah," Nikki smirked. "She *definitely* knows now."

After getting back to the room, Nikki snuck off to make a phone call to Jay, explaining that she'd need to stay one more night to support her best friend. She conveniently left out that it would basically be a night out at a bar while he wrangled their two wild children.

Kate used the opportunity to check in with Sydney, since she was a night owl and would likely be awake. Curled up with a blanket on her porch lounger, Kate waited as the familiar FaceTime ring started up. It occurred to her that she hadn't thought about Chris in what seemed like days—that was new.

The rings abruptly ended as Sydney's face popped up on the screen, in full LED light therapy face mask and glass of red wine, looking like a futuristic, sophisticated villain.

"Where have you BEEN, I feel like I haven't heard from you in days!" Sydney exclaimed, muffled behind the mask.

Kate laughed out loud at the ridiculousness of Sydney's look, and the role reversal. Here she was just getting back from making out and a bitch fight on the beach and Sydney was at home doing a skincare routine. "Syd, it's only been like two days! And you told me to detox from my phone."

"I said to lay off *social media*. Where are you?"

"Back at my hotel room on the porch. Nikki's here for a couple nights."

"Oh fun! The more the merrier!" Sydney replied, still looking incredibly silly in her self-care get-up. Kate thought it was a weird response, but then again, it was 11 p.m. and Sydney may be half into a bottle of wine.

"Let me guess. You're watching a true crime documentary and drinking that bottle of Stag's Leap I bought you?" Kate asked with a knowing smirk.

"How can you even tell what wine it is from the phone! Unreal," Sydney responded, probably smiling, though it was hard to tell. "Hey, wait. Where were *you*? What are you two getting back from?"

"So actually...you're probably going to be proud of me in a weird, very inappropriate way. I have a lot to catch you up on."

"UM, spill," she said, ripping off the mask and bringing her face dangerously close to the phone. "Was it a lobsterman?! Was he jacked and scruffy? Did he look like one of those guys from Yellowstone?"

"Stop!" Kate said, laughing at the same time. "Not one of those guys. Think...younger." She made a playful cringe face, fully anticipating the reaction.

"Wait, younger? How much younger? Start from the beginning."

Kate did her best to catch Sydney up on the whirlwind of scandalous events since she arrived at the Chatham Bars Inn. She had no fear of judgment; Sydney loved her the way Nikki did—flaws, questionable decisions, and all. The only thing she left out was the blow-up with Lindsey. Sydney and "Aunt" Lindsey had always got along well, much to her surprise.

"He's twenty-two?! You absolute COUGAR! I'm dead. For real. I knew you had it in you!" Sydney squealed with delight. "This is like a total rom-com. Like that one with Anne Hathaway where she falls in love with the young singer at Coachella! Is he a musician?"

"I don't think I can be a cougar at 44, I'm still verifying that. And I don't think he's a musician, as far as I know." A faint memory lingered in her mind. Even if this ended up being a makeout on the beach, she was glad he wasn't a musician.

"Well. It's still early summer and you're already contributing to the feminist agenda by demonstrating that women have as much right to date younger as men do. You're like Cape Cod's Madonna right now."

"It's probably not going to turn into anything. But it feels nice. I feel like a different person here. It's weird."

Sydney smiled. "I'm not sure I've ever seen you like this. I like it."

Sydney's comment made Kate wonder if she had underestimated how closed off and rigid she'd become.

"Anyway, I've got to go and make sure I fall asleep before Nikki starts snoring."

"Yeah, I need to figure out where the killer hid the sawed-off body parts before I go to sleep."

"Bye Syd, love you."

"Love you, too."

She didn't fall asleep as quickly as she'd hoped. As she lay there, listening to Nikki lightly snore beside her, her thoughts wandered. At first, they drifted to Aiden—the spark, the thrill, the way he made her feel visible again. It had been fun. Sexy. A reminder that she was still capable of wanting and being wanted. But deep down, she already knew it wasn't what she really needed.

What *did* she need?

No matter how hard she tried to redirect her thoughts, they kept slipping back to Matt. It was like there was some magnetic force tethering her to the past, pulling her back to him the second she let her guard down. Since she'd arrived, it had been happening in flashes—songs, the ocean, the way the night air smelled. And tonight, on the beach with Aiden, it was the strongest. She couldn't shake the memory of what it had felt like to be loved by Matt—it had been so perfect, so real.

Until it wasn't. Until she discovered the lies. Until she realized everything she'd believed about their love, about the future she thought they were building, had been balanced on a foundation of shifting sand—beautiful, but never solid enough to last.

Kate turned onto her side, pulling the blanket up around her shoulders, and squeezed her eyes shut.

Sleep evaded her, but the memories stayed. Stubborn and heavy. Refusing to let her escape.

Chapter Eighteen

2002

Kate was practically clawing her way to escape the bar, and Matt. But the late-night crowd at The Squire had other ideas. Drunk, sweaty, and completely oblivious to personal space, they bounced off her like she was trapped in some alcohol-fueled game of human pinball.

She couldn't take the humiliation—not here, around a bunch of people she knew. Maybe no one else noticed that Matt had acted like she didn't exist. They didn't know that just twenty-four hours ago, she'd been tangled up naked in his apartment—on his kitchen counter, his couch—making love.

Or maybe it was just sex to him. Tonight, she was just another stupid girl chasing after the lead singer.

Kate had nearly reached the door when Nikki materialized in front of her, blocking the way like a bouncer.

"Where do you think you're going?" Nikki asked, half-laughing. "Don't tell me you're already drunk enough to forget about the oath!"

The playfulness drained from her face as she caught sight of the tears shining in Kate's eyes.

"What happened? Was it someone from work? Or a rando? Do I need to bitch slap someone here?!" She furiously scanned the bar looking for targets.

Kate let out a shaky breath and tried to steady herself. "No," she said, forcing a smile. "I mean... watching you bitch slap someone would be entertaining, but— it's Matt."

"If he's being a little bitch, I do not discriminate which gender I slap."

"He was just talking to Jessica and basically acted like I was invisible. He brushed me off. He clearly doesn't love me like I thought he did. I just want to go, ok?"

Nikki's expression turned stern. "Ok, first of all, I know Jessica is naturally gorgeous, with that stunning blonde hair and brown doe-eye combo, and she's smart—"

"Nik, *really* not helping," Kate muttered.

"Let me finish," Nikki said firmly, grabbing Kate's shoulders. "There's a reason Matt was into you from the first day he met you. You're amazing in all those ways and more. She can't just waltz in here and have any guy she wants. That one's *taken*."

Kate's throat tightened. "Is he, though?" she said softly. "Because he sure didn't act like it. He acted like I'm just... a summer fling. A secret. I was naïve to think it was ever more than that."

Before Nikki could respond, Matt was making his way over, his brow furrowed with concern.

"Kate, wait," he called as he approached, his voice urgent. She wanted to storm out and have him feel a fraction of the hurt and confusion that she just felt, but Nikki was standing in her way. Probably to keep her from running.

"What's going on?" he asked, his voice low, glancing over his shoulder toward Jessica and the others, who were laughing and carrying on like nothing had happened. "Why did you take off like that?"

Nikki gave Kate's shoulder a reassuring squeeze. "I'll go get drinks at the bar," she said, casting Matt a critical glare before slipping away. Kate nodded, then crossed her arms over her chest, trying to keep her emotions in check.

"I get it now," Kate said, struggling to keep her voice steady. "This was just a casual summer thing. Something you'd rather keep quiet." She swallowed hard. "I came here tonight thinking we could actually be together—*out* together. But you barely even looked at me until now. If this is just some fling that you're embarrassed about... I have a little more self-respect than that."

Matt's eyes widened, genuine shock flashing across his face. "Kate... you really think that? That I'm ashamed of you?"

"What else am I supposed to think?" she said, her voice cracking. "It's hard enough when you pretend we're not together when we're at the restaurant. I thought tonight would be different, and you'd be okay to be seen with me. But I guess not."

He looked pained, and that surprised Kate.

Is he seriously this clueless?

Matt stepped closer, reaching for her hand. His touch was warm and grounding, but she didn't relax.

"Kate," he said, his voice low and earnest, "that couldn't be further from the truth. I'll admit... a part of me didn't want to let anyone into this little world we built. It felt so special, so *ours*."

He shook his head, frustrated with himself. "But I didn't think about how that might look—or how it might make you feel. I'm so sorry. I was being selfish. And stupid. That all stops tonight."

He drew in a deep breath, staring directly into her eyes with love and concern. "Come with me."

She wasn't sure she fully bought his explanation — not yet — but something in his eyes chipped away at her defenses. She let him take her hand and lead her back toward the bar. Despite everything, the feel of his fingers wrapped around hers still made her heart flutter. She loved him. Naïve or not, she did.

As they reached the others, Matt suddenly stopped.

Before she could say a word, he turned her toward him, cupped her face in his hands, and kissed her — right there, in front of everyone. Including Jessica.

It wasn't a quick, casual kiss. It was deep, unguarded, claiming her in a way that left Kate breathless. He pulled her against him, wrapping her in his arms like he couldn't stand even an inch of distance between them. It made her entire body melt.

Nikki let out a whoop from the bar. "Finally!"

That signaled the crew around them whistled and clapped as Kate broke away from the kiss, catching her breath and smiling at Matt. Out of the corner of her eye, she searched for Jessica to gauge her reaction, but she was nowhere to be seen.

Matt didn't look away from Kate, his eyes filled with affection and a hint of mischief. "See?" he said softly. "Now everyone knows. And I'm glad they know I love you."

The words hit Kate like a wave, and she was pulled under, overwhelmed with feelings. Joy, disbelief, hope — and beneath it all, a fierce, aching love that had been growing inside her all summer.

He loved her. She wasn't imagining it. It was real.

Nikki reappeared at Kate's side, pressing a vodka lemonade into her hand, her grin practically splitting her face.

Matt leaned in, his voice low and warm against Kate's ear. "I've got to get back on stage for the next set," he murmured, pressing a lingering kiss to her cheek. "Don't go anywhere, ok?"

Kate could only nod, still floating, her whole body buzzing with butterflies.

As Matt picked up his guitar and stepped up to the microphone, the entire bar buzzed, waiting for the music to start again.

"This is one I've been working on," he announced, his gaze settling on Kate. "It's our first time playing it. I learned it to impress a girl who likes '90s alt rock. Or who *said* she did, anyway. Maybe she was trying to impress me. I don't know for sure." The crowd laughed and clapped in anticipation. "This is for Katie."

As Matt started strumming the familiar chords in G minor, the opening of *Follow you Down* by the Gin Blossoms, the bar erupted with cheers, and Kate felt a jolt of electricity surge through her. Something fluttered in her chest as she recognized the song. It was one of her favorites.

Did you see the sky, I think it means that we've been lost?
Maybe one last time is all we need
I can't really help it if my tongue's all tied in knots
Jumping off a bridge, it's just the farthest that I've ever been

He stood on the stage, illuminated by the hazy lights, his gaze occasionally flicking toward her as he sang. Kate grabbed Nikki's hand and pulled her toward the front as Matt's voice poured through the speakers. Kate danced without reservation, her hair falling in loose waves around her face, and as Matt's voice soared through the chorus.

"He's totally in love with you," Nikki shouted over the music. "I can see it from here!"

"I love him, too!" Kate yelled to Nikki with a smile that could not get any bigger.

For the next hour, Kate and Nikki drank, danced, and laughed, joining in on the singalongs. The band's energy was infectious, and it seemed like the entire bar was having the time of their lives. As the set ended and the band took their bows, the DJ took over to keep the party atmosphere going.

Kate made her way back to the bar, still buzzing with adrenaline and tipsy from at least four very strong vodka lemonades. She figured she should ask for water as she anxiously waited for Matt to reappear from loading up the band equipment. She couldn't wait to kiss him again and to tell him that she loved him, too. She'd never meant anything more.

As the minutes ticked by, Kate realized that Matt was taking longer than usual. Kate began to scan the crowd, searching for his face among the sea of people. Her gaze wandered across the dimly lit bar, but there was no sign of him. The lingering euphoria started to wane, replaced by a twinge of unease.

Jessica's waitress friend Allison stumbled over to Kate, looking like she was going to order another drink but probably shouldn't. "Looking for Matt?" she slurred, her eyes glassy and unfocused.

Kate managed a smile. "Yeah, have you seen him?"

Allison leaned in closer, her breath smelling of tequila. "I didn't realize you guys were hooking up. Look at you making moves," she said, her voice heavy with alcohol and mischief.

Hooking up suggested her relationship with Matt was casual and unimportant. Not that they had fallen in love. But it didn't seem worth correcting someone who was clearly one drink away from blacking out.

"Feel bad for Jess, though," Allison added, stirring her margarita casually with her straw.

Kate's causal smile faltered. "What does that mean?" she asked.

Allison raised her eyebrows in faint surprise. "Oh, you didn't know?" She let out a small laugh, followed by a hiccup. "They were dating this spring. Things got hot and heavy. But you guys are together now, so Jess will just have to let him go, I guess." Allison hiccupped again and covered her mouth, unable to stop herself from giggling.

Matt and Jessica? In the spring? That was barely a month before she met him.

The realization hit hard, leaving a sick twist low in her stomach. He had never mentioned anything about it, not even once. Something like that wasn't a minor oversight. Dating a co-worker prior to her was something that *should* have come up. He had clearly, purposefully, chosen not to tell her.

Whether it was the alcohol or the new information, the room seemed to spin around her. Kate didn't respond to Allison as she turned on her heel and started pushing her way through the crowd for the second time that night. She needed to find him. She needed answers.

Kate shoved her way toward the door and burst outside. She scanned the crowded patio, where people were smoking, chatting, and saying long, drunken goodbyes. Her eyes swept across the scene until she finally spotted him.

Matt stood near the corner of the patio, his arms wrapped around a girl who was clinging to him, her head buried in his chest.

It was Jessica.

The sight of Matt holding Jessica hit Kate like a punch to the gut, making the ground feel unsteady beneath her. The sticky summer air clung to her skin, thick and suffocating. She could still hear the thump of bass from inside, muffled by the heavy door, and the chatter of patrons spilled out around her, mixing with the smell of sweat and spilled beer.

Her mind raced, trying to process what she was seeing, and she felt a mix of shock, betrayal, and nausea swirl inside her.

But he told me he loved me.

Yet here he was, his arms around Jessica. His ex-girlfriend.

She couldn't hear what they were saying over the background noise. But it didn't matter. The way Jessica clung to him told her enough.

He lied to me. He lied.

She wanted to scream. She wanted to ask why. She wanted to cry somewhere safe, somewhere not here.

Why did he make her fall in love with him? Why did he do the big romantic gesture? Was that song just a well-crafted move? Why was he so cruel?

But she couldn't speak, couldn't confront him. She felt numb.

Matt made eye contact with her, immediately stiffened and Jessica quickly turned around. Jessica's expression was one of stunned guilt, while Matt's face twisted into sheer panic. He stepped back, letting go of Jessica.

"Kate, this isn't what it looks like," he started as he took a few steps closer, his voice placating.

"The fuck it isn't," Nikki piped in angrily from behind Kate, looking like she might kill one or both of them. Kate was thankful Nikki had followed her out. She wasn't sure if she could handle this on her own. She could feel the eyes of other people on them as curious glances drifted in their direction.

"Here's what it looks like to me," Kate replied, her voice full of hurt and barely contained anger. "It looks to me like you were just wrapped up with your ex-girlfriend." An intense ache was growing in her throat.

Jessica's eyes darted to Matt and then to Kate. She bit her lip, seemingly unsure whether to stay or leave. She took a step back, muttering, "You should have told her. I told you this would happen. I should go."

"No, wait a minute, Jess," Matt said, putting his hand on Jessica's arm, but turning to Kate. He was visibly flustered. "Kate, let me explain."

She didn't need him to explain anything. Regardless of whether it was or wasn't what it looked like, he was previously—or currently—hiding something. She was certain of that.

"Whatever is happening here, you kept it from me," Kate's voice cracked, and she felt her cheeks flush with a mixture of hurt and fury. "This whole time, everyone knew you two had dated. *Everyone knew.* And no one told me I was the rebound. God, what an idiot I have been to think you were different."

The look on his face was one of shattering regret. But that didn't make it hurt any less. Kate took a step back toward Nikki, who was standing angrily with her hands on her hips.

She wrapped her own arms around herself, trying to hold together the pieces starting to crack apart.

"Did you even mean what you said?" she asked, voice barely above a whisper. "Did any of it mean anything?"

Matt took a step closer, trying to bridge the small gap between them. "Of course I meant it," he said desperately. "I love you. I'm madly in love with you."

There was something raw in his voice, and his eyes looked suspiciously watery. But she didn't know what to trust anymore. *If that was true, why keep his relationship with Jessica a secret?*

Out of the corner of her eye, she saw Jessica wipe a tear from her cheek, then turn away, moving quickly toward the parking lot, digging for her keys.

Don't, Kate pleaded silently. *If you go after her, it's over.*

But Matt pivoted toward Jessica.

"Jess," he called out, frantic. "Jess, wait—please."

Kate's heart dropped, and she shook her head slowly with a painful realization. "No, Matt. I'm done. We are done."

He turned back to her, the words tumbling out in a rush.

"She's pregnant, Kate. It's mine. She just found out a couple weeks ago."

The world seemed to tilt sideways. The noise, the lights, the people—it all faded. She stood there, frozen, struggling to breathe.

He's known for weeks, she realized.

And he said nothing.

He touched me. He kissed me. He told me he loved me.

And the whole time, he kept this secret. And kept it easily, as if it were nothing.

Matt's voice broke into her spinning thoughts.

"We broke it off before you even got here. We didn't know about the baby. I was going to tell you tonight, I swear. I was just... scared to lose you. But Jess—she's pregnant. I need to be there for her. There's nothing romantic between us, but... I care about her."

Kate's gaze flicked to Jessica, who stood there frozen, head bowed, looking utterly wrecked. There was *something* still there for her Jessica— no matter what Matt said. And now, they'd be bound forever.

It was too much. Tears burned in her eyes, but she refused to let them fall here, in front of everyone.

She turned to Nikki, who was uncharacteristically silent, completely shocked. *Let's go,* Kate mouthed. Nikki gave a tight nod.

"Katie, wait!" Matt's voice rang out, raw and emotional. "You have every right to be upset. But we can figure this out. *Please.* I love you."

Kate stopped, but didn't turn around.

"Don't call me that," she said, voice steady, each word slicing clean. "You lied to me. Call me old-fashioned, but that's not love. I deserve better."

She drew in a breath that felt like it might break her ribs. "I'm going back to New York in a couple of weeks. I won't be back to the restaurant. And I never want to see you again."

They disappeared into the summer night before he could hear her sobs, her vision blurred with tears and her heart utterly broken.

Kate held true to her word. She never spoke to Matt again.

* * *

The next morning, Nikki called Tara and told her they wouldn't be finishing their shifts at The Salty Anchor. Despite Kate's protests, Nikki quit in solidarity, choosing to spend her time helping heal her best friend's broken heart.

Matt called. Every day. But Kate blocked his number. When he called Nikki's house, they didn't pick up. Eventually, the calls stopped.

Nikki distracted Kate by talking about their final year at NYU, about how many handsome, strait-laced finance grads would be lining up to date Kate, and how much better it would be to move on. Only once, as they sat on the beach, the waves crashing steadily against the shore, did Nikki ask, "So he's an idiot, no question. But... I don't want you to leave with regrets. Are you sure you don't want to talk to him?"

Kate's gaze lingered on the horizon, but her voice was flat. "What would we talk about? The relationship is not going to work. I should cut my losses now."

"Fair enough," Nikki replied, putting her head on Kate's shoulder. "Just didn't want you to have any doubts."

The drive back to the city came quickly, which Kate was thankful for. She couldn't help but feel the bittersweet weight of leaving the Cape. This summer had been the best and the worst of her life.

Nikki pulled something out of her bag. "I got you something," she said, passing her a small box.

"What? Why?" Kate asked, tilting her head as she took the box.

"Do I need a reason? I love you, and I want you to know that no matter what any guy does, that will *always* be true," she said with an unexpected hint of emotion in her voice.

Kate opened the box and gasped, seeing the gold and silver bracelet from Eden Hand Arts inside. "Nikki," she whispered, fighting back fresh tears. "This is too much. It's beautiful. How did you even *get* this?"

Nikki sniffled, wiping her eyes as she settled back into the driver's seat. "I'm sneaky. And I got one for myself," she added, lifting her wrist to reveal a matching bracelet.

"And one more thing..." Nikki added with a grin.

"There's more?" Kate laughed incredulously, wiping her eyes.

Nikki pulled out a newly minted mix CD—*Boys Suck Volume 1-2002*—and popped it into the car stereo. The opening chords of Michelle Branch's *Goodbye to You* filled the car, and for the first time in weeks, Kate felt a shift. The pressure in her chest loosened if only a little.

But it was enough.

Chapter Nineteen

2025

"I think like two hours here is enough," Kate warned Nikki as they pulled into the packed parking lot of The Squire. She hadn't been sleeping well. Tossing and turning through vivid memories of her past, and when she finally drifted off, her dreams were chaotic and too emotional to find rest.

"You always *say* that" Nikki said, grinning as she threw the car into park. "But after one drink and a few songs, I'll be dragging you out of here at 1 a.m. Or someone will." She winked playfully.

Kate pretended not to notice the not-so-subtle hint about Aiden. As they stepped out into the cool evening, the faint strains of a familiar yacht rock classic floated through the air.

Hall & Oates, she thought, smiling despite herself. Damn it, she did love live music—and whoever the band was, they were already hitting all the right notes.

Tonight, Kate put less effort into her outfit than she had for the bonfire. She'd gone simple: a long white linen skirt, a chocolate-brown crop top, and wedge sandals. Next to Nikki, who was wearing a black leather skirt, a vintage Guns N' Roses tee with the sleeves hacked off, and a Gucci belt, Kate felt like her Amish cousin.

As they headed toward the entrance, Nikki shot her a mischievous look. "You ready to party?"

"Yeah, but I feel like the oath applies here," she said, half-joking. A strange anxiety fluttered beneath her words. Probably all the Matt-infused dreams.

Nikki bumped her shoulder. "Please. That oath was from twenty years ago, when horny guys were discovering roofies and we made way worse choices than we do now. You're allowed to have a little fun, you know."

Kate wasn't entirely convinced she was making better choices this time around. "I know," she said. "It's just... I've been feeling this insane sense of déjà vu lately. It's like I'm slipping back in time. And now here we are at The Squire..."

Nikki gave her a knowing smile. "Tonight can be whatever you want it to be. *You're* in the driver's seat. He knows your age, you know his. Just don't overthink it."

Kate nodded, trying hard to push the feeling aside. Inside, The Squire was packed. The scent of beer and fried food mingled with the warm, heady atmosphere of laughter and music. It was exactly like she remembered it.

Kate spotted Aiden almost instantly, leaning casually against the bar like he owned the place. The dim light gave his skin a golden glow, highlighting sharp cheekbones and the easy tilt of his head as he chatted with the bartender. He looked completely at home in the chaos of the bar—and that laid-back magnetism had drawn a small crowd of *very* pretty women who were clearly auditioning for the role of "one night stand." They looked like they were in their late twenties, maybe early thirties, and they were working extra hard for his attention.

Her first instinct was to judge them for being so thirsty—hovering around Aiden like moths to a flame—until she caught herself. Wasn't she doing the same thing? Wanting his attention, craving that spark of validation? Even showing up tonight felt like part of the same chase.

The realization made her uncomfortable. But maybe this was proof she wasn't the cold, calculated ice queen Chris had once accused her of being (if not in words, then in tone). Because standing in front of her was someone who offered none of what she was supposed to want. No stability. No future. Just chaos. Maybe sex. Almost definitely a mess. And still, here she was. At this bar, about to walk right into it.

Aiden's face lit up the second he saw them. He waved enthusiastically. "Kate! Nikki! Over here!"

They wove through the crowd, and Aiden greeted Nikki first, kissing her on the cheek. "Nice to see you. You look stunning, as always."

Nikki gave an exaggerated little swoon, pretending to fan herself.

Then Aiden turned to Kate, his expression softening. "And you," he said, voice dropping a little, "look beautiful."

He kissed her cheek too, lingering just a beat longer than necessary, and whispered, "I'm really glad you came."

"Thanks," she said, smiling. "Nice to see this place hasn't changed one bit."

Aiden grinned. "Some things get better with age. Speaking of, can I get you both a drink?"

Nikki didn't miss a beat. "Two vodka lemonade. Heavy on the vodka, light on the lemonade."

Kate laughed. *Some things really didn't change.*

Aiden returned with their drinks and a beer for himself, and they moved closer to the stage. "I know these guys," he said, nearly shouting to be heard over a Goo Goo Dolls cover. "They're pretty good, huh?"

"Yeah, they're great!" Kate shouted back.

After another song, their drinks were already empty. *So much for pacing myself,* she thought. Nikki was quick to grab their glasses and offer to pick up the next round. She reappeared, balancing their drinks and a tray of shots Kate was pretty sure no one had ordered.

"Now it's a party!" Nikki declared, passing the shots around to Kate, Aiden and a couple of Aiden's friends standing nearby. "Here's to you, and here's to me! If by chance you don't agree... fuck you, here's to me!" She toasted gleefully before they all knocked back their shots. The tequila burned Kate's throat and warmed her chest, and she grimaced slightly. Tequila was not her favorite.

After handing them the drinks they actually *had* ordered, Nikki vanished again, ferrying the rogue tray of shots back to the bar.

Aiden's grin turned mischievous. "You like '90s rock?" he asked, out of nowhere.

Kate arched an eyebrow. "I was alive in the '90s, so...yes? Why?"

"Well...I play sometime with the band." Aiden's sheepish grin reminded Kate of a kid caught sneaking dessert before dinner. "Didn't mention it because, well... saying 'I'm in a band' feels like peak douchebag, right?"

He gave a playful, apologetic wince, rubbing the back of his neck. "Don't worry, I just dabble. My dad taught me, but he's miles better. Anyway, stay here. If you're horrified by what you see, no hard feelings if you bolt."

His grin widened, and before she could fully process his words, he leaned in, brushing her cheek with a sultry kiss and then disappeared into the crowd. She blinked, trying to recalibrate, but her thoughts spiraled as her past began to claw its way to the surface.

Matt played 90's rock here once upon a time. Given their similar look, it didn't feel all that different that night in 2002.

Aiden weaved his way toward the stage, greeted by a flurry of high-fives and cheers from his friends. He reached the lead singer, exchanged a quick fist bump, and ceremoniously accepted the guitar, its strap slung over his shoulder like he'd done this a hundred times before. The crowd buzzed with anticipation.

"Where's your boy toy?" Nikki's voice jolted Kate from her trance. She turned to find Nikki holding two drinks and eyeing her suspiciously. "You look kind of terrified right now—what'd I miss?"

As the pieces flew together, Kate was frozen. Words wouldn't form. Instead, she turned back toward the stage where Aiden stepped up to the microphone, testing the strings with a few strums.

"Hey all!" His voice rang out, confident but casual. The chatter in the bar softened, and the crowd pressed closer. "Big thanks to the band for letting me crash their set tonight. They slay, right?"

A ripple of applause and whistles broke out. A group of girls at the bar—part of a raucous bachelorette party—raised their cans of White Claws, catcalling their approval of the attractive new addition to the band.

Nikki's head whipped from Kate to the stage, where Aiden stood. "Wait...I was only gone for like five minutes. What is he doing on stage?"

"This is one of the first songs I ever learned to play," he continued, glancing toward Kate as if searching for her reaction. "It's special to me, and I'm dedicating it to someone I'm trying to impress tonight." He gave a small, self-effacing laugh. "Fingers crossed. And, uh, hope you all like '90s rock."

Kate's stomach clenched as the first familiar chords rang out. Her body tensed, as though bracing for impact. *No. No. No. It's not possible. It can't be.*

Then the drums kicked in, the lead singer joined with a harmonica that seemed to materialize out of nowhere, and the crowd erupted. Cheers and whoops echoed across the room, but Kate barely registered them. Her world narrowed, her heart thudding so loudly she couldn't hear the music.

"Oh my *God*," Nikki said, her voice a breathless gasp. Both glasses slipped from her hands, shattering on the floor. Neither she nor Kate flinched.

Kate stood rooted, heat prickling her skin. Her breathing quickened, and her vision blurred as the song she knew all too well enveloped her. This wasn't a coincidence. It *couldn't* be.

The flash of familiarity when they first met. The relentless memories crashing over her, constantly. The eerie déjà vu she couldn't shake.

It all snapped into place with brutal clarity.

She knew exactly who he was.

Chapter Twenty

2025

The person standing on stage, singing "Follow you Down," was not the same person that sang it for her over twenty years ago.

It was his son.

Kate's heart hammered against her ribs so hard it felt like it might burst straight out of her chest and land on the bar floor—currently sticky with spilled beer and scattered with shards of broken glass.

She tried to steady herself, inhaling a few yoga-style breaths as Aiden and the band wrapped up their Gin Blossoms cover to raucous applause. The noise around her was muffled and distant, like she was underwater.

"Listen," Nikki said, finally finding her voice. "You didn't know. I mean—*how* could you know? Seriously. This is fucking *wild*. I can't even process this." She was more rattled than Kate had seen her in a long time. Maybe ever.

Kate stared straight ahead, willing herself to stay calm even as her insides flipped and twisted.

"I knew it," she said, her voice eerily steady despite the chaos inside her. "I knew something was off—the way the memories kept coming back every time I was near him. Like I was missing a giant, flashing neon sign."

"I mean... you could just ghost him like the kids do and skip the Jerry Springer-level awkwardness," Nikki suggested nervously. "And honestly, you didn't do anything wrong. You only kissed him. *You only kissed him*, right?"

"Yes," Kate replied. A fresh wave of nausea hit her.

Thank God. *Thank God* they hadn't gone any further.

Aiden hopped off the stage, guitar still slung over his shoulder. His grin was broad and boyish, and he made a beeline for Kate, completely unaware of the emotional earthquake he'd just set off.

"So?" he asked, looking directly at Kate. "How'd I do? Was it painful?"

Kate's arms were crossed tightly, her fingers digging into her sides as if to physically hold herself together. She exchanged a brief, panicked glance with Nikki, who stood next to her looking as unsure as she did.

"It was good," Kate managed, her voice uneven.

"Good?" Aiden's smile turned teasing, but there was genuine curiosity in his tone. "Oof. If it sucked you can tell me, I can take it."

Her face softened with guilt. There was no reason to upset him when he was completely clueless, and his earnestness was disarming. "No, it was great," she said, forcing a brighter tone. "I love that song." She smiled, but it didn't quite reach her eyes.

"Good news," Aiden beamed, leaning in slightly. "Because there's more mediocre covers where that came from." He winked, adding with a flirtatious lilt. "Maybe we can head to the beach later, and I'll take requests. Or... whatever you want to do."

It occurred to her that ghosting Aiden would not be an option. If she disappeared without an explanation, he'd just come after her with even more determination. People usually pursued *him*. Brushing him off would only make her more appealing. The last thing she needed was him chasing a fantasy she couldn't possibly let happen.

"Hey, so there's something I need to tell you—" she started carefully.

"Oh! There she is!" A girl's voice called out, approaching from across the bar.

The interruption was loud, insistent, and unmistakable. Kate knew that voice. She was beginning to wonder if the universe hated her for some reason.

Nikki's eyes widened, mirroring Kate's unspoken *Are you kidding me right now?*

"Kate!" Sydney called again, waving with excitement. "Surprise! "A wide, dimpled smile lit up her whole face as she maneuvered her way to Kate, unaware that she was about to walk straight into a minefield of buried secrets and high-stakes drama.

The color drained from her face as Sydney wrapped her in a tight, enthusiastic hug.

"Syd. Hi," Kate said, trying to sound cheerful and normal. "Oh my God, wow. What are you...what are you *doing* here? I thought you were in Boston?"

"I was!" Sydney said, pulling back just enough to beam at her. "But I wanted to surprise you! My boss has a house here, so she offered to drive me and let me crash with her for the weekend."

Kate blinked, her head spinning as she tried to process the mounting chaos. "That's... great," she managed.

Oh no. She knows about Aiden. Worst timing ever. Think, Kate, think...

Sydney's sharp eyes flitted toward Aiden, lighting up with amused recognition. She turned back to Kate and mouthed, *He's a SNACK.*

Then, with a grin, she addressed him directly. "So, you must be the lifeguard-slash-bartender? And apparently, a cover band singer, as well?"

Aiden chuckled, throwing Kate a knowing glance. "Guilty. Word travels fast around here, huh?"

"Oh, she undersold you big time," Sydney said conspiratorially, nudging Kate. "I'm Sydney." She extended her hand, the picture of confidence.

"Aiden," he replied, shaking it with his trademark easy charm.

"Huh. Funny," Sydney said, tilting her head thoughtfully. "My boss's son is named Aiden, too."

The ground shifted beneath her. The air grew heavy, and her pulse quickened. *It's a coincidence.*

"Fairly common name," Aiden said casually, but his shrug did nothing to dispel Kate's growing dread that there was yet another surprise in store.

Nikki, sensing the tension, jumped in. "Your boss at the internship—the fashion designer in Boston? I've heard amazing things about her lines. I'd love to meet her."

"She's incredible!" Sydney said brightly. "Oh, there she is!" She waved enthusiastically toward the bar. "Jess! Over here!"

Time seemed to slow. The air was thick, pressing in on Kate from all sides.

The woman emerged from the crowd, looking like she'd just strolled off the cover of *Town & Country* and onto the sticky floor of The Squire, two drinks in hand.

Her blond hair gleamed in glossy, effortless waves. White flared trousers that looked like they'd been hand-stitched in Paris clung to her mile-long legs. A navy lace bodice hugged her figure with the kind of precision only achievable through a personal stylist and tailor.

She looked airbrushed. Untouchable. Intimidating as hell.

Nikki audibly sucked in a breath beside her, her wide eyes snapping between Kate and the approaching woman like she was watching a slow-motion car crash.

The woman slowed, a slight frown creasing her perfect forehead as realization sparked behind her brooding brown eyes.

"Kate," Jessica said, her voice soft but laced with tension. "Wow. It's been a while."

Kate's entire body locked up, her tongue heavy and useless in her mouth, her palms clammy. She couldn't move—only stand there, like some wax museum version of herself. She managed to nod a hello.

Jessica turned her gaze to Nikki next, her tone clipped but polite.

"Hi, Nikki."

Nikki, normally the queen of smart comebacks, looked like someone had hit her with a stun gun. She blinked twice, her face a frozen mix of horror and rapidly dawning understanding.

Sydney, still cheerfully oblivious to the emotional carnage unfolding around her, beamed. "Wait—you know my stepmom? And, Nikki too?"

Jessica's lips curled into a wry, almost imperceptible smile.

"Turns out," she said coolly, "I know *everyone* here."

Before anyone could say a single word, Aiden swooped in, leaned down and kissed Jessica on the cheek with easy affection.

"Hi, Mom," he said casually, like this was the most normal night of his life.

"Hey, sweetie," Jessica replied, her voice softening immediately. "I didn't expect to see you until tomorrow."

Kate pressed her fingers against her thighs, grounding herself, trying desperately not to vomit all over her wedges.

"Me neither, but—what a nice surprise," Aiden said, grinning, blissfully unaware of the emotional nuclear fallout around him. "I was gonna introduce you to Kate and Nikki, but... looks like I don't need to!"

Jessica nodded slowly, her sharp eyes connecting dots in real time—Kate, Nikki, Sydney, and Aiden—a messy, tangled constellation she was clearly trying to map.

"Well," Aiden said, oblivious to the live wire crackling between them all, "maybe you can catch Sydney and me up on how everyone knows each other. Kate—vodka and lemonade?"

His hand brushed lightly against the small of her back, a casual, almost imperceptible flirtation.

Jessica saw it.

And in that instant, Kate knew—*she* knew.

The blood drained from Kate's face so fast she nearly swayed.

"Wait..." Sydney piped up, motioning between Aiden and Jessica. "Lifeguard-slash-bartender is *your* son, Jess?"

Even if Sydney didn't have the whole picture, she felt the tectonic plates shifting beneath them.

"Ohhhh boy," she muttered, instinctively moving closer to Kate like she was bracing for impact.

Jessica set her drink down on the table next to her with a soft *thunk* that somehow sounded like a gunshot.

"I'm sorry," she said, her voice even but razor-sharp. "Let me get this straight. Are you here *with* Aiden?"

Kate flushed crimson, mortified. She had known—in the hazy, back-of-her-mind way she knew not to touch a hot stove—that whoever Aiden's mother was, she'd have an issue with the age gap. But it was just a *kiss*! A stupid, ill-fated kiss. She didn't expect to have to meet his *mother,* for Christ's sake. Or that it would be *her.*

"I didn't know..." Kate stammered, her throat tightening painfully.

"Didn't know he was twenty-two?" Jessica snapped, incredulous.

Aiden cut in, his voice calm but firm. "OK, enough. I don't know how you two know each other, but whatever is happening I'm not digging it. I'm an adult. So is Kate."

Sydney, still recovering but trying her best to de-escalate, chimed in, "We're all adults here. Now we all know each other...so, maybe we just, like, have a drink and move on?"

Kate loved her for trying. But she didn't think Jessica was going to shrug and carry on. There was too much history, and it wasn't forgotten in the past. It was right here, standing in front of them at five-feet-eleven inches with the same deep brown, soul-searching eyes as his mom.

Jessica's gaze never left Kate. She ignored Aiden. Ignored Sydney.

Zeroed in, all sniper focus.

"Is your type just *any* man connected to me? Did you tell him about Matt?" Jessica asked, her voice even but charged with emotion.

The words hit like a slap.

"Who is *Matt*? What is going on?" Sydney pleaded, clearly uncomfortable about the tension between her stepmother and her boss.

Nikki silently put her hand on Kate's arm, a simple gesture that was slightly comforting as they stood in a metaphorical dumpster doused in gasoline. Jessica held the match.

"Why are you bringing up Dad? What does he have to do with anything?" Aiden demanded incredulously.

Jessica didn't break her gaze from Kate. "I know you're smart, Kate. You've put all the pieces together, I assume. Do you want to tell him, or should I?"

"Tell me what?" Aiden asked, his voice tinged with unease as he turned to Kate. "What's she talking about?"

Kate couldn't find the words. The room felt suffocating, like every pair of eyes were on her.

"She didn't know," Nikki said quietly to Aiden, her voice steady but firm, like she was trying to anchor the room. "Not until about fifteen minutes ago."

"Didn't know *what*?" Aiden asked, frustration sharpening his voice.

A new voice cut cleanly through the tension behind Kate—casual, upbeat, and completely oblivious.

"Didn't know what?"

Aiden's eyes shifted past Kate, and confusion slid over his face like a fog.

"Dad? *You're* here too? What is this—some kind of intervention? What the fuck is going on?"

Kate's stomach dropped. Cold sweat broke across her back. Her legs felt like they were underwater.

She didn't want to turn. Couldn't. But she had to.

She turned slowly, Nikki instinctively moving with her like they were bracing for impact together.

And then—there he was.

Older, yes, but unmistakably *him*.

Her breath caught as her eyes landed on him.

His hair was shorter, the rich dark now threaded with silver at the temples, but those blue eyes—those goddamn eyes—were exactly the same. Piercing. Hypnotic.

He wore a soft gray t-shirt and jeans—effortless, familiar. The boyish charm that once made her weak in the knees hadn't faded; it had just grown up. Standing there, older and real and *here*, she was caught in a dizzying paradox—like decades had passed and yet they'd just seen each other yesterday.

For a moment, the entire bar blurred. Her ears rang. Her knees buckled, and the world narrowed to the space between them.

"Kate...?" he said, voice barely above a whisper. His face had gone white.

The years, the spinning mess of this night—they all crashed over her in one dizzying wave.

She barely felt Nikki's hand on her arm.

Everything went dark.

Chapter Twenty One

2025

Kate's consciousness surfaced like a swimmer breaking through deep water.

Distantly, she heard voices calling her name. One warm, familiar voice murmured, "Kate, wake up," while another, laced with a mix of urgency and care, pleaded, "Kate, can you hear us?"

Her eyes fluttered open, and the concerned faces of Aiden and Matt hovered above her. For a moment, she wasn't sure if she was dreaming or having a nightmare. Past and present, standing side by side in front of her.

Her heart pounded as the memory of the evening came rushing back. She'd come to this cursed bar of bad surprises to see Aiden—against her better judgment. Then Aiden got on stage and played the same oddly specific Gin Blossoms song that Matt played for her back in 2002. Cue the overdue, jaw-drop realization: Aiden is Matt's son. Sydney showed up, completely unannounced, with her new boss. Who turned out to be Jessica, Aiden's mother. Then Matt himself walked in, because of course he did. And that's when she fainted. All caught up.

I guess fainting is a fun new thing I do now, she thought absently.

Out of the corner of her eye, she saw Nikki kneeling by her side. Her hand was resting underneath Kate's arm, steadying her, and she felt relieved that it looked like maybe she caught her before she hit the floor. Sydney was also close, propping up her other side, her wide eyes filled with concern. "Oh, thank god," Sydney sighed with relief.

Kate's face felt cold and wet, but thankfully, nothing else on her body was damp. Jessica was standing on the other side of Nikki, clutching a glass of ice water, her poised demeanor cracking with a look of genuine concern on her face.

She pieced together that one of them splashed ice water on her face to wake her up. Probably Jessica, if she had to guess.

"Are you ok? Should we call an ambulance?" Aiden asked anxiously, his hand brushing her shoulder as she started to slowly stand up.

She swallowed hard, trying to shake off the lingering disorientation.

"I'm ok. Don't call an ambulance," she managed, as her gaze landed on Matt, whose expression was a kaleidoscope of concern and confusion. She was probably the last person he expected to see tonight. She knew the feeling.

"Are you sure you're ok to stand?" Matt asked, stepping closer. His voice was warm and full of that unmistakable something that had once unraveled her so completely.

There was a hum between them, some unshakable frequency that brought it all rushing back—bonfires, bare skin, whispered secrets and dreams. And now here he was, older, steadier, and unfortunately a part of the world's most humiliating reunion.

"Yeah, I can stand," she repeated faintly, her legs still shaky but stabilizing. She couldn't look away from him. After so many years, he still enchanted her.

Nikki leaned in and turned Kate's face toward her, snapping her out of the trance. "Are you good?" Nikki asked softly, her voice full of love and worry. "That was scary."

Kate nodded, her voice steadier. "Sorry, I don't know why that keeps happening. I'm good now."

Sydney stepped closer, huddling with them like a protective cocoon. "I'm not *entirely* sure what just happened," she said, her voice low, "but I think I'm starting to get an idea. Do you want to get out of here, Kate? We can go. The three of us."

Kate nodded again, feeling a rush of gratitude for these two women who loved her so fiercely.

"Kate." Matt's voice pulled her back like a tether. He was staring at her, those blue eyes scanning her face, searching. "Why...what are you doing here?"

Fair question. Kate let out a breath. "I don't know, exactly."

And that was the truth. She had no idea which decisions she'd made over the last few months were the ones that landed her in this emotional demolition derby.

"Aiden is your son. With Jessica." It came out more like a question than she intended.

Matt nodded. "Yes."

The weight of twenty years pressed down on her. She couldn't stop the reel of thoughts:

They had the baby.

He and Jess weren't together.

Aiden said he never settled down. Why?

Did Jessica break it off with him, or was it mutual?

Did he ever think about that summer? About her?

Did she want to know? Yes. No. Well...maybe.

All these thoughts, at the same time, in only seconds. She was spiraling.

"Sorry, I'm still lost," Matt said, eyes locked on Kate. "I came to catch the band and hang out with Aiden, and somehow, after twenty years, you and Nikki are standing here with him? And Jess—what are you doing here? You *hate* The Squire."

Kate didn't want to be the one to unravel this disaster. But no one else was talking. Jessica shot her a look that said, *Don't look at me. This is all you.*

Matt's eyes settled on Kate, quietly asking for the truth.

"I'm here for the summer," she said, carefully. Not technically a lie. "I met Aiden. He invited us out tonight. That's all."

Matt processed that. He looked like he was about to speak when Aiden's voice cut through the awkward silence.

"Wait—let me get this straight." He looked baffled, not angry. "*My dad* is the guy who broke your heart?"

Matt flinched at Aiden's words—just slightly—but Kate caught it. And with it, a wave of guilt she didn't expect. The same feeling she'd had after snapping at Lindsey: like she had made accusations that were true, but somehow in a way that was unfair. Like part of it was her fault. But it wasn't her fault.

"Yes," she said, voice steady but thin. Matt had broken her heart. Worse—he'd reshaped it. Hardened it. Turned her from someone who lived in the moment to someone obsessed with controlling the future. All to avoid pain like *that* ever again.

Matt's jaw tightened. "Is that how you remember it, Kate?" he asked, his voice rough. "I *loved* you. I would've done anything for you. And you just... left. The second it got hard. The second I needed you."

No. That wasn't fair. He was making it seem like she ran away for no reason. She was twenty-two. He was about to be a father. She did what she *had* to do. But then again...he obviously did what he needed to, as well. He needed to be there for Jessica and the baby, because that was the kind of guy he was.

And I left him. No. He could have told her the truth voluntarily, instead of getting caught. He could have given her the choice. Maybe things would've been different.

"You lied to me," she said quietly. "That's not love."

"I MADE A MISTAKE." His voice rose, cracking with emotion. Like this breakup happened yesterday, not decades ago. "You think running away when something doesn't go your way is better? When things are hard, you can just disappear? Build an easier life with even higher walls?"

His tone softened. "I never loved anyone the way I loved you. And you just... walked away."

Kate stood frozen, overwhelmed. Maybe it was the alcohol. Or the fainting. Or the fact that the boy she loved was standing in front of her as a man, saying things he wanted to say years ago. But the feelings were still there. Not dead. Not even dormant. Just buried deep—and now wide awake.

I never loved anyone like I loved you. She thought it, but couldn't say it. She wasn't ready to admit maybe *she* made a mistake, too.

The bar kept buzzing around them like none of it mattered. But Nikki, Sydney, and Aiden were completely still, watching the scene unfold. Jessica, previously cool and composed, looked visibly agitated.

"So sorry to interrupt," Jessica snapped suddenly, her voice tight. "I know I'm the bad guy in your love story here, but I'm not going to stand here while you both talk around me. *Again.* I existed in this story too, remember? Neither of you cared much about *that* back then."

Kate flushed. Jessica was right. She'd never stopped to think about what it had been like for her—pregnant, scared, watching the man she still had feelings for fall for someone else and then nurse a broken heart. It must have been truly awful.

For the first time, Kate began to see herself not as the innocent bystander, who'd been hurt. She'd caused hurt, too.

Jessica straightened. "I have a great son, a successful business, and—thankfully—a solid co-parent." She nodded vaguely at Matt. "But I have *zero* interest in being part of this drama. Aiden, I'll see you tomorrow. Sydney, you're still welcome at my place, but I don't want to discuss anything that happened here tonight."

With that, she turned and walked out—head high, not looking back.

Kate felt the weight of it all settle on her chest like a brick. She turned to Nikki and Sydney.

"I want to go now."

Nikki moved instantly. "Say no more. Let's go."

She and Sydney flanked Kate, linking arms to escort her away from all of the chaos.

"Kate—" Matt's voice was low but urgent as he stepped toward her.

She turned to face him. There was so much in his eyes, she knew he wanted more from her, needed more. She didn't want to leave, she didn't want to run away, but she couldn't do this. Not tonight. Not like this.

"I can't," she said, her voice barely more than a whisper. "I just... I can't right now. I'm sorry, Matt. I'm so sorry. For everything."

The words hung there between them, suspended in the thick air. They began to move toward the exit.

The door swung open, and the cool night air wrapped around her like mercy. It didn't fix anything—didn't make the past less complicated or the future more certain—but it was enough to help her breathe again. And for now, that was all she could manage.

* * *

Later, curled up in her hotel room between Sydney and Nikki like she was enclosed in emotional bubble wrap, sleep came fast. Dreams came fast.

A dizzying blur of faces, voices, memories—past and present. Lindsey and Jessica, telling her she messed everything up, she was an awful person, she needed therapy.

Two men faded in and out, pulling her in opposite directions.

One with warm brown eyes who wanted to kiss her, impulsively and recklessly.

One with piercing blue eyes, who held out his hand, asking to love her again.

Chapter Twenty Two

2025

The soft light of the rising sun stretched lazily across the porch of Kate's room at the Inn, bathing the weathered wood in a golden glow. She sat tucked in a blanket, her hands wrapped around a warm mug of coffee, the steam curling up lazily into the still air.

The dunes stretched out in front of her, their tall grasses almost motionless in the calm morning. A few gulls called in the distance. Their cries were sharp but not unpleasant against the serenity.

Kate took a slow sip of the coffee, savoring the bittersweet taste, her gaze fixed on the horizon.

Last night felt like a fever dream she'd only just stumbled out of. Inside, Nikki and Sydney were still asleep, evidenced by Nikki's unapologetic snoring carrying over to the porch. An empty bottle of 2019 Cakebread Cabernet sat on the counter. She'd been saving the well-aged red for a special occasion. She decided a crisis was special in its own way.

She drew the blanket tighter around herself and exhaled deeply. This summer was supposed to be a chance to sift through her life and rediscover what really mattered. Instead, she felt more lost than ever.

She had a life plan—a solid one. For a while, it even looked like she'd pulled it off: the prestigious job, the picture-perfect marriage to a stable, kind man, all framed by the glittering skyline of Manhattan.

I was happy, wasn't I? She used to think so. She hadn't been unhappy, exactly. She'd been... content.

But had she really been living—or just avoiding everything hard?

Her whole life, she'd dodged confrontation. With Lindsey, she swallowed resentment instead of speaking up. What if she'd just said how she felt—really said it? Could they have had something closer to friendship than rivalry? Something built on mutual respect?

And Matt. Last night, he told her she ran when things got hard. And she did. She ran away. Yes, the situation was complicated. Yes, he'd lied. But she hadn't even tried. She didn't ask for an explanation or offer forgiveness. She just shut the door and locked it behind her. Chose the safe path, the clean break, the tidy life.

How many times had she done that? Cut off people or possibilities the moment they strayed from her master plan?

How many experiences had she skipped—not because they weren't right, but because they weren't easy?

It was sobering. She could see the cracks now—hairline fractures in the life she had meticulously sculpted. And she couldn't unsee them.

Her heart tugged, unexpectedly, for Chris. He hadn't been perfect, but he'd wanted more for both of them. Not just stability—joy. Passion. Something *real.* He'd tried to shake her out of autopilot, and she'd dismissed him for it. Blamed him, absolved herself.

The truth was, she didn't know what she wanted anymore. Her instincts had split in two—one part of her still clinging to the structured, measured life she'd built in New York; the other gravitating to the messier, more free-spirited decisions she seemed to make in Chatham.

She closed her eyes and let the rolling waves carry her back to last night, and to when they were in love. She could still *feel* him—the weight of his gaze, those piercing blue eyes that always seemed to be reading her soul.

The way he'd pull her in, arms wrapped around her tightly like she might slip away. The feel of his hand in hers on those sun-drenched summer days, the ocean biting at their ankles. The desire that burned within her when his lips brushed the back of her neck. How he held her after they made love, caressing her skin gently and her all over.

Maybe he did love her the way he said he did. Maybe it *was* real. But she couldn't stay. How could she stay?

Her mind drifted to that one song that kept drawing her back to him.

I'll follow you down, but not that far.

It had always been there, hidden in the lyrics. She never really stopped to consider what the Gin Blossoms meant—but maybe it was that love, and life, was kind of like a black hole. Deep, dark, unknowable. You can't see the bottom. You jump in, hoping for beauty. Bracing for ruin. You only find out if you're brave enough to leap.

Is the best kind of love the one that you let consume you? Where you risk everything? And even if it breaks you, you're still glad you jumped—because you weren't alone. They were falling with you.

I wasn't willing to go that far, she realized. *But maybe Matt was.*

Kate heard a light knock at the hotel door and froze, her coffee mug halfway to her lips. She glanced at her watch. 8:00 a.m. Awfully early for housekeeping.

Tiptoeing to the door, she turned the knob carefully, trying not to wake Nikki and Sydney in the bedroom. When she cracked it open, she was greeted by Aiden.

Tousled hair, a hoodie, and joggers. On any other day, he would have looked kind of sexy, like he was about to head to a Vuori photoshoot. But now all she could see was Matt's son.

He shifted his weight awkwardly, looking uncharacteristically shy.

"Hey. Can we talk?"

Kate hesitated for only a moment before nodding.

"Sure, but we need to be quiet. Nikki and Sydney are still asleep." She stepped back to let him in. "Coffee?"

"Yeah, that'd be great," he said, following her into the kitchen. A few minutes later, they were sitting on the porch, French doors closed behind them.

Kate broke the silence first. "So. I'm kind of surprised you're here. I didn't really expect to see you again. I planned on high-tailing it out of here to avoid any awkward run-ins."

Aiden's lips twitched in a small smile. "Good luck avoiding me. I'm everywhere, remember."

"That's true, you do hold every job in town."

He took a sip of coffee then leaned back into his chair. "I wasn't sure if I wanted to come either. But I was up all night. Thinking."

Kate's stomach knotted. "And?"

"And I felt like you needed to hear this from me. You didn't know, I didn't know. We're good."

An unexpected wave of relief washed over her. Just to hear him say that she didn't need to feel guilty or ashamed—it meant more than she realized.

"Thank you, Aiden," she said quietly, taking a sip of her coffee to steady herself. "Don't take this the wrong way, because you're very attractive, charming and all that—but I'm glad we only kissed."

He smiled, his trademark cockiness slipping back into place. "You say that *now*."

The tension eased and Kate cracked a smile. "I don't want to be the main character in your future therapy sessions."

Aiden's expression softened. "Listen. I want you to know I think you're beautiful and sexy. In the short time we spent together, I could see you relax a little, get lighter. I know you're going through a lot. It would be easy to use what happened last night as an excuse to shut people out. I guess...maybe consider *not* doing that."

Kate blinked, caught off guard by his mature assessment and complete honesty. "Thank you. I'll consider it."

"The past is always part of us, but you can't let it define you, you know? Breathe in the good energy and breathe out the bad."

She nodded in agreement, continuously surprised by his extremely high emotional IQ. He was going to make some lucky girl happy one day.

"I'm sure you, your mom, and your dad had a lot to talk about after last night." She wasn't sure she wanted an answer to that, but she couldn't help herself.

He chuckled. "My mom will be fine. She doesn't always react well in the moment and the local bar scene isn't really a place where she's comfortable, anyway. I called her last night. She admitted it was a funny coincidence that we met."

"And... what did you tell Matt—I mean your dad?" Kate asked tentatively.

"I told him the truth: that I pursued you relentlessly, we had no idea there was a connection, and nothing really happened."

Kate exhaled. "Ok. Thanks."

Aiden seemed to sense her unease. "Listen. My dad is a pretty open guy, and while he didn't get into a ton of detail, he was honest with me about your past. For what it's worth, I'm sorry for the way it ended with him. It sounds like he really loved you. He asked a lot of questions."

Her heart fluttered, taking her by surprise. Despite the hurt he clearly still held on to for how things ended, he was asking about her.

"I think he'd like to reconnect and talk more. If you're up for it."

"I'm not sure I'm ready for that," she said softly.

"I get it," Aiden said knowingly. "Anyway, I should get going. But one last thought. You should stay. Here in Chatham. Finish your summer. I promise I won't make it awkward."

He leaned in, giving her a heartfelt hug and kiss on the cheek before heading to the door. Kate walked him out, and as the door clicked shut behind him, she let out a long breath. She felt more at peace than she had earlier. That was a start.

She scribbled a quick note for Nikki and Sydney: *Going for a morning swim. Will not get eaten by sharks (probably). Back in time for mimosas. XOXO Kate*

Chapter Twenty Three

2025

"I'm glad you decided to stay in Chatham," Sydney said, slicking on lip gloss and adjusting her phone for better lighting. She was prepping for a date at some hip Mexican place in Boston's Seaport.

It'd been about a week since Kate told them she wanted to stay through the summer, and they both left to carry on with their own mercifully calm and consistent lives. It was almost as if they hadn't left though, given the daily check-ins and pep talks from them both. While the care and attention were appreciated, the truth was, Kate felt surprisingly good.

"Yeah, something in my gut told me to stay," Kate reflected, raising her glass of Avaline rosé to her lips. Cameron Diaz, turned out, knew her way around a grape. She deftly plucked another spicy tuna roll from her takeout container—her third sushi order that week—and gave it a satisfying dunk in soy sauce.

She had started a personal journal the other day, and the pages were already filled with things she hadn't let herself say aloud in years: musings on childhood, marriage, regret, ambition. New career ideas—some safe, some unhinged. All of it spilling out. She still wasn't sure exactly what she was going to do with her life, but she was trying to be more introspective about how her own behavior might be contributing to her life not turning out the way she hoped. These dramatic outcomes weren't just happening *to* her. She was not an inactive participant to her life, and her reactions when things went wrong could be making things even worse.

"I feel like you still have a summer glow-up coming. It would be delulu to bail now, halfway through the summer."

Mouth half-full, Kate nodded. "Totally." She wasn't exactly sure what Sydney was talking about, but it sounded positive.

"*Kate*," Sydney interrupted, mascara wand frozen mid-air. "Is that takeout sushi again?"

Kate gave a sheepish shrug.

"Have you even left the property all week?" Sydney asked.

"I picked up sushi," Kate replied, like it was a solid defense. "And I went to the wine shop down the road. Got snacks at the general store."

"So... you haven't been more than a mile from the Inn?"

Technically true. But she hadn't been wallowing.

She'd started waking early—not out of duty, but for the quiet magic of watching the sun rise over the ocean, slow and golden. She ran along the shoreline after coffee, the waves syncing with her breath. She'd begun wine journaling again, too—pairing memories with each bottle: a buttery chardonnay over scallops with Chris; a velvety pinot and fries with Nikki's feral honesty; a chilled rosé on a rainy Manhattan night, curled beside Sydney.

In the afternoons, she'd lounge with old biographies from the Inn's dusty library. Evenings: takeout, wine, and black-and-white movies. It had been healing, restorative. It was what she should've done in the first place.

"I'm feeling rather attacked right now," Kate muttered, grabbing another roll.

"You *are* being attacked," Sydney said with a hint of exasperation. "Lovingly, of course. But come on, you can't stay cooped up all summer. You won't find love in a pile of sushi in your room."

"You don't *know* that. One of the guys at the sushi place is kind of cute."

Sydney smiled, but her voice softened. "I'm serious. Watching you break up with Dad was hard. Then all the Aiden and Matt stuff... it's a lot. It kind of makes me worry about love in general."

Kate looked up, surprised. This was the first time Sydney had said anything like this.

"I guess..." Sydney hesitated, swallowing. "I need to know that when love falls apart, someone as strong and amazing as you can be okay. You're like my mom. I need to know that things falling apart doesn't mean *you* fall apart."

Kate's heart clenched. She hadn't seen it—how much Sydney had been quietly struggling with the divorce. She'd been so focused on shielding her from the mess, she forgot Sydney wasn't a child anymore. She saw *everything*. And what she needed wasn't protection. It was permission—to be hurt, to heal, to keep going. But Kate herself wasn't exactly doing that, or doing it well.

"I'm sorry," Kate said quietly. "I didn't know you were feeling this way. Are you okay?"

"I didn't want to add to your stress," Sydney said, wiping under her eyes carefully to preserve her mascara. "But yeah, it's been hard seeing you so... closed off. I know it's probably unfair, but I'm looking to you. I want to know how to handle things when life doesn't go as planned."

Kate felt tears prick her own eyes. Sydney didn't need her to be perfect—she just needed her to be real. To show her how to learn from your mistakes, not run from them.

"I love you, Syd," she said, voice thick.

"I love you too." Sydney dabbed her eyes again. "And, for the record, your generation's weird resistance to therapy is annoying. Go to therapy."

Kate laughed, wiping her own eyes. "Noted."

"Okay, I have to go," Sydney said, adjusting the phone. "But before I do—please, for the love of brunch, *leave* the Inn. Take a walk. Get happy hour oysters at another bar. Join a bonfire. Just... exit the premises."

"Maybe."

"*Promise me.*"

Kate smiled. "Fine. I promise."

* * *

Kate spent the next week consciously expanding her world beyond the safe walls of the Inn.

She ventured out for sunrise runs on more unfamiliar paths, skirting the coastline in quieter, more residential neighborhoods where she could breathe and think.

One afternoon, she had ice cream for lunch, just because she could. Black raspberry soft serve in a cone, eaten slowly on a park bench facing the bay. It felt indulgent and oddly defiant, eating ice cream in the middle of the day with no hint of a to-do list calling.

She avoided the usual Chatham hotspots—the bustling seafood shacks, the local bookstore, the harbor. Instead, she opted for the random, the obscure: out-of-the-way walking trails, tucked-away coffee stands, uncrowded beaches. Places where the odds of running into Matt felt lower.

In her journal, she admitted that she was actively avoiding him. And that it was progress to recognize and question it.

She didn't know what she'd say if she did run into him. Could a conversation with Matt untangle some of the questions this place had stirred up—questions about who she had been, and who she was now?

She wasn't sure. But she *had* been thinking about him. A lot. More in the past few weeks than in the last two decades combined. But still, she told herself she wasn't ready. Not yet.

Aiden, on the other hand, had remained a constant presence around the Inn. More in the background now, but present, nonetheless.

True to his word, he'd kept things easy between them, their interactions turning into something that resembled an actual friendship. He was still charming, still the guy who could make women from sixteen to sixty pause mid-step when he walked by. But now she saw him as her unconventional and unlikely friend and nothing more. He didn't bring up his dad, and for that, she was grateful.

A few days ago, she sat down to have coffee with him after a run, and he filled her in on his plans to move to Boston to join his mother's company full-time. She wished him well, and she meant it.

After an early dinner at the bar of a nearby bistro, Kate returned to her room and kicked off her sandals. The windows were cracked open, the sea breeze drifting in. She poured herself another glass of wine, sat on the edge of the bed, and stared at her phone for a long minute before scrolling to Chris's name.

She hadn't spoken to him since leaving the city, though it felt like a lifetime had passed. In the swirl of reflection and upheaval over the past month, something unexpected had happened—her resentment had quietly faded. The sharp edges of blame had softened, replaced by a deeper understanding. She saw him now with clearer eyes, not as the villain in their story, but as someone who had simply wanted more—for both of them. And for the first time, she felt something else too. She missed her friend.

She pressed call. She figured Chris might still be at work, but he picked up after a few rings

"Hey, Kate. Everything okay?"

"Yeah," she said. "Everything's fine. I just... felt like talking."

There was a pause. "I'm glad you called. It's been a while. How's Cape Cod?"

"Quieter than New York," she said, settling into the armchair by the window. "It's weird not hearing sirens every hour. Nice, but weird."

He chuckled. "Little siren lullabies. You're not missing much—hot, sticky, everyone's miserable. You sound good though?"

"I am," she said. And meant it.

"Are you relaxing? Or already deep in business planning mode?"

She'd forgotten she'd told him that little white lie.

"Mostly relaxing," she said. A month ago, she might've felt the need to prove something—to sound accomplished, thriving. But she didn't feel that way anymore. "Actually... I don't know what I'm doing next, Chris. I feel kind of lost."

It was quiet for a few seconds. When he spoke, his voice was soft. "I know this is fucking hard, Kate. I really am sorry."

"I know," she said. "And... I'm sorry too. I spent a long time blaming you, holding on to this narrative where I was the one who got hurt. That this happened to me, that none of it was my fault. I feel like I've been carrying around this version of myself I thought I was supposed to be. But I think maybe it's been holding me back. I don't know."

"You're a beautiful, brilliant person," he said, emotion edging his words. "And there's always time—to change, to be happy, to come back to yourself. I'm trying to do the same. It's not easy."

"Yeah," she said softly. "And before you say it—Sydney already told me to get a therapist."

He laughed. "She found mine, actually. When did she get so wise?"

"I know. We did something right there."

She could hear his smile through the phone. "Yeah. We did."

"Chris?"

"Yeah?"

"I'm selling the condo."

A beat. "Really?"

She nodded, even though he couldn't see. "It's beautiful, and I'm grateful for all the memories. But it feels like it belongs to the person I *used* to be. I'm not sure who I am right now, but I know I'm not her anymore."

"Are you sure?" he asked gently.

"I know. It was my safety net. But it was also part of the life I curated so carefully I forgot how to live in it. I thought if I kept everything just so, nothing could hurt me. But that was not true. And I think... I think that's what you were trying to tell me. I just wasn't ready to hear it."

"I'm sorry," she added. "For acting like the victim. For making you the villain. You weren't."

He cleared his throat. "Kate... thank you. That means more than you know."

"I want you to be happy," she said softly

"I'm trying. I'm getting there. And I want that for you too. Even if it's messy. Especially if it's messy."

She smiled. "No more five-year plans."

They both laughed, the sound light and easy.

"Any idea where you'll go next?" he asked.

She looked out the window at the swaying beach grass, the sun gradually starting to set in the picturesque landscape. "Not yet," she said. "But I'm okay with that."

"Kate," he said after a moment, his voice kind. "I'm proud of you."

She closed her eyes. Let it land. Let it mean something.

"Thanks, Chris."

There was nothing left to say, and somehow, that felt like peace.

"Goodnight," she whispered.

"Goodnight."

She ended the call and let the phone fall into her lap. The room was quiet except for the sound of waves in the distance. She scanned her cozy little room. It was still early. The beach was magical at night, it wouldn't hurt to go enjoy it.

She threw on a pair of worn denim cutoffs, her old NYU sweatshirt, and tossed the open bottle of wine and a glass into her tote, her sights set on Lighthouse Beach.

Chapter Twenty Four

2025

The sky was vibrant with streaks of rose gold, indigo, and soft apricot stretching across the horizon, dipping into the sea like brushstrokes from an unseen hand. The sun hovered just above the waterline, casting one last warm glow across Lighthouse Beach before it surrendered to night. A salty breeze curled around Kate as she stepped onto the sand, her tote bag bumping gently against her hip.

Her sandals sank with each step, kicking up soft sand. The beach was dotted with its usual Friday night charm: a few low bonfires burning in the distance, casting halos around clusters of locals and late-summer vacationers. Laughter carried on the wind—soft, companionable, forgettable. She was already glad she came.

Kate kept to the edge of it all, scanning the dunes until she found the perfect spot: a quiet patch where the sand rose just slightly, shielding her from the nearest group and offering an unobstructed view of the ocean. She laid out her blanket, a navy throw she'd found in the closet of her suite, and pulled the wine and glass from her bag.

She smiled to herself as she poured a generous first glass. The rosé was chilled just enough. She held it up briefly in salute and took a slow sip.

It was nice here. Peaceful.

She tucked her knees under her sweatshirt and stared at the horizon, the sky now deepening into a watercolor wash of lavender and steel blue.

Am I crazy?

Selling the condo felt like the right thing to do, but also like cutting off a limb. Where would she live? More importantly, what would she do? She was leaning toward walking away from her career in marketing; from the grind, structure and shiny title. It was terrifying to write off the career she'd been building for so long. But also: exhilarating.

She considered that maybe she didn't want to climb the corporate ladder anymore. She wanted to build something. She didn't know exactly what yet—but she wanted to be connected to something on a deeper level. She wanted something that felt more like her. And she was trying to trust those new feelings.

She closed her eyes for a moment, letting the breeze play with the ends of her hair.

Then—footsteps.

Slow, steady. Stopping just behind her.

Kate tensed. She opened one eye, already annoyed. *Great.* Some drunk college kid was about to stumble over, ask for her name, maybe a glass of wine, and she'd have to awkwardly shut it down without sounding like someone's cranky aunt.

But when she turned her head, the air snagged in her throat.

It wasn't a college kid. Not at all.

"Hey, Kate," Matt said softly.

He stood a few feet away from her blanket, just outside the boundary of whatever this moment was supposed to be. It was dusk and light was fading quickly, but she would have recognized him in the dark, blindfolded. Her whole body did.

His fitted navy t-shirt clung to his broad shoulders and chest. His khaki shorts were worn in and sun-bleached, his legs tan. Leather sandals—scuffed and well-loved—sank slightly into the sand, and a faded Red Sox cap shaded the face she knew too well. In completely laid-back attire, which likely took no effort at all, he looked more handsome than he did when he was in his twenties.

His eyes locked onto hers. Still that same impossible blue. Still warm. Still mischievous. Still Matt.

Of course he's here. Of course.

He ran a hand through his hair—a nervous tic she remembered all too well. In his other hand, he held a bottle of Sam Adams, the condensation glistening in the fading light.

"Hi…" she managed, though her voice came out barely above a whisper. She cleared her throat, trying to reclaim some measure of composure.

"It's nice to see you're still always prepared with a real wine glass for any occasion," he said, a gentle smile tugging at his lips.

Kate lifted her glass tentatively. "What can I say? I like to drink my emotions with a stem."

He laughed, low and warm, and just like that, a tiny bridge began to form across the canyon of years between them.

"May I join you?" he asked, the hope in his eyes almost too earnest to bear. "It's ok if you say no. You looked deep in thought."

"Sure," she said. He sat down on her blanket. Close, but still a respectable distance.

She'd been expertly dodging him for two weeks, only to fold like a beach chair the moment he appeared. Everything in her wanted to be near him, even if she had no idea how to navigate what came next.

"How did you know I'd be here?" she asked, trying to strike a tone that was both casual and not accusatory. She hadn't told anyone she'd be here tonight. The whole thing had been spontaneous.

"I promise I'm not stalking you," he said, reading her mind with unsettling accuracy. "I come here most nights. Just to walk. Clear my head. I guess... part of me was always hoping I'd run into you."

Her heart kicked in her chest. "Oh," she said, warmth blooming across her collarbone. "Well. You knew where I was staying. There were easier ways to find me."

"I know," he said, pausing to take a sip of his beer. "But I didn't want to pressure you. I figured if I saw you here, maybe it was for a reason."

She looked at him, trying to read his expression, but it was soft, open—unguarded. The wind picked up a little, brushing her cheek and stirring her hair. She glanced down at her half-full wine glass, then back at the man she hadn't been ready to face. Until now.

She didn't know exactly what to say next. They were essentially strangers. Strangers who had known each other very intimately a long time ago. Who'd been brought back together by forces unknown in dramatic and chaotic fashion.

Matt sat beside her, legs stretched out, beer now resting in the sand. She swirled her wine out of nervous habit. She wasn't ready to look into his eyes just yet.

They didn't speak for a long moment, just sat there, side by side, watching the last blush of sunset fade into the vast, waiting dark. She was full of anticipation of what might be said next, but the sitting felt...nice. Unexpectedly comfortable.

"Kate," he said, his voice turning serious. "I was hoping to run into you because...I didn't want to leave things the way we did."

The air between them shifted slightly. It felt heavier. He grabbed the beer bottle from the sand, seemingly just to have something in his hand. A lump rose in her throat—whether from embarrassment, longing, or something far more complicated, she couldn't tell.

"I wanted to say I'm sorry for the way things ended back then." He exhaled, running a hand through his hair again. "I should have told you about Jess the second she told me she was pregnant. It took us both by surprise. We had stopped dating before I even met you. And I was so scared of losing you, I thought if I just found the right moment, I could convince you that it would be ok. I could convince you to stay, to be with me. But there was never a right moment. And then I lost you anyway."

Kate tried to absorb the context that she ran away from all those years ago. She continued to stare down at her glass, turning it in her hands. Finally, she lifted her gaze and locked eyes with him. She didn't know what she wanted to say to this man. But the words just poured out of her.

"Every part of my heart, my soul and my body was in so deeply love with you," she said, her voice thick with emotion, raw and unfiltered. "I made myself vulnerable and opened my heart. And it was shattered. *Completely.*" Her voice broke slightly, and she swallowed hard before continuing. "I thought that what we had was real. But all along, you were keeping such a big secret. It made me question ever trusting my heart again."

She held his gaze, even as her eyes shimmered with the threat of tears. He didn't flinch. He let her words land, let them sting.

"I am so sorry, Kate," he said quietly. "I didn't know how to be there for Jess and a baby and still be the man I wanted to be with you. I tried to fix it all instead of being honest. And I've regretted it ever since."

He paused, then added, "Jess and I tried—for Aiden. But it wasn't right. She wanted something else. And I still loved you. I think I always have."

Kate's body surged with raw emotion, firing chaotically from her chest to her brain, back again and firing to all her limbs. After all these years, after the boyfriends, the heartbreaks, an entire marriage—Matt admitted that he still loved her. His eyes glistened, deep and unguarded, revealing everything else between the lines.

The way he looked at her now, it was like no time had passed at all. She wondered if deep down, she had never moved on from him, either.

"It's been over twenty years, Matt," she said, trying to breathe levity into the moment. "I'm sure we're both very different people. I don't know anything about your life. You could be a convicted felon, for all I know."

He laughed, breaking the tension. "Only if they're prosecuting people for never using Instagram. But I did check in on you from time to time."

She gave him a faux glare. "So, you're a lurker?! You know that by law, if you look up old flames online, you're required to pitch them an MLM?"

"Damn. So, this *isn't* the right time to sell you collagen supplements?"

She laughed, and it felt real. Easy.

He looked at her again, quieter now. "I assumed you wouldn't want me to reach out. You were married. You had a family. I didn't want to disrupt your life for my own selfish desire."

At the word *desire*, something tightened low in her stomach. It was crazy to think she could still desire someone she no longer knew. But her body was reacting to him in ways her mind couldn't justify.

"Well, I was married," she said, staring out at the ocean. "But I wasn't particularly happy. And now, I'm not sure what I am. Except maybe...free."

They sat in silence again, the surf crashing softly in the distance.

"So, you're not freaked out by this whole situation with Aiden?" she asked, realizing she probably did not need to go there. Too late now.

Matt grinned. "Not really. I mean, if Aiden saw the same things I did when I fell for you, who can blame him? You've always had this light. And, not for nothing, but you still look about 30. So that's kind of on *you*."

She blushed and was grateful for the cover of twilight. Then he added with a sly smile, "That said, he does look *exactly* like me. I'm choosing to read something into that."

It was so surreal to be sitting next to him, listening to him very clearly flirt with her. She had spent a long time trying to hold on to the fleeting memory of what he looked like, felt like, in the years following that summer. And now she could reach out and touch him.

She really wanted to touch him.

"Well, if you knew me, you'd know how out of character this entire summer has been for me. I'm saying and doing things I can't explain."

"Well," he said, softer now. "I'd like to get to know you again. If that's ok."

Kate swallowed hard, struggling to steady herself against a tidal wave of emotions. He was a stranger now—someone she barely knew. And yet, it didn't stop her from wanting to throw her arms around his neck, to close the distance, to taste the memory of him on her lips. She felt almost dizzy as she tried to balance the magnetic force drawing her in.

"I'd like that," she whispered.

"I'm not expecting anything," he added gently. "If we just come out of this with a friendship, that's ok."

A thought burst into her mind with blunt force, as if her heart pulled an override switch from her brain. *I don't want to be friends.*

Every action, every moment thereafter, was steady and decisive, as if she was on autopilot. She carefully wedged her glass into the sand and turned and faced him.

He met her gaze, and despite his attempt at friendly reconciliation, there was raw desire and passion in his blue eyes. And love. She could still see it there, too. Like a not quite-extinguished flame, burning.

And then—without a word, without permission from her better judgment—she leaned in.

Their lips met in a hesitant brush, featherlight. It was tender, tentative—years of dormant longing distilled into a single, fragile moment. His hand cupped her cheek, reverent and shaking slightly, as if afraid she might vanish again if he wasn't careful. He pulled back slightly for a moment, a recalibration. She felt his breath, warm and uneven, against her skin.

The second kiss came with more certainty, the dam breaking. Their mouths found each other with a hunger that startled her—urgent, unfiltered, real. She gasped softly as his hand slid into her hair, his fingers threading through it like he was relearning her by touch alone. Her arms wrapped around his neck, pulling him closer until there was nothing between them but heat and memory and want.

Time ceased to exist. Twenty years collapsed between heartbeats.

Her body awakened in ways that made her feel lightheaded, weightless—like every sleeping nerve was suddenly and wildly alive. Her skin tingled, her chest tightened. She clung to him, breathing him in.

He broke away again, his forehead resting against hers, both of them panting and stunned by the force of it.

"I forgot what this feels like," she whispered, almost involuntarily.

"Tell me," he murmured, his voice low and rough with want. "What does it feel like?"

Her lips found his again, more desperate this time; less about remembering, more about *reliving.* His hands were on her waist, her ribs, her back, and then lower. Their mouths crashed together with need, their kiss deepening, raw and almost chaotic. It was messy and perfect. Her body arched against him, and he groaned into her mouth.

She reached down and tugged at the hem of his t-shirt, sliding her hands underneath to feel his skin—warm and taut, alive under her touch. When her fingers made contact, he shivered and exhaled.

Without thinking, Kate laid back on the blanket, pulling him with her. The forgotten wine glass tilted in the sand beside them. The stars above swirled in a blur of heat and heady emotion. The wind off the water cooled her flushed cheeks, but it couldn't temper the fire burning in her blood.

Matt hovered above her, his eyes scanning hers, asking a silent question—one that didn't need words. He wanted to make sure this was what she wanted.

She nodded. "I need this," she breathed. "I need *you.*"

He lowered himself slowly, his weight settling onto her, solid and grounding and electric. Her hands roamed his back, his shoulders, memorizing every inch, rediscovering the man she once knew through the body he had become. He kissed her neck, her collarbone and jawline with complete adoration.

They were both trembling; whether from nerves or need, she couldn't say. Their bodies began to move together instinctively, syncing like waves meeting shoreline—surging and retreating, testing and claiming. Their rhythm was breathless, imperfect and intoxicating. She moaned softly into his ear, feeling every inch of him against her, her legs wrapping around his waist as he pressed deeper into her, still clothed but aching.

Emotion cracked open inside her like lightning across a night sky. She wanted to cry. She wanted to laugh. She wanted to lose herself in this man, in this moment, until the rest of the world faded to nothing but heat and memory and the sweet ache of longing finally met.

It was like coming home.

Chapter Twenty Five

2025

It was 7:00 a.m. Sunlight filtered through the slatted blinds, painting soft gold stripes across the sheets. Kate lay still, eyes open, her body exhausted but restless. Sleep hadn't come easy—not with the rush of adrenaline, memory, and sensation still coursing through her like electricity.

She kept replaying the night before.

His hands on her skin.

His mouth tracing long-forgotten paths.

The way it felt both wildly new and deeply familiar, like muscle memory.

The simple intimacy of him holding her hand as he walked her back to the Inn as if no time had passed; as if they'd never stopped holding hands.

Then his voice—low, careful, sincere—when she'd pulled him close and whispered, *Come back with me.*

"If I were listening to my body, we'd already be there," he'd said gently, thumb brushing her cheek. "But something tells me you might need to sit with this. I want to know all of you, not just this part."

Her body had throbbed with the ache of unfinished desire—the tension of kisses that lingered, hands that wandered but never crossed the line. But her heart exhaled.

He was right, of course. The night had been a fever dream charged, sensual, and dizzy with nostalgia and possibility. But in the quiet morning light, excitement tangled with more consideration.

She was following her heart and gut for once, but she didn't want to rush it. To be too impulsive. There should be room for some degree of careful consideration in this new life of hers.

It's not like this was the same clean slate as when they first met. They weren't twenty anymore. In a weird twist of fate, they both had twenty-two-year-old adult children, even if Sydney wasn't technically hers. And Kate didn't live here. She didn't even have a damn job. Her future was a mosaic of maybes and unfinished thoughts.

Matt likely had a life rooted here. Friends. Routines. If he was still the man she remembered, city life wouldn't suit him. Then again, she's not sure if it suited her, either. Not anymore.

She stared at the ceiling, the silence loud with questions she didn't know how to answer. Laying here and letting her thoughts run wild wasn't helping. She threw off the covers, pulled on her running gear, and laced her sneakers. Her runs had become therapeutic, and there was certainly a lot to work through.

The Inn's lobby was serene as she made her way toward the door, with just a handful of guests milling about. Just as she reached for the handle, a voice called out behind her.

Kate paused before turning around. It was a familiar voice.

She turned and was startled to see her sister standing near the reception desk. Her run-ins with Lindsey always seemed to be this way: unexpected and usually unwelcome.

Lindsey looked unusually casual in ripped boyfriend jeans and a cropped sweatshirt. Her hair was tied back in a loose ponytail, a look that made her seem younger and, for once, somewhat approachable. She held up two Starbucks iced coffees with a small smile that looked almost like a peace offering.

"Good morning. I brought you one," Lindsey said, wiggling the cup slightly.

Kate raised an eyebrow. *Is this the twilight zone?*

"I was just heading out for a run. What are you doing here?"

Lindsey hesitated, her smile faltering. "Oh, well, mind if I join you? Could we walk instead?"

Kate sighed, already mourning the quiet reflective run she'd been craving.

"Sure," she relented. "I'll take that coffee though."

As they walked toward the beach, the early morning air was still cool and briny, with the soft murmur of waves rolling onto the sand. The cloudless sky promised a perfect Cape summer day ahead. Kate sipped her iced coffee, while Lindsey trailed beside her, uncharacteristically quiet.

"So," Kate began after a stretch of silence, "are you here to dig for information on Aiden, or are you here to lecture me on my poor life choices?"

"No," Lindsey said, shaking her head. "I actually...came to apologize. For that night."

Kate stopped abruptly, turning to face her sister. She hadn't heard from her sister in weeks, and that had been perfectly fine by Kate. In fact, Lindsey left with the family almost two weeks ago. "Let me get this straight. You came all the way here from Duxbury on a Sunday morning? Did you get up at 5 a.m.?"

Lindsey shrugged sheepishly. "Pretty close to that. I wanted to catch you, and with the kids' activities, Sunday morning was the only time I could get over here. I'm sorry, I should have texted."

If she had texted, Kate would have told her not to come. She probably knew that.

"Did Mom put you up to this?"

"No! Not at all. She keeps calling for updates on you, but I've been sending her straight to voicemail."

More surprising behavior.

"You passed up the opportunity to share juicy gossip about me being seen with a younger man? Who are you, and what have you done with my sister?"

Lindsey winced. "Ouch. I just wanted to say, in-person, I'm sorry for how I reacted when I saw you on the beach. I was caught off guard, and maybe a little resentful that you were there with a hot new guy. My therapist says I need to work on being less…"

"Bitchy?" Kate offered.

"I was going to say self-involved, but yeah. That too." Lindsey was not looking her in the eye. Her voice was remorseful.

Kate's expression softened. "Well, I'm sorry for what I said. I was feeling vulnerable that night and you hit a nerve."

"No," Lindsey said earnestly. "I deserved it. Honestly, I was kind of proud of you for standing up for yourself. You've never done that with me before."

Kate blinked, taken aback. Where was all this self-awareness coming from? Therapy was a hell of a drug, apparently.

"I've been trying to figure out why I've always been so hard on you," Lindsey continued. "And I think it's because I was jealous."

Kate frowned. "Sorry, what? Jealous of *me*?"

Lindsey nodded, kicking at the sand. "You've always been the smart one. You knew about fancy wine, you traveled, you were sophisticated, you lived in New York City. All I had were my looks and popularity, and even I know those things don't last forever."

Kate was stunned, both by the admission and the unexpected compliments. "I had no idea you felt that way. And trust me, you have very little to be jealous of currently."

"I had been hoping we could spend some time together this summer," Lindsey continued. "Reconnect. I know it's been a rough year for you, and I'm sorry I haven't been there. I haven't been a very good sister."

Kate swallowed the lump forming in her throat. "That means a lot." What a wild turn this morning had taken. "And just so we're clear, I'm going to be furious with you if this is some sort of bait and switch…"

Lindsey lightly nudged her. "It's not. But speaking of switch. They upgraded your room, right? I never got the confirmation."

Kate's stopped in her tracks. She had forgotten all about that. And she had found it odd that Nikki never mentioned it. "That was *you*?"

"Guilty," Lindsey said with a grin. "Figured you could use a little extra luxury. I was trying not to make it about me, so I didn't say anything."

Kate shook her head incredulously. "Well, thanks. That was generous. The room is beautiful."

"And by the way, I'm not surprised that stupidly attractive man was into you. You seem to be completely oblivious to how alluring and mysterious you are."

Kate sighed. "Oh, that. Well, funny thing... turns out he's the son of a guy I dated in the summer of 2002."

"WHAT?" Lindsey nearly choked on her coffee.

Kate nodded gravely. "And his mom is the girl I caught him with one night out in the parking lot, right before I left to go back to school. Jessica Johnson."

"The *designer*?" Lindsey's jaw dropped.

"Apparently. They all showed up at The Squire a few weeks ago and we had the lucky experience of putting the pieces together in real time. It was kind of a disaster."

Lindsey gawked, then burst into laughter. "Kate, this is *too much*! You're like a walking soap opera."

Kate rolled her eyes dramatically and let out a big sigh. "Lucky me."

Kate stopped at the edge of where the dry beach met the ocean-soaked sand, letting the salty air fill her lungs. The quiet expanse of smooth shore in front of her was barely touched by footprints. The tide whispered as it crept up, the only movement in the stillness of the morning.

For a moment, she let it all soak in—the cool breeze brushing her cheeks and the simple, unhurried beauty of the Cape before it was overrun by beach umbrellas and sunbathers. The unexpectedness of her sister's company, which shockingly didn't feel awful.

Without thinking, she sank onto the sand, taking off her shoes and cathartically plunging her feet in. It wasn't a sweaty, healing run, but the results of this walk were remarkably similar. Instead of reliving every moment from last night and overanalyzing her future, she had a different distraction to work through.

Lindsey dropped down beside her, cross-legged and casual, brushing a stray strand of hair from her face.

"What's next for you?" Lindsey asked with no judgment, only genuine curiosity.

Kate watched the tide, the water creeping up slowly before pulling back. "I don't know, honestly. This so-called sabbatical summer of finding myself wasn't what I thought it would be. On the plus side, I realized that Chris was right all along, and that we are better as friends. That feels healthy, I think."

Lindsey nodded thoughtfully. "Yeah, I think so."

Kate considered telling her about Matt but then decided against it. This bonding was still very new, unfamiliar territory.

"On the bright side, I guess I'm not an old hag that no one is going to want."

Lindsey gave a soft scoff. "You're delusional if you thought that."

"All that aside, I don't feel any closer to knowing what's next."

Lindsey arched a brow. "Did you really think you were going to figure it all out in one summer? Rebuild your confidence, reimagine your career, and find passionate love—all before Labor Day? That's a year of therapy. Minimum. I'd know."

Kate shrugged. "In hindsight, yeah, it sounds ridiculous. But I did come here thinking I could sort it all out. I used to believe I could do anything if I just worked hard enough."

"I think both things can be true," Lindsey offered. "You can be open to something new—even something uncertain—and still be the kind of woman who makes shit happen when it counts. Have you thought about leaving New York? Starting fresh somewhere else?"

Kate pushed her toes into the sand, flicking at a shell. Of course she had. She was selling the condo.

She'd already considered starting over somewhere wildly different—Lisbon, maybe, or some coastal town in California.

But ever since last night, since Matt, she'd been wondering what it would mean to stay. Not as a vacationer. Not as a woman hiding out. But as herself. For real. Maybe Cape Kate could just become... Kate.

Still, reality tugged at her. "Thinking about where to live without knowing how I'll make a living feels a little backwards," she admitted. "I don't think I want to go back to corporate marketing. But I'm not ready to retire, either."

Lindsey's expression turned thoughtful. "Well," she said, leaning in, eyes gleaming, "I might have an idea."

* * *

After walking back to the Inn together, Lindsey gave her a quick hug and said she needed to get back to the family, promising to call and visit more often. It wasn't a grand gesture, but it felt like a beginning—something softening between them.

Kate felt energized. Present. Capable. More pieces of her new life were starting to click into place, and she was curious—almost excited—to tug on the thread of Lindsey's idea.

But first, there was one important thing she needed to do.

Morning :)

Matt's reply came quickly.

Hey – good morning :) Sleep well?

Not exactly lol...lots to think about. Last night was amazing. But you were right. The way we are drawn to each other is coming from our past. I want us to discover who we are now. I need just a little time. There's something I need to take care of first. Is that ok...?

The three dots seemed to linger for far too long as she awaited his response.

> Take all the time you need. I will always wait for you.

Chapter Twenty Six

2025

The sun hung high in the sky, basking Old Wharf Road in pulsating summer heat. Tourists bustled along the street laughing, car doors slamming, children laughing, dogs barking.

The Town of Dennis was very different than Chatham. It wasn't as manicured, or quiet, or sophisticated. There was a mix of vacationers and locals. If the Cape had boroughs like New York City, Dennis would be Queens. Kate kind of liked that.

She stood by her car, taking in the view. Somehow, the summer had unfolded just as she'd imagined when she left her condo in June, a lifetime ago.

In the week after her walk with Lindsey, her sister returned with the kids for a beach day. Her niece and nephew shrieked with joy as Aunt Kate jumped waves with them, then got to work building sandcastles while Kate and Lindsey sat nearby, talking in a way they never had before. They weren't best friends or anything—years of resentment and misread intentions didn't vanish overnight—but something real had shifted between them.

Sydney came for the weekend, and they spent lazy afternoons bouncing between coffee shops and boutique stores. Sydney casually offered her unsolicited but astute advice about marketing her new business venture to a younger generation. "You need a stronger Instagram presence. Be funny, but don't try that 'Gen Z wrote this' thing—it's over. And post reels. Old people are obsessed with reels." Kate rolled her eyes but made a mental note. She *did* love reels.

She kept her promise to herself, and she hadn't seen Matt in at least two weeks. But they did text each other sweet check-ins and traded daily photos—his soft-serve swirl with chocolate sprinkles, her glass of wine against a fiery sunset. Most of their messages were wordless, yet somehow said everything. She hoped the space wouldn't cool what still lingered between them, but she also knew better now than to rush. She could only make one big decision at a time. If he was truly the one she'd been waiting for all along, a brief pause wouldn't change that.

And now, here she was in Dennis, about to take a massive leap.

Kate took a deep breath, adjusting the tote slung over her shoulder. The rich leather handle was soft against her sun-warmed skin, and the iced latte in her other hand cooled her, if only slightly. A simple sundress swayed around her legs, and her hair was twisted into an easy updo. She felt good despite the stifling New England humidity.

She turned toward the building in front of her—small, historic, and radiating the charm of an old New England pub. The paint on the shutters was chipping, and the wooden sign above the entrance was so faded it was barely legible. It had been a pub once but hadn't been anything in at least five years. It needed work, but Kate had seen potential. She saw possibility.

Pushing open the heavy door, she stepped inside. Sunlight pierced through the dusty windows, illuminating the rich mahogany of the old bar. The space was eerily quiet, the only sound the faint rustling from the kitchen. Moments later, a woman appeared, her arms full of paperwork. Jeanie, her real estate agent, was sharp and efficient but carried an air of warmth that Kate had come to appreciate. They had made this happen faster than she thought possible, and she had Jeanie to thank for that. And Chris, for helping her put the condo on the market while she stayed in the Cape.

"Today's the day!" Jeanie said brightly, placing the papers on the bar. "Are you ready to sign?"

She glanced around once more, taking in the rustic beams, the scuffed floors, the worn-in tables and chairs scattered about haphazardly. It was imperfect, but it was hers. Or at least, it would be in a few minutes.

Kate took a deep breath, setting her things down on the bar. "I think so."

Jeanie smiled knowingly. "It's going to be so nice to have a cute little wine shop and bar here in Dennis. People are going to love this. Personally, I can't wait to see what you do with it."

Kate traced her fingers along the edge of the old wooden counter. "It's going to be a lot of work, but I'm excited, too."

She thought back to when Lindsey first suggested she follow her passion.

"Running things on your own terms. And wine," Lindsey had said, without missing a beat. "That pairing list you made for Mom and me last year? I sent it to some wine-obsessed friends. They *loved* it. Still talk about it. You don't just pair wine with food—you pair it with people, with moods. That's a gift."

The idea had taken Kate by surprise. Sure, she *loved* wine, but it was a hobby. A side passion. Surely, she was not a savant.

But the more she mulled it over, the more excited she became. Maybe, for the first time in her life, work wouldn't feel like work. Maybe this could be different.

When Lindsey sent her the link to a spot she knew in Dennis that could be perfect for a wine shop and bar, Kate figured it wouldn't hurt to check it out. She had toured it with the real estate agent, and from the moment she stepped inside, she *knew*. There was a quiet but resolute voice in her gut. And maybe her heart, too. And she listened.

Kate looked down at the contract in front of her, the weight of the moment settling in. The divorce was final. The condo was selling. This signature would officially be the start of a completely new life.

With a steady hand, she signed her name. *Kate Walker.* Owner of this unkempt building. Professional wine lover. Newly minted risk taker. Born-again dreamer.

Jeanie clapped her hands together. "And just like that, you're a business owner!"

Kate let out a slow breath, a wide smile spreading across her face. She felt excited. A little terrified, maybe. But mostly excited.

Jeanie handed her the keys, apologizing for rushing off, and hurried along to her next appointment. She promised to be in touch soon with condo and house listings, given Kate would now need to be a full-time resident of Cape Cod.

She found herself alone in the property she officially owned, taking in the moment. The restaurant was more or less a blank slate, save for a few tables, chairs and stools in various stages of disrepair.

Kate could already see what it might look like in six months. The shelves lined with an interesting mix of red, white and rose varietals. Rare finds tucked between old favorites. Small, candlelit tables where couples lingered over a second glass, where strangers struck up conversations about wineries they'd visited, travel plans and great food.

There would be a sleek but welcoming tasting bar with her behind it, choosing the exact right wine for those that wanted to try something new. Maybe there'd be live acoustic music in the corner—something low and bluesy, not too polished, just enough to make the air hum.

She smiled to herself, lost in the vision, running her fingertips along the aged bar top that was now hers.

The door creaked open behind her.

"Are you here to tell me I made a huge mistake?" she called over her shoulder, half-laughing, fully expecting to see a frazzled Jeanie searching for her misplaced keys—again.

"Is it ok if I come in?"

She turned, and there he was—Matt—standing in the doorway. Her heart skipped a beat.

She smiled and nodded. "Yeah," she said softly. "Come in."

He stepped inside, slow and deliberate, his eyes sweeping the empty space before settling on her again. Their eyes met—comforting and familiar—and suddenly she could breathe again.

"It's not much to look at yet," she said shyly, suddenly aware of the questionable smells, uneven lighting and dusty, abandoned furniture. It wasn't exactly the Chatham Bars Inn. Or even The Squire, truth be told.

He turned in a slow circle, taking it all in with a thoughtful smile. "I think it's perfect. Congratulations."

Her eyes welled unexpectedly. Of all the people she wanted to share this with, she realized he was at the top of the list. And here he was, like he just *knew*.

"Thank you," she managed. "I'm probably clinically unwell for doing this, but no turning back now."

She tilted her head, still trying to make sense of him being here. "I'm confused. How did you find me here? I'm starting to feel like I emit an undetectable sound for people to pop up and surprise me at random places."

Matt grinned. "Yeah, it's like a dog whistle. We have meetings. Take turns tracking you down. I was up."

She shook her head, laughing. "Ok, ok. Seriously, though. Did Nikki call you?" She was definitely going to scold her best friend for meddling.

"No, not exactly," Matt coyly admitted. "Word travels fast here in Dennis, and I caught wind that this place was selling to some cute, young 'New York City' woman who was going to make it a wine bar. I took a good guess who that might be. And I might have done a *little* digging to know you'd be here today."

"Is that for me?" she asked, nodding toward the bottle of pink wine in his hand.

He lifted the bottle. "It's a Wölffer Estate Rose from Provence. I've never tried it, but it's called 'Summer in a Bottle.' It seemed like the perfect one for you," he said, and she detected a touch of sentimentality.

"I know you said you needed some time. I Just came here to congratulate you. Welcome you to town, officially."

He handed the bottle over to her gently. She turned it over in her hand and admired its design—a kaleidoscope of delicate wildflowers, butterflies, and vibrant hues that danced across the glass. Somehow, the bottle was a time capsule of her summers here, both past and present. The label, "Summer in a Bottle," felt like an open invitation to embrace the spirit of those summers and carry it forward into this next adventure.

He was right. It was perfect.

She was about to take his hand, to feel the warmth of his skin against hers, but something stopped her. She glanced down at the bottle, her fingers lingering on its smooth surface as a thought surfaced in her mind. She walked over to the bar, setting the bottle gently on a small shelf against the mirror, as if it had always belonged there. The spot felt almost intentional, like it was waiting for this moment.

"You don't want to drink it?" Matt asked, curiosity in his voice.

"No," she said, turning back to him. Her gaze softened as she spoke, something deeper than words in her tone. "I know this might sound strange, but I think there's a little magic in this bottle. I want to keep it here. As a reminder."

"A reminder of what?" he asked, stepping closer. His eyes, full of that familiar mix of tenderness and gravity, didn't waver.

She met his gaze, heart full. "That no matter how far down I go—I'll always find my way back. To myself. To what matters. To...you."

He didn't say anything at first. He just looked at her like she was the answer to every question he didn't know he was asking.

And then, without hesitation, she closed the space between them and kissed him—deeply, wholly, like a woman who finally knew what she wanted.

He kissed her back like he'd been waiting his whole life.

And in that moment, everything else slipped away. The doubts. The what-ifs. Even the noise of the world outside the door.

The kiss didn't feel like a perfect ending.

It felt like a beginning.

For the first time in a long time, Kate wasn't chasing someone else's idea of happiness.

She was choosing her own. And she was exactly where she needed to be.

The future was unwritten.

And she couldn't wait to begin.

Dear Reader

Thank you. I am truly honored that you read *Follow You Down*, my first novel. I hope you enjoyed reading it as much as I enjoyed creating it! If you liked the novel and want to support me as a new author, here are some suggestions:

- **Review it.** Reader reviews are one of the best ways to share your views on a story, and help buyers make an informed decision. Consider posting your review at Goodreads or your favorite online retailer, like Amazon.
- **Share it on social.** Word of mouth is so important! If you could share that you read and recommend it, with the link to where to purchase, that would be amazing. There are also some great forums and groups to post on.
- **Share it with your book club.** I love a good book club. In fact, I was "NH famous" for a minute in my early 20's because I started a book club that had three generations, as it included my mom and grandmother, and the *Concord Monitor* wrote a lifestyle piece on it! Book clubs are powerful!

Happy reading, and I hope I can catch you on whatever my next novel will be!

Acknowledgments

Dan said I should start with the viral Snoop Dogg quote "I want to thank me, for believing in me. I want to thank me for doing all this hard work." I laughed it off, but Dan is usually right, so. It's unreal that I am writing an acknowledgment page for a novel I completed. Amid a demanding full-time job, raising two kids and managing a household—this was an insane hobby to pick up. I could not have done it alone, obviously. So there are some people I do need to thank (not everyone can be Snoop).

Madeline, thank you for that one conversation that opened my eyes to wanting to do this, for real. Kids have a funny way of showing you truths you can't see on your own. Jackson, thank you for always asking "is that your book, mommy?" when seeing Emily Henry and Abby Jimenez books around the house. Not yet bubba, not yet. And for Madeline proudly telling her 4th grade teacher her mom wrote a beach read and letting me know her teacher wanted to read it. That was both cute and terrifying. Thank you both for letting mom skip bedtime every once and a while when I was on a roll downstairs, typing away.

Speaking of skipped bedtimes, I can't imagine that this would ever have happened without a supportive partner, and I picked the best one there is. Dan, even though you may never read this (though I suspect you will), you never once questioned this endeavor. You gave me space and time to work on this, and didn't bat an eye when I told you how much the developmental edit cost. You always want me to do what makes me happy, and I cannot thank you enough for that, or love you more because of it.

Kate J., I'm also not sure this would have ever happened without you. You have been one of my biggest cheerleaders. You have given so much of your time, experience and expertise helping me figure out what the hell I'm doing. You were my first beta reader, when I only had a few chapters. This book is SO much better with your guidance and copyediting. Your feedback on my writing makes me so proud.

Kayla B., thanks for indulging me in such a random request, and for creating such fun and perfect cover art. You are so very talented. Thank you.

Thank you to Kate A. for a robust and thoughtful developmental edit. This story needed to change, and though it was hard work, you helped me get there.

Thank you to my beta readers (who are also my family and closest friends). Katy, my key demo and the first to finish an early draft. Beth, Cindy, Cailey who let our Provincetown weekend become partially Katie's soft book launch. My mom, my biggest fan, who was so excited to read that she finished it in one night. Nicole U., who not only read an early copy, but was totally ok with me basing a character on her. I hope I did you justice!

Thank you to almost everyone I know who I talked about this to, for well over a year. I'm sure some of you were just being nice, and I'm grateful for that.

While no other character was 1:1 based on anyone I know, there are certainly situations and character traits from my past that I pulled from. I used to give myself a really hard time for what a train wreck I was dating in my 20s (I've come to realize, I am certainly not alone). But as I've gotten older, I've come to appreciate some of the wonderful and cringey moments that have shaped who I am. What a boring life to have always picked guys that were right for you, to always be in control and to have everything go to plan. Take a lesson from Kate Walker, it's better sometimes to be open to new experiences, to learn from them, and to let go a little. I'm not always great without a plan or agenda, but every so often, you'll catch me going out to dinner without a reservation. You have to start somewhere.

About the Author

A lifelong bookworm, she spent her New Hampshire childhood reading everything she could get her hands on while her sister tried to coax her outside. She now lives in Westwood, Massachusetts, with her husband and two elementary school-aged kids. After a few oddly specific dreams and a heart-to-heart with her daughter, she finally decided to chase her longtime dream of writing fiction.

When she's not writing, she's building over-the-top charcuterie boards, planning her next trip, or daydreaming about owning a wine cellar. She's a romantic comedy fan in every form—books, shows, or movies. *Follow You Down* is her debut novel.